Adolescence in Orphalese

Chapter 1: A December night walk

That bright sunlight, I couldn't stop thinking about it. When it has been this cold and snowing for so long, all you can think about is the sun shining and the sunrays warming your face. It was a cold yet cozy December night. The last few days had been very windy, and I had been in a hurry all the time.

Sometimes I think I stress too much. I had even reached a state of mind where I didn't enjoy Christmas a single bit anymore. I kept trying to convince myself that it was because Christmas nowadays is something centered around the children and consumerism, but I couldn't make myself truly believe that it was only that.

Tonight, though, was quiet. It was snowing a little, but I didn't mind, as I was appropriately dressed. I was crossing the snowy street and walking silently. I could hear the sound of a busy buzzing city in the distance, but focused on the pleasant sound of snow being trodden under my boots instead. Despite all the stress lately, I was actually able to enjoy this late December walk. Walking there like that made me able to process a lot of the stuff that had been going on lately.

Usually I like to go away from all the people and the noise when I have to think. To places that remind so much of nature, that I can make myself believe that I am far out in the real nature. I guess the transcendentalism in my English class did have some effect on me after all. This night, however, I didn't. As I tell you this, I still don't know why; I guess I just didn't feel like it or something of that sort. I bet you know the feeling, doing something and not knowing why.

However, I walked towards the city center. You always see some exciting things there at night, and I had nothing better to do at the time. After all, being home around that time never was that pleasant for me. I always looked forward to it, but it never met my expectations.

As I walked there, I began to watch the snowflakes as they tangled and danced around in the yellow light from the lampposts. It suddenly struck me, I had walked down this street once before. Man, I tell you, it was a lousy street. The snow scenery here at night had definitely raised it many grades on the beauty scale.

It was sad for the dumb ass real estate guys. I'm telling you, if they had seen what I saw, I bet they could've doubled the prices if they had brought customers there that night.

I walked on and started to open my mouth to catch snowflakes with my tongue, just like you did when you were a child. It was too difficult, and made me wonder if maybe I just forgot the technique.

As I was turning the corner of the street walking onto a bigger street, I passed this very cute couple; they were cuddling and smiling as they walked down the street.

It made me feel a little lonesome, and my mind began to process the potential girls that I could've walked with like that. I couldn't think of many, but my mind did come across one, old Atika, who is a girl I once met, and I mean it literally; I only meet her once.

We came across each other on a vacation some time ago. It's actually a long time ago by now. It was on a family trip out on the countryside. We didn't live too far from the sea, and Atika's family lived a couple hundred meters down the road. The only reason I met her was that the youth out there made a campfire on the beach every evening after dinner, and strangers were allowed to join. I think it was some kind of tradition.

I didn't feel like going just to meet a bunch of hillbilly strangers, but my sister talked me into it. That is where I meet Atika, and this girl just intrigued me like crazy with her stories, knowledge, awareness about people, and kindness towards them. She was nothing like the girls that I am usually surrounded by, like all the girls from school. Actually, I don't want to talk about her, but whatever. She was great, poor shame that there aren't more girls like her around.

The street I was on led directly towards the city center from one of the many suburbs, and I was somewhere in the middle of it.

As I walked on that street, I looked inside every house I passed. It was an experience watching how so many people had bought the same idea of a happy life. All the houses were like they were copies of each other, just with different humans living the exact same life. They all had either a Ford or a Toyota parked in the driveway, a big decorated Christmas tree in the living room, and the TV was busy broadcasting some major sports event, which they all thought meant the world, but in reality didn't mean shit.

I was thinking about them and the values they had chosen for their lives. It made me sad that my prejudiced perception of what some people call the middle class was confirmed.

I stuck out my tongue and drove it around my lips and felt that they were beginning to rip open, but that wasn't my concern anymore. There was starting to be too much activity around me to be focusing on ripped lips. There are all kinds of strange sounds and people in the city, especially at night.

I was turning yet another corner. It let me out onto the street that would eventually lead me to the area of the city center where you want to be at night. The ambience that I had walked to before, the noise from my shoes compressing the snow between the sole and the pavement was no longer significant enough to be heard.

In here it's the drunks and pimps buzzing and yelling that gets heard. When I had passed another two traffic lights, more people started to be around, and as I was among these different people, I began getting in a mood. I didn't think that it was anything special at the time, just a feeling of not going home before 01:00 AM.

Restlessness began grabbing me. I wanted something to happen and thought of how nice it would be to get away from this place, away to someplace happy. I began thinking about nature and that I shouldn't have walked into the city, but I also started to picture all the beautiful places on this planet that I know of. My daydreaming got interrupted by a girl that bumped into me. "*Watch out, kiddie,*" she said in an angry and sarcastic voice. "*Kiddie,*" I thought, how dare she call me that?

I hate people judging by looks like that. Yes, I know that I'm not twenty-five like her, but it still doesn't give her the right to be like that. Technically I'm an adult and fuck that, I know people at the age of sixteen who are more mature than some thirty-year-olds. So I hate people pulling something like that on me. Basically I was just so concentrated and lost in my own thoughts for a while that I lost attention on the road. I would always apologize if it had been a nice person, and it usually is, but maybe that's because I mostly come here in the daytime. It's a funny thing how bumping into someone becomes a whole different thing after eleven o'clock. Whatever, I didn't say anything to her and she was already a hundred meters down the road before I'd even processed what I wanted to say to a person like that, in such a situation.

I began to get really cold as I walked there looking into all the closed shops. All the mannequins, especially the men, looked pretty scary, even psychopathic while standing there in a dark room only lighted by the glow from the lampposts. It freaked me out a little.

There was a little street coming across and interrupting the street that I was walking on. It was a negligible street only containing the ventilators for the shops' air-conditioning and a few windows. It didn't look like a place where people would go through, and it wasn't. There was, however, a taxicab driving rather quickly down the street. I actually had to run a few meters to cross it in time. The taxi driver was too busy and didn't even pay attention to me even though I had to run a little because of his crazy driving. I really hate things like that.

Just as I crossed there was a small convenience store on the right-hand side. I was almost out of cigarettes so I went inside. It was a regular-looking Indian-owned kiosk, the kind of store where the only employees are the family members. This evening it was a young man around my age that was behind the checkout counter.

I walked straight to the counter and asked for a package of my favorite cigarettes. The first thing the guy did was ask for my ID. I reached in my left pocket where I always keep my light brown leather wallet; it hurt a little because my hands were so cold and the pockets in the jeans were very tight. I struggled a little to get it out, and as I got it out, my hand had gotten totally red on the upper side. I opened my wallet and took out my school ID card.

No more than a few seconds after I handed it over to him he said, "I don't believe this is yours, sir. I'm afraid that I cannot sell you cigarettes."

I was a little surprised with his hostility and just looked at him in silence.

"What? Why? Do you think that I have faked it?" I said in the most serious voice I could muster.

"Yes sir, I do, or maybe borrowed it from your brother," he said in a voice that really wanted to be authoritarian but wasn't. I didn't understand him, why the fuck would he care whether I smoked or not? Hopefully he could see that I was old enough to make my own decisions. I began to complain a lot, and then it wasn't too long before his father came out from a room in the back.

A middle-aged Indian man in an old yet well-ironed blue shirt with some white print on it. He had pants that looked like they belonged with a tuxedo, old leather shoes, and a golden watch. No doubt that he once had been a handsome man. He took the ID out of his son's hands and put on his square-shaped glasses that were hanging in a strap around his neck. He looked at it, then at me, and asked "you're from down South West, huh? How's that?"

"It's okay, sir, I guess."

"Well, my son here goes to school on the other side of town. You know the schools there?"

"No I don't really, but I've heard that there's some good schools there." I was playing it cool, but it seemed a little weird to me.

"There is, isn't there?" he said and looked at his son.

"Yes, yes, they're good," the son replied.

The father then informed his son to sell me the cigarettes. It made me very glad and confident. I felt that justice had been served, and I nodded to the father as a sign of thankfulness before I left the store. The nice thing was that it didn't seem like anyone did anything wrong. The father was happy with his son's skepticism and I with my cigarettes.

I turned onto the street and ripped open my new pack of cigarettes, reached in my inner pocket for my lighter, and lighted a cigarette.

I was thinking of the son's behavior. I clearly sensed that that young man would never live up to his father, but the father was still trying his best to let him. Not that his father was a big shot or anything, but he was just better doing what he did. Better with people. I was thinking that the problem with that guy was that his father probably led him onto a life path that reminded him of his own, but didn't fit the son. I think that's the only reason why people fail at something. It's because they choose the wrong path.

Instead of finding that guy's real talents; I mean, he must have some. It's funny how some parents fail to raise their children well, even though they are good people, but I guess that that's just the way it is. He was still in school, though, so maybe there was still hope.

I was getting close to the bar area and I already had the place that I wanted to go to in mind. I had never been inside before, but I had walked past several times during the daytime and heard a lot of good things about it, which means that I've read it on the Internet.

The city was buzzing around me and I could feel how people had so many and yet very similar purposes here at night. I was getting very close to the place now, and the timing was great because I finished my cigarette just outside the entrance. The bouncer looked skeptically at me, but he didn't say anything as I walked past him.

I got down the stairs into this mysterious room that was full of decoration. The furniture was old and all different, there were globes with lightbulbs in them hanging from the ceiling as lamps, a long aquarium covering part of the far end wall, those light chains that remind me of those from circuses, and all kinds of different stuff from old ship models to African tribe masks. The place had a great and cozy atmosphere and was also almost full of people. Luckily I managed to squeeze in between a lot of people and find a seat on the end of a long table.

I liked this bar for that, having big and long tables, some of them even round. It forced strangers to sit together, and a lot of the time their separate conversations would unite and become one. There was only one seat left, and that's probably why it wasn't taken. Most people don't go out alone.

"Is this seat taken?" I asked the three ladies that sat there.

"No, feel free, young man," they said.

I took off my jacket and hung it on the old and very heavy wooden chair, then I squeezed back in between all the people to order something at the bar. There was this one guy talking with two girls. He didn't move until I had asked him very loudly for the third time. I had the feeling that he heard me even the first time I asked, but that he was the type of guy that had created a belief of himself being someone special. Someone that didn't have to move for anyone. On top of acting like a douche bag, he also looked corny as fuck. God, I hate people like that.

I managed to get to the bar and find me a good spot. Usually I would go for beer, but as I looked around and saw almost everyone drinking cocktails, red wine, or some foreign beer that I had never heard off, I realized that I probably shouldn't order a regular beer. I looked through the drinks menu and had no clue what 90 percent of the cocktails were. The place had, of course, for who knows what reason, not written the ingredients in the menu. The price tags were my primary guideline, and my eyes fell upon one specific cocktail that wasn't that expensive, but neither was it one of the cheap ass drinks. The Ramos Gin Fizz.

There were people all over the bar and the three bartenders were very busy, but I just stood there silently trusting that they knew that I had waited longer than some of the inpatient dickheads that kept calling for them while they were busy doing other stuff. I thought that it had to be a pain in the ass working under such conditions, but again, someone has to do it. It made me a little upset when one of the younger bartenders attended to a guy two places down the bar beside me that had almost just arrived, but I figured that I would just keep on waiting. A short while after, the oldest-looking and most classically dressed of them came to me and asked, "What can I do for you, sir?"

"I would like the Ramos Gin Fizz, sir," I said.

"Excellent choice," he said with a smile. It made me glad that I had picked something that he liked, even though I afterwards thought that he might say that to every young bastard.

Whatever, I reached for my wallet and found enough money to tip him around ten percent. He was, after all, a pleasant-mannered, nice guy to receive a compliment from. One minute later I got my cocktail and I gave him the money, he quickly counted them and said, "Thank you," before he rushed on to the next guest.

After some time I managed to squeeze myself back to my seat, and that's when I began to overhear other people's conversations. There was a couple behind me. I couldn't figure out whether they were dating or just friends, but I liked their discussion. They discussed the unbelievable scale of consumerism that is associated with Christmas nowadays. I couldn't agree more, but the conversation wasn't too interesting as it went on. It was like they kept talking about the same stuff in different manners.

So instead I turned my attention on the three women sitting next to me. I had one on my left and two on the opposite side. They were scouting the room for guys, more specifically partners. What was special was that it wasn't partners for them all, as it usually is. No, it was only for one of them, and it seemed that they very well could have been three generations going out together. A daughter, mother, and grandmother.

It freaked me out, and I started realizing how they didn't fit in at all. Why would you do such a thing, go out with your mother and grandmother? I began to picture this young girl's entire life story. How she had a boyfriend from the early teenage years until the early twenties and how he had left her because he finally found out that it wasn't what he wanted. How she had cut off her friends because of him so that she now only had family to support her. It's kind of a sad story.

All three of them were dressed in their finest clothes, but it couldn't cover the yellow skin and teeth on their suffering unhealthy bodies. It was so obvious which type of people they were. The worst part was that the daughter wasn't very motivated, but that her dumb ass mother was on behalf of her. She kept pointing out guys that she thought had potential to the daughter. It was relatively discreet, but I saw. The grandmother gave second opinions and encouraged her granddaughter to make contact.

I tried to imagine how they ended up here, how the mother and the grandmother agreed on helping her and her to receive help. It's fucked up, but it's not what's important. She would never engage in a conversation with anyone, and even if she did it wouldn't lead to anything. Why do I say that? Because it would either be way too awkward with two fucking family spectators, or just uninteresting because of her persona. I bet her mother was single and the only reason her grandmother still had a husband was because of the marriage norms of her generation.

It actually made me irritated to sit beside them; people like these get me in a bad mood. Though most of all I just felt sorry for them and wished them the best, well, maybe only that they knew better.

The Ramos Gin Fizz was good, though. I sucked through it like a madman. I finished it within a few minutes, and then I leaned back and lighted a cigarette. It wasn't too comfortable leaning back on this very old, hard wooden chair, but I didn't mind.

I decided that I would leave, as I didn't want to be around these kind of people. Not with so many other way more interesting people in the city. I also figured that it would be rude to change seats while they were here, and actually also virtually impossible with all these people that had entered the already densely packed place.

I stood up, putting my jacket on would be too much of a struggle with so little space, so I waited until I got up the stairs and outside. On the way out I got a rather joyful "Good night to you" from the bouncer that previously had been a little skeptical towards me.

"Likewise," I answered in a surprised voice. I didn't know whether he had been watching me or if his mood just had changed a little. Actually I didn't care as long as he was friendly. But then it struck me, he was a very big guy and mood swings are a common side effect of unnatural testosterone usage. He seemed just like the type, and it explained everything to me.

I began walking down the street. The skin on my face began to prickle because of the cool air. Judging by its surroundings and looks, the street with bars and restaurants was a charming place. It had a buzzing and new feeling of life in old surroundings. It certainly was a beautiful place.

The only thing disturbing was that some of the people around there began to change that. They had gotten too drunk already, and there were only more of them appearing as the time went by.

As I got more and more fed up with drunks, I began searching for a more quiet part of town. I knew that it was my own mistake. I knew that I didn't like big open spaces as it is. Especially when they are crowded with drunks, then it sure as hell is not a place for me. Unfortunately, though, that's exactly what that part of town was at that time of the night.

I was thinking of places or just areas in town to go to. Some of the places I thought about were too far away, but then again, I thought, the night is still young.

So I decided to go to the Latin Quarter a little farther down south. I knew that it would be calm and prestigious in a cool way. Okay, to be honest, it can get way too pretentious sometimes, and then it's just an obnoxious place, but I really felt like it tonight, especially because it holds all kinds of places and people. Everything from the finest restaurants and bars, to chill places with students from the university to homosexual-bars and even combined art galleries, bookshops, and bars.

I think the reason why it's so diverse is because the rent down there isn't so damn expensive. I mean, it probably is, but it's not sky-high like the city center. It's a nice part of town and I really like it. Sadly, though, I don't go there enough, and actually almost never at night. I think the only reason is because it's on the complete opposite side of town. As I thought about it, it really made me sad. The fact that I miss out on such a lovely part of town just because I'm too lazy to get my ass on a bus, tram, metro, or whatever, is kind of sad. It was kind of dumb when I think about it, but it cheered me up knowing that I was going there now.

I had gotten off the main nightlife streets and was walking in the quiet part of the city center now. I was headed for the closest tram stop that I knew of. Despite the fact that we moved here three years ago, I hadn't become too familiar with the layout of the city yet. It was actually quite funny because I didn't even mind whether I had to walk half or two kilometers. I didn't have anything to stress about. I knew that I could have taken the bus in the city center, but I didn't want to. It would include a fifteen-minute trip with a lot of drunks, and that I wasn't interested in. Besides that, I also love the trams. They have a whole other feeling to them compared to the busses. I mean, the trams here are mostly old and they have such a beautiful feeling and look, it sometimes makes me feel like I'm living in another time or even starring in a movie. Even though I know that I don't, I just find the trams the easiest place to dream. They make me want to get my dad's old trench coat out of his closet, put on some classy leather shoes, and get a classy haircut. I guess that I, at that point, was too nostalgic about the world; just because they dressed different didn't mean that it wasn't the same bullshit.

As I got closer to the tram station, the city began to get quieter around me. The thing I observed was that the people at the tram station were mostly the people who had to stay up at night rather than the people who stayed up by choice. As I got on the platform, I immediately lighted a cigarette and placed myself on the far end of the platform. We were something like seven souls standing on the platform that night. Five of them looked like tired nightshift workers and they didn't take much of my interest. The other two looked like they had left some kind of occasion early for who knows what reason. Well, basically it didn't matter at all.

The man I would have guessed to be about thirty, and the woman close to forty. It didn't seem like they were together or anything, but they were both noticeable as they were neatly dressed. The woman had a long fur coat on, high heels and bare legs. In this cold she must have been wearing skin colored pantyhose, but I couldn't tell from that distance. Given the bare legs, she most likely had a dress underneath the coat. Without doubt a beautiful classy dress. I didn't like fur too much after some of the videos that I had seen showing fur production, but I got to admit that it looked gorgeous on this lady.

The guy was dressed just as classy, the only difference being that he was a man, a gentleman. He almost looked the same way I wanted to look like riding the tram. He had the classical leather shoes, suit and tie, and a 1920s' haircut. He didn't seem like an anachronism, though, and he lacked the trench coat. This guy looked so badass, I hope he was. The sad thing about this look nowadays is that it's mostly nobodies that look like that; not that they are worth less, but back in the days it was gangsters, businessmen, regular laborers, and artists who had that look. It wasn't pretentious. Nowadays it's people working in hair salons, fashion and furniture stores, which are not even close to being badass professions. For some people it's enough if other people just think they are something that they're not.

I felt a soft wind blow on my cheek as the sound from the approaching tram entered my ears. It was definitely music time, and I took my headset out of my pocket.

The cable on it was all entangled. It was like that every time, and every time I complained to myself and thought of storing it in a different way in the future, but it never happened.

I detangled it and plugged it in my phone. I felt like putting on jazz to keep the old school feeling alive, but I couldn't resist the temptation of just one Frank Ocean track first. I don't remember which track it was; well, it doesn't matter, most of them are pretty cool.

I ended up entering the same wagon as the classy-dressed lady. The wagon we entered was quite empty; we were about ten souls in there. The lady was still the one who had my attention, and at one point she caught me looking at her, and I promise you it wasn't a smile that I got for that. She left the wagon after only two stops, and by that time I had gotten carried away staying on Frank and enjoying it.

Two stops was a relatively short ride, I would have walked that distance, but, well, she was a lady in high heels; it was fair enough. The problem was that as she left, a drunk entered the wagon and that was exactly what I didn't want.

This guy was out for trouble, and he made a shitload of noise, so much that I actually wasn't able to enjoy my Frank anymore. What a bastard. Okay, that's rough, but turning into a jerk or a fool seems like the norm for people who are too drunk. I don't like it.

The ride was quite long, and as always I was reading something on my phone. I'm always reading an article or something similar on Wikipedia that I saved to read earlier. Most people just play games and waste their time.

For a long time I thought that smartphones and the new wave of technology was a really bad thing, but I really enjoy it and appreciate it. I know that looking into your phone closes you off from the world, but as long as you know it does, then it's all right. My smartphone is kind of like heroin to me, but still I use it for actual purposes, like reading stuff. At least that was better than playing some random and time-consuming game, I think. Sometimes I kind of wished we didn't have this culture.

I looked up, but the problem was that everybody was on their phones. Even if I wanted to strike up a conversation with a stranger, it would still be very hard. Looking into empty space was less interesting than reading about artificial intelligence and how it is developing, so once again I became part of the smartphone zombie herd.

Finally, I reached the station where I had to get off. My mood was weird and I had changed my music accordingly. Going with some dark grunge always accompanies moods like this pretty well. Really I just didn't want to be here. I really hadn't felt happy for a long time, and even worse I didn't really know what to blame.

Basically I had felt very different and constantly changing the last couple of years. I really couldn't think of what to do, but I just wanted to do something. Dark grunge almost always fits my mood, but right now it didn't. I changed, but the next thing I found didn't work as well. It kept going like that with me not being able to find anything that I wanted to listen to. That was new; it had never happened to me before.

The architecture there was very beautiful. I took a look back at the subway station; damn it was gorgeous this time of night. Once again I tried to wrap my earphones so they wouldn't tangle, yet still I knew that they would.

I was on the main road heading for an area that was well known for its late-night cafés. The main road was the only way I knew, but suddenly I felt an urge to take a different route on some of the streets that I didn't know.

I looked out for cars and crossed the road. The streets I got into were quiet. There were no cafés, restaurants, or bars. They were the kind of streets that would be vibrant and alive during weekend daytime, given that it was an area for city people living and raising families. It still felt good on my mood to walk there.

I looked up in search of stars, but couldn't see any with the yellow light from the lampposts illuminating my eyes. I looked down and around, just enjoying the quiet ambience.

It wasn't long before I entered the café area. At the first café I passed by, a young man was stacking chairs. I took out my phone and looked at the time. It was getting late.

That was when I realized that I actually went all across town just to see a bunch of cafés closing up. Few people on the street and cafés closing down, it was the same as I walked along. I passed one café that was still open and felt relieved. I could take a stroll around, but no matter what, I had this place.

It was a beautiful café with kind of a French design. It was casual, but still the tables had white tablecloths and shit. The people here were very different. It was the kind of people who went out with friends.

They were couples, a mix of girls and guys. No one in there seemed to be looking to talk to strangers. Sure, most of them would talk to me if I started, but I didn't feel like interfering in their social lives. They were probably all working, and this was their time off to meet with their friends.

Taking a walk around, I quickly realized that there was no other place. I walked back, went inside, and ordered a beer. It was clear that I didn't quite fit the picture, but it was late and they didn't care. People were aware of me, but I felt like a fly on the wall. I was just sitting there overhearing different conversations.

Most of them were discussing work and making jokes about different things. They seemed like the kind of people who were interested in the world and would discuss politics, ideas, and human life, but that was four hours ago. They were part of the organism and needed to blow off steam. They had brains, but needed some alcohol and humor for a break. I don't blame them; they were probably doing better than I would.

The café was decorated with class, and a lot of the posters were actually interesting. It seemed like the owner or whoever designed the place was actually interested in other things than serving beer and making money.

It wasn't a bad place, but there was something inside me that was smoldering. Something had to happen. I don't know if you can call it wanderlust, but I had been going against something inside me for too long.

Hikikomori is a Japanese word for social isolation that I came across some time ago. I haven't been a hikikomori, but I sure as hell had a long antisocial period in my life. I had always been social, but things had changed the last few years. Friendships were few, and it had all come with new knowledge. I learned some things that I will tell you more about later.

The last sip of beer was a little too tepid, but at least it went down. I got up and walked out the bar. It literally felt like everybody was looking at me as I left. I know me being there might have seemed a little weird, but still they should just mind their own business.

The streets were almost empty, but I really didn't mind. There is always a lot of possibilities in the world, it's just about seeing them, but there at that time there weren't many. I began walking along with the few people that were actually on the street. It was like four people, but they were walking towards a part of town that I didn't know.

Chapter 2: A gentlemen's place

As I was let through the door and came into what seemed to be a normal apartment building, the shady voice behind me in the doorway told me to go up the stairs, and that's what I began doing.

What was I thinking? I asked myself that, the streets were empty, but it was like they led me here. The stairs were beautiful. There was a red carpet on the steps, it reminded me of something glamorous, like the ones they have at movie premiers. Of course, it's a corny feeling to have, feeling like a movie star, but I didn't really. I just have to admit that I think red carpets are really beautiful.

The railing, walls, and ceiling were white. It was an old building and you could see how the railing had been used for many years. It was a beautiful one with volutes on the end of each part of the stairway. The railing was cold and smooth as I dragged my hand over the lacquered wood on my way to the second floor.

My ears got more and more filled with music with every step I took up those stairs, and my stomach was starting to act strange. It tickled in there, in a way that it never had before.

Nervousness, I think it was, because I crossed my own line with such great extent that I felt that way. Still to this day I'm wondering what dragged me in there. Maybe having very few possibilities makes it easier to choose.

As I turned to the last part of the stairway before the second floor, I began seeing the lights that shined from that place where it all took place. I'm telling you, I was so intrigued by then that I didn't know whether to follow my instincts and walk away, or follow my curiosity and go on. I did the latter.

As I stepped on that second floor, four eyes were meeting me already. It was the last security check. Really it wasn't actually a security check. You just had to walk by two guys to get inside.

The place was set up in an old luxury flat that had been reshaped, but you could still feel the old atmosphere. It gave a very special feeling of intimacy.

As in almost any other apartment, you enter the hallway and there are some rooms on each site. On the right side there was a toilet and to the left a bedroom and kitchen beside it. The toilet was for everybody, but what I suppose was the old master bedroom and the kitchen was for the staff. There was a very lousy-made sign on the first door saying "Staff only" and the kitchen was covered by these curtains which had an oriental touch. They were red and looked heavy as they were folding and covering the door frame. I was vaguely able to sense some people behind them. I suppose it was the part of the staff taking a break from work.

As I walked down the hall towards the place where everything seemed to be happening, I passed the bar on my left. It had once been a room, but was now opened up to an open bar. It was just outside the door that led to the living room, which now was the place of action, so to say.

The girl behind the bar welcomed me, and with her head signaled for me to go on. She told me to continue straight ahead.

As I walked in that hallway, the shaping of the room in front of me began to hit my cornea. I cannot remember focusing anywhere else than on that small gate. That small gate towards mystery.

My heart was pumping. I definitely didn't feel comfortable, but the voice of my gut was stronger than the one of my mind. It's quite a rare case for me.

Before I knew it, I was situated in a chair in the corner of that once upon a time normal living room. It was in line of the door to the hallway and sure was a strange room to enter.

Entering it, you would walk between two lines of sofas and then you could walk to the right entering the rest of the room or walk straight towards the seats where I was located. Once upon a time it was a well-sized living room, but by now it had a well-sized stripping plateau in the middle of it.

All the furniture was classical and red. The girls were all sitting on the two couches that you had to pass on your way in, and many of them were very attractive.

Whenever someone walked through the door and entered the room, they were all looking. When you had passed them, you would find that there was always a girl who was performing a show, except for the short breaks for shifting dancers.

It kept everybody busy looking at the stage kind of thing, and waiting for the next girl. I, however, tended to pay more attention the girls sitting on the two couches by the entrance.

They were all chatting and also giggling once in a while. I observed them and their behavior and tried to figure out who played the different roles in their group and, more importantly, how they all winded up here. I mean, they were young, some of them maybe not even that much older than me. Were they still in school and was this maybe just part-time work for them?

My head kept spinning around those thoughts for a minute or two, until a girl walked towards me in one of the sexiest ways I've ever seen. The way her long legs were crossing each other as she walked, they were distributing the movement perfectly throughout her entire body. Her body was only covered by a very thin classical black set of underwear, and she walked with an intense look on her face. She did not take her eyes off me one single time as she walked there.

When she was right next to me, I was looking at her in a way that felt very strange. When she bent down, she was sitting in a position that most of all reminded me of when girls pee outside in nature, but that didn't matter. This girl did it in a sexy way.

I was so overwhelmed and intrigued that I could barely articulate a civilized answer to her request for an order. I couldn't think of anything that I wanted, but I thought that it would be cool if I had my own drink, instead of taking her suggestion, so I ordered a Ramos Gin Fizz. She didn't know it, but she took the order anyways.

It wasn't too long before she was back with my Ramos. She threw a trivet on the table and put the drink on top of it. It was a small Ramos compared to the one that I had earlier on. I grabbed the straw and tasted it. Horrible compared to the one that I had earlier. I figured that they didn't know the recipe and probably just went and googled it. The result was disappointing, but I kept it with a smile anyways and figured that it was probably my own fault for ordering something off the menu.

She smiled, turned her back on me, and walked away. The way she walked away was in just the same sexy way that she had approached me with, the only difference being her very sex butt. I felt really bad for having looked at her ass, but it wasn't strange in here. It really didn't feel good to me. I don't like women being sexual objects like that. Of course, if they choose it, but not when they are paid for it.

As I began looking around the room, which only held a handful of guests, I asked myself what kind of fucking person I had become. I shared the corner, which consisted of three chairs and two couches, with one other guy. He seemed like a strange guy. He greeted me by making a modest nod with his head when the waiter left. Afterwards, he was just sitting there. His chair faced towards the room so that he could overview the entire room. Compared to mine it was a nice position. I mean, if you wanted to look at girls, it was.

I slightly faced the other way and had to look to my left to follow the performance on the plateau. I did that sometimes, but a lot of the time I was just looking slightly to the left so that I could observe the girls sitting on the couches. When I did neither of those, I would be observing the man sitting in the corner.

He was so strange and I couldn't place him in a final box. I know it sounds fucked up, but that's one thing that I like to do, place people in boxes. I love to predict what type of person someone is by his or her looks and behavior. Actually, I consider myself quite good at it. I mean, I get it right a lot of times. Of course, I'm also wrong a shitload of times, but the funny thing is that most of the times it remains a mystery because I never get to speak to the person. Well, whatever, that's the way it is. I find interest in way too many people in this city to spend time on all of them. This guy sitting in that chair could be anything from a truck driver taking a break after a long run, to an American dad kind of person taking a break from a life that he begins to realize is way too shallow and trivial. Hell, he might as well be a CEO of some company, who knows? He was acting so calm and dressed very normal in black clothes, yet it seemed a little classy. He was a very complicated guy. He didn't say anything to me even though I showed interest in talking to him. Maybe I was just bad at it.

I was sitting there leaned back in the chair with both my hands around my Ramos and my legs far under the table that we shared. He was an interesting guy, but something is only interesting until something else becomes even more interesting, and that is what happened to me that night.

This one girl that I had not seen before came directly in through the door and walked on the plateau. I actually didn't see her coming through the door, she only caught my attention when she was already on the plateau. She was an unbelievably beautiful girl, even made the girl that had served my Ramos seem average. I don't even want to explain her looks to you, because I know that you can imagine the beauty. Everyone has a perception of true beauty, and she fulfilled mine.

Many of the girls were kind of Barbie, but she seemed rather natural looking, especially when you take her profession into consideration. The strange thing was that a majority of the crowd seemed not to like her that much.

Before I knew it, I was turned 90 degrees on my chair watching her closely. The show was breathtaking. I had never experienced something like it. I mean, I have seen a girl naked, but it was nothing like this. Suddenly my thoughts kind of broke and I was thinking, how the fuck I could get attracted to a girl showing her entire body including her most sacred parts to total strangers? Some part of me really thought it was disgusting, but it didn't make me look away.

As she finished up and walked down the stairs, a guy from the opposite side of the room walked after her and tapped her on the shoulder.

I couldn't hear a single word, but I saw her smiling briefly just before he handed her a note. Then she grabbed his hand and began walking. She led the way and he walked with his arm stretched out after her. They turned right just outside the door and left me wondering. Was this only a strip club, or also a brothel? That's the thoughts that were going through my head.

"What the fuck! Why did I walk into a fucking brothel?" I thought to myself. I was disgusted with myself and remember sitting there and getting even more disgusted with that beautiful girl giving herself away for money.

Before I knew it, the guy came back. It had only been around five minutes or something. I was a little amazed about how fast it went, but then I thought twice. She is stunningly beautiful and he probably thinks so as well. I myself probably wouldn't even last two minutes. A minute later the girl came back as well.

Even though I was disgusted with what was going on, I couldn't help myself feeling a little funny about how everybody in the room knew how long the guy lasted. Then again, not that I would last more than five minutes with a girl like her, but just the fact that everybody knew seemed quite funny to me.

Now I was just sitting there. The worst part was that even though I felt disgusted, she was still only unattractive to me for a few minutes. She had placed herself calmly on the couch with the other girls and they were just sitting there continuing with their conversation.

That is when the shock of the night happened. One of the other guys from the back of the room walked up to the girls and was standing there talking for a few seconds. That's until that same girl stood up and walked him the exact same way. I think my jaw dropped. I couldn't believe my own eyes. I think I'd misinterpreted the crowd. They seemed to like her a lot. That guy, like everybody else in the room, had just seen the girl leave with the other guy a few minutes ago. I mean, if he was not fucking blind or anything, he couldn't have missed it.

I was speechless, not that I was speaking or anything, but my mind couldn't process what just happened. I was sitting there totally disturbed over what was going on in this place and was seriously considering leaving. I actually wished that I were far, far away. Somewhere else, a place where stuff like this doesn't happen.

I was thinking for a while, but couldn't think of a place, but I convinced myself that it did exist somewhere. I guess that it's just a big part of every culture. Actually, I even read once on this iPhone app I had called Cool-facts or something that it's the oldest profession in the world. It was a bit shocking to me, but hey, we humans are a fucked-up species.

Even though it's all over this goddamn planet, I still wanted to escape to someplace else. It wasn't the first time tonight that I felt like that, and I was beginning to think how it would be to travel away right now. It's really funny and really sad at the same time, how one night out in the city where you live can give you an eager desire to just leave the place and never come back. I guess that I don't live the place that suits me the most.

Actually, it wasn't even funny at all; what it was really was fucking miserable. Living in a city that you want to turn your back on forever each and every time you walk out onto the streets of it, if only you just could. Life is definitely too short for that, but with my age in the world today you have almost no chance of relocating and living a decent life without economical support from your parents, and my parents definitely weren't up for that.

Still, I was thinking of possibilities. Usually I kill them inside my head, but something was different that night.

Vacation was coming up in a week and it was flu season. It meant that I could easily take some days off pretending to be sick. I liked the thought.

I was thinking of all kinds of places around the world. All cool places that everybody is talking about. All the great wonders of the world, all the big cities each with their own special vibe, the vast forests, the quiet and calm countrysides; actually all the places that are so different from this shitty place where I'm located.

I wanted to sniff in the scent of great foreign cultures both temporary and distinct. I was also thinking of whomever of my friends that would possibly be up for a trip like that. Couldn't think of many. Truth be told, I couldn't think of any.

The thing is that I didn't manage to build that many strong friendships here. I have a few guys from school that I consider friends, and then I have guys from the place where I lived before. Those were my real friends, but things happened that made us grow apart. Really, I think it was more me that grew away from them, but I'll talk more about that later.

There was also the fact that my family and I moved, but honestly it suited me quite well. I'd really differed between being really extroverted and introverted for a while. I was very different back then. I was a kid that I'm not anymore, but basically I changed many times.

Now I really only had one close friend, but luckily I still met people that I cared about from time to time. I would just rather call them acquaintances than friends.

Thinking back to when I was in that strip club, I remember not wanting to travel without a companion. It wasn't like it is today. Nowadays I enjoy traveling alone. It was a big problem for me that I didn't have strong friendships, but I figured that I would rather be alone, feel lonely sometimes, and still be true to myself. Instead of being like the majority of the guys from school, all not knowing themselves truly, half of them cared about sports and parties on Fridays, the other half about computer games and Hollywood blockbusters.

To me those are all very superficial interests. Most of them also only cared about the everyday life banalities. Like whether they got a B or B+ in English class, which girls they would have a chance of kissing on Friday night, or if their parents' car had got a scratch while they borrowed it and parked it on the school parking lot.

All of that has always seemed so ridiculous to me. I mean, I think of a car as a tool, like your jeans. You use them and sometimes they get scratched, that's just the way it goes, and yeah, I know that a car costs way more than a pair of jeans, but who cares? It's a fucking tool.

On top of that they were all very insecure and the type of people who try to make themselves look good by bringing other people down. One of them once did the worst and most cruel thing to a girl from our class.

Marvin was his name. The girl was in our biology class. She was pretty clever and worked hard, and so she did very well. It seemed that she had somewhat of a rough background. No one knew anything about her father, well, maybe some of the girls did, but the boys and I didn't. Her mother was very kind. I met her once or twice and it wasn't hard to sense that they were very poor.

That was the thing with our school. It was mostly regular middle- and upper-middle class children like myself, but we also had some students from very rich and very poor families.

This guy Marvin was from quite a rich family, but didn't do too well in school. It didn't seem to me like he had anything against Hannah. She was a quiet girl, a little weird sometimes, but still very sweet.

What Marvin did was something that only a few people should have found funny, as there are always some pricks that will. Unfortunately, people were drunk at the time it happened. That meant that their moral codex that was already childish and bad was even worse than usual.

As far as I know Hannah's mom was unemployed, but she knew how to play some instruments. I think it was guitar, piano, and some other stuff. She was teaching whomever she could for money, and on top of that she played different gigs such as parties and festivities on weekends. It was for the extra money, and she probably didn't report it for tax, but I didn't care, they had so little.

So back to what Marvin did. He hosted a school party on a Friday night, and of course he invited a lot of people to his awesome house, which of course was his own.

It was on his parents' property, but he still lived in a building all by himself. He had hired Hannah's mom for a fake gig and asked her to wear a red dress. You can guess how the rest played out, and how Hannah and her mother's night was ruined.

The worst part was that it wasn't just that night that was ruined. The rumor, of course, spread as it does in a school. People in our school weren't responsible and mature enough to turn against Marvin and help Hannah. Instead they all talked and made fun about it.

By the time it happened, I think it had been more than a year, and Hannah still had trouble finding her place and trusting people. The worst part was that I didn't stand up for her as well. I was just like all the other dickheads. I let it happen and I haven't even tried to support her until today. I figured that I would find a way to ask her out for coffee or maybe even a Ramos someday. That is because I still feel sorry for her and I hate myself for letting a dick like Marvin make fun of her and her family like that.

Another thing I hated about the guys like Marvin was that they really thought that their parents' wealth did reflect directly in their own success or something.

So yeah, now you've heard a little about the guys and how they are, except one of them, of course; there's always a good guy. I mean, they can't all be bad. It might come as a surprise to you, but they can't. What might come as an even bigger surprise is that I'm not the good guy. No, there actually is someone else, and I will tell you more about him later.

Apart from the boys, of course, there were the girls. Most of them had stereotypical and superficial interests like the boys. Even though there were a few girls that had interests that rooted a little deeper than makeup, image, clothing, and pop music, it wasn't much. Subjects like philosophy, art, and politics were an interest of some, but sadly I didn't get along very well with them. Actually, I was like that with many girls. I had always been bad at maintaining my friendships with them. It's not that we got cross with each other or anything. No, we just slowly fell apart. It actually made me pretty sad.

Luckily there was this one guy in my class that I got along with pretty well. His name was Calvin and was what I considered my only true friend. Calvin was all into music. I would say that we got along pretty well, the two of us. I had a music interest, yet nothing like Calvin's.

He played piano, guitar, and a little sax. I think his father forced him through a lot of musical training when he was little, but his father didn't have to anymore. At the time, Calvin would gladly spend all his spare time from school on music. As long as I was willing to talk about music or anything related to it, then we would have a good time hanging out. We used to say that everything would have been better if we were young when Billy Corgan had hair. I don't even remember which one of us originally said that, but it was an on-going joke, well almost a motto, we had.

I liked him, but we couldn't get along in the long run. I always ended up figuring that we probably would be very good together if I could play an instrument. We probably would have had a lot more in common and way more stuff to do together if that had been the case. After all, most of the time we just listened to music and found new tracks on Soundcloud or some hipster blog.

Calvin was a nice guy, but my conclusion was that not even him, my best friend at the moment, would be in consideration to be invited on a trip like the one I was imagining. When I thought about it, I realized that he would probably even refuse if I asked him. It meant that he was definitely out of the picture as well.

I felt a little lonely, as I had thought my entire friendship situation through. It happened once in a while, but I had learned how to deal with it. I was good at finding meaning in stuff that didn't involve other people. I could just read for myself and then create something with my imagination, newly obtained knowledge, and my hands.

That was enough to make me feel happy. If I could just create something every day, or work a bit on a bigger project, then I felt that I had served. Not served for anybody else, just for my ego, my self-realization needs, and myself. It felt good doing stuff like that. I didn't care if people thought of me as antisocial, but what did bother me was that I rarely created new acquaintances because I was such an enclosed individual. The funny thing was that everything that I ever tried to create was made for other people to see. The problem was that I didn't feel like having people see it.

That is why that night became very important to me. It was the night that I had the guts to live out the thoughts that I was thinking, well, maybe even dreaming.

It's just when you stand there on that cliff and you have to jump, it's not even half as easy as it was in your head. It's like when you imagine how you're going to play out a conversation or discussion that you're planning for in advance, and it ends up turning out completely different from the script in your head. Or when you wish you had said something different than what you actually said. You even rile for some time and swear that if it happens again you will act differently, and then it does happen again someday and you still don't act differently. All despite the fact that you want to so badly, but there's just something that still keeps you from acting differently. It can be a hundred different things, but for me it was the fear of the unknown, strangers getting close to me, and me leaving my comfort zone.

What I was thinking that night is what I want to tell you now. It was something that really pushed my boundaries, and I didn't feel sure about it at all. I just decided that if I wanted to be a different person, the person I always imagined and dreamt myself to be, then I had to act. No more postponing and thinking that I would do stuff someday. It had to be tonight, that night. It was the night that I decided that I had the guts. I could dream no more.

As I was sitting there, I felt more and more cool, like Tom Cruise in that very sexual movie he starred in. God, I can't remember the name of it right now. He played alongside Nicole Kidman. Whatever, actually I know it's a shame only remembering a film for its actors and not all the people behind it. It's like thanking the girl at the checkout counter for ringing the groceries even though she's just the last link. I know that the actors play a vital role and that they are very important, but still there's so much more behind it. I guess there is behind everything. Whatever, I felt like Tom Cruise's character in that movie with all the red lights around me. It was a pretty awesome feeling.

I had been lost in my thoughts for a while. My Ramos was getting dry, and the dancers had switched two or three times, I think. The surroundings felt like a different world. Different guys still went with the girls, and I had started counting.

It sounds stupid, but I was betting with myself about who lasted the longest. I was actually disgusted with myself for some time, but like everybody else, alcohol helped move boundaries. I'll tell you more about my moral issues of that night in a short while.

The funny thing was that they all came back in around the same time. After a total of six, I got pretty sure that they either put a fixed clock on the time of the intercourse or just gave them some kind of private dance show.

I wanted to know for sure, but I had my inner fights about asking. What was the worst that could happen? A lot, but after all, everyone that surrounded me right now were strippers, hookers, and perverts. Not exactly the kind of people that I wanted to ask a question. Questions that clearly would give away that I definitely don't visit places like this regularly. Of course, when I thought about it, everybody could properly tell by my looks and behavior, but the fact that I hadn't blown my own cover still gave me coolness in a way.

The chair had gotten really hot around me, and when I finally got out of my dazed condition, I realized that I was about to take my last sip of the Ramos. That's when the plan just fell in place.

When I finished my Ramos, I would sit for a second and try to get eye contact with the special girl, the one who had been taken away twice in a row. I would then ask her the question about what they did when they went away for five minutes. Then I would hope to start a conversation, and if it didn't work, I could order another drink. If she told me, and it wasn't going for a fuck, then I would ask her to take me. It was the ultimate way of inviting her.

Well, it was definitely the way I was going to do it. I thought about what I would say to her in my little speech. I tried with all my abilities from school to find the perfect balance between ethos, pathos, logos, and in this case also Eros. It was a good plan. Instead of taking the dance or fuck like every other pervert, I would make her sit down and then explain my plan to her. How I wanted to travel and how I would pay for everything if only she would come along. When the tape rolled inside my head at the time, I couldn't even hear how desperate it actually sounded. I guess it was good, if I had it might never have happened. Actually, I was already shaking with the plan as it was. It was so far outside my comfort zone, but I was sure that this was the ultimate way of inviting her. This could make things happen.

She was busy talking to the other girls, but she didn't seem like she was prepared for another dance on stage or anything. After all, she pretty much sold herself, didn't need any advertisement.

They were interesting as they sat there. She looked happy, and I didn't understand why. She was smiling and laughing discretely with the other girls, and when she finally decided to stand up, she walked out the door. As I was looking at her, one of the other girls stood up as well and she was coming towards me.

As soon as I realized it, I didn't know what to do. My plan had failed. I tried to think fast, should I take the conversation with this girl and ask her to go get the other girl, or should I ask for the other girl immediately and not use my script on her? When she was in front of me, I had not decided anything.

"Would you care for another drink, sir?" she asked in a way too sensual voice.

I was thinking that I probably had to order another one. "Another one of the same?" she continued.

God no, I thought to myself.

"No, no, please just surprise me," I said while trying to make a natural smile. She nodded her head and turned around. I think she thought I sounded really whack, but I didn't even look after her. All I was thinking about was that other girl. I just hoped that she would be the one bringing me my new unknown drink.

I felt good as I sat there. Didn't have much to care about. My family was home safely asleep or having a good time and probably not even knowing that I wasn't in my bed. It all felt so very perfect and relaxing.

As I was sitting there hoping, I had some time to think, and again some part of me began to work against my actions. Did I really want to talk to her? Wasn't this just some silly drunk idea? It's Christmas; shouldn't I just spend it in an ordinary way? I hate myself for that. Letting myself control myself with fear, even after I know that it exists in me.

I was setting myself up, but when my drink came back to me it wasn't the right person carrying it. Again my script kind of fell apart, but I figured that it was kind of now or never. Wow, stop, that sounds way too corny and it's also a phrase from that pop rock song. I fucking hate that kind of music.

I had to do it, and it had to be this night. I had tried something similar a couple of times before and I always chickened out. I was a little fucking pussy with a lot of opinions and a minimum of action. It was actually pretty damn terrible. I tried so hard to act, and some part of me just refused. I guess some would even call it pathetic.

I don't know if my denial part had a meltdown that night, but it was that night that I had the courage to ask the waitress if she could go get the other girl. When I asked, she looked at me in kind of a surprised way. At first she didn't know which girl I was talking about, and she gave me a very distinctive look. The kind of look that says, "Okay, you're cute but lost, young but old enough, and you look kind of cute in a childish way."

I didn't like it even though the cute youngster card seemed to be a good card to play. The smile didn't stay on her face and her voice wasn't smiling either.

"Which girl, sir?"

Sir? I'm no sir, but of course I didn't say so. Which girl? The beautiful one, who else could it be, I thought to myself, as if it was the most natural thing in the world. My head finally stopped playing tricks on me and I answered.

"Ehmm, the one who just left the room. She has dark blond hair and looks very cute," I said in a calm voice.

Cute, I said that. Oh, that sounds childish. I probably wouldn't use that word today, but back then I did. I actually think that it was what convinced the waitress girl that I was somewhat close to a child. I wasn't, though.

"I think I know who you're talking about, I'll go get her for you, but it'll be a minute."

"Thanks," I said. This was when I realized that it was too late. It was too late to do it over. This wasn't the hard part, not even close. This girl was getting her to come right over to me. Hopefully it would be the right girl. I couldn't imagine how awkward it would be if it wasn't. There was no turning back, though. I had to make this work.

I still don't know what made me ask. The courage didn't really feel like it was there, but still I asked. This is what panicked me. Just because I prevailed over my control freak brain part once, doesn't mean that I will do it twice. I seriously considered warding her off by saying something lame, but I couldn't think of anything, and she really had an aura that didn't deserve something like that. Then again, I was thinking, wasn't this what I wanted?

My anticipation rose by the second. I was shivering and began to feel sweaty as well. Another minute of really hard physical anticipation and panic passed before she entered through the gate of mystery. Luckily it was her and not one of the other girls. God, she was beautiful. She didn't waste time but did chatter a little with the girls as she walked past the couches.

I didn't like that. It really felt like everyone in the room had their attention turned on me in those seconds. Guess it was karma with the way I had been a part of the crowd with the other guys. It had now come to me. It was my time to stand alone in front of the crowd. I didn't like that it was like being on a stage; it wasn't nice at all.

She looked a tiny bit curious even though she was smiling. When she stood in front of me, she leaned on her one leg so she stood slightly to the side. Gosh, it was like she knew everything about body language and posturing.

"You called for me?" she asked in a fresh almost eager voice, actually way too fresh at that hour.

"Yeah, yes I did." It was already going bad.

"I suppose you want me to dance for you?"

Dance, she said it. She was a dancer and not a hooker. That did cheer me up a little bit. Still, I didn't know whether to say yes or no, whether to reveal my motive immediately or save it for later. I decided that later was the best, well, not the best, but maybe the least wicked.

"Yeah, if you could, I would be glad." I know that I was talking in a pretty formal language, but I think that was part of my identity back then. Just when I said it my body temperature doubled and I just sat there in that red chair and felt like I was one fire with it.

"Let's go then," she said after something that felt like ten seconds of awkward silence.

As I rose from the chair, reality hit me again. I think it was one of the most uncomfortable moments of my early life. Worse than being introduced in front of a new class in school, worse than the biggest humiliation I had ever tried. I felt eyes following me as I walked over the floor behind her. I was concentrating so bad to keep my eyes straight at her neck. I must have looked like a freak walking there, but I simply couldn't bear the thought of an eye contact situation.

It wasn't many meters, but I managed to break it. It was at the critical point, the couches. One of the girls there said something to the girl I was following as we walked past. It totally broke my concentration and made me look. I think my cheeks were just about the same color as the interior of the room when I made eye contact with the girl talking.

She was seated in the couch right next to me and still I didn't hear what she said. Luckily it was just small talk and the girl taking me didn't stop to talk. She did laugh shortly, though, which made me a bit frustrated. I hated myself and couldn't stick to any plan anymore. I felt so embarrassed. I'll go so far as to say that dragging me naked through a public space only would have been slightly more humiliating. Okay, it wouldn't, but my boundaries were being pushed drastically.

Having middle-aged, nasty men and strippers look at me while walking into a private show felt like the worst thing. It once again made me sick and I just wanted to leave it all behind at once. Places like this didn't suit me, and I sure as hell didn't suit them. When we got out the door everything was quieter. The girl turned right to walk down towards the room. Suddenly she made a pirouette and looked at me.

"We just have to wait a minute," she said with a smile on her face.

"All right," I answered while trying not to act weird. I could see that they had two rooms down the hallway. I began to doubt the authenticity of her smile.

Were they instructed to always smile like that? It seemed to me that there really wasn't much to smile about at the time, but then again, without exaggerating, I can say that I'm not the most positive of humans.

I looked her dead in the eyes and she looked back. Eye contact scares me, but I read a bit of psychology and learned that it's an important factor for building trust on a subconscious level. If I were to judge, which I am because I tell the story, then I would say that it's one of my most well-developed social abilities. It took me a lot of practice to overcome the awkwardness of prolonged eye contact, but I did it. Actually so much that I started enjoying it though it still felt too intense sometimes.

Really it's not only just having eye contact. You also have to practice on cultural differences. When you live in a multicultural society, as almost all of us do today, then you have to know how different cultures interact with eye contact. That's not even the hard part. The hard part is decoding specific individuals and to find out whether it will attract or frighten and repel them. Eye contact can be intimidating. I of all people know that. Still, I believe that the eyes are the way to a person's soul.

If there is one thing about humans that I generally enjoy then it's the eyes. The reading about psychology thing was part of something I used to do a lot. Reading about stuff. Reading is important, but my problem was that I was forgetting to see the things with my own eyes. A good mix is essential.

The girl seemed pretty darn confident, or at least acted like it, and that's why I did it. I couldn't tell if she even wanted to talk to me or not, but my plan could never get anywhere without a conversation. I figured that I might as well just begin it before we would enter the room. We were standing there kind of alone so it wasn't that bad, and I had the nerve to ask her, "What's your name?"

She didn't stop smiling, but her smile changed to a more subdued one. I liked it, it seemed way more natural than before.

"Valerie," she said in a soft and calm voice. "What's yours?" she continued.

"Let's keep that a secret for now," I said.

She looked a little disappointed or maybe just surprised. I don't think she expected me to answer like that. Also I couldn't tell if she found it intriguing or just douche. Silence occurred, and I couldn't think of what to say.

Just as I was about to ask her something personal, she said, "Its gonna cost you forty."

"That's all right," I answered.

I think I was lucky that she said something just before I did. It was good that it didn't get personal right there in the middle of the hallway.

We stood there in silence and I felt like it was getting more and more awkward, but I had a hard time finding out if she felt the same. She was smiling and acting cool, being very hard to read.

I took a step back towards the door so that I could use the loud music as my cover. Maybe she sensed my insecurity, but nonetheless she didn't mention anything that implied it. I realized that the music wasn't that loud, as I could hear the sound of an old wooden door creaking open around the corner.

A second later she reached out her hand and said, "Come with." I felt embarrassed about her holding my hand. My palms where so moist from sweat, and it didn't help at all that she grabbed it.

It was about a five-meter walk before we reached the door to the private room. Walking out and past us came a girl and a guy whom I hadn't seen in the main room. On top of that he didn't look like any of the other guests in the place.

He wore a suit with a vest underneath. He seemed like a pimp to me, way too confident in the surroundings. That's despite the fact that he didn't look like a criminal. I guess that it might have had something to do with my stereotypical perception of a pimp. A perception that was primarily conceived through Coppola's and Scorsese's work, and of course also all the shitty gangster movies that were broadcasted randomly throughout my childhood.

My father always watched shit like that, but he did have a little taste as *Taxi Driver* was one of his favorites. The guy could also just have been a business kind of guy just like the guy in the main room. A guy who got fed up with the monogamous lifestyle that almost everyone strives towards these days.

Whatever he was, he did seem skeptical about my presence, like I really didn't fit in, which I guess didn't at all. Maybe he just didn't like me knowing he was there. He probably didn't regret anything to this day, but the thing is I still don't know. Like so many of my peeks into other people's existences, I didn't know how they turned out.

When we turned and entered the room, I was shivering. It was the same feeling as when you have to do your first presentation in front of a big crowd. It feels so nerve racking, even dangerous.

The room had a red glare from the lights mounted around the top of the couch that was winding all around the room. She sat me down at the back of the room, turned around and closed the door. She turned towards a little table in the corner where they kept a really small and outdated stereo.

She clicked a few buttons and played the CD from the top. I was sitting there trying to gather myself, trying to get myself to say something. It had to be now; it had to be before she turned on the music.

"Don't," I said. Valerie turned the upper part of her body around to the left and looked at me in an asking manner.

God, she was gorgeous.

"What?"

"Don't turn on the music."

"Why?" Her voice raised a little, like she was getting aggravated or something.

"Ehmm, I want to talk to you. I mean, I didn't come in here for a dance. I want to ask you something."

I remember trying my best not to stutter out those words. You could see that she considered calling the bouncer for a second, but she didn't. Either was she a little too curious, or maybe it was me not being very intimidating.

"What do want to ask me?" Her facial expression turned more serious.

"The thing is, I'm … I wanna travel."

She kept quiet.

"Yeah, so I wanna travel. I've have had this feeling all night, and as I'm saying this it feels kind of crazy. I'm not drunk, and I have thought this through. Well, kind of."

She looked very skeptical by now. She had even moved her right hand to the door handle, but she hadn't opened it. I guess that it could only mean that I had caught her interest.

"I'm not fucking with you. I have got some time off from my everyday life, and I want to see some part of the world that I haven't seen before." I stopped, but the silence told me to keep going.

"And see, now you think something like 'well good for you,' but the thing is that traveling alone doesn't seem very appealing to me. Now do you see what I'm getting at?"

"I think I do, but I'm not sure," she said in a nonplussed voice. Her being bewildered was kind of a good sign to me, and I decided to try to be really honest with her.

"The thing is that I don't have a single person in the world that I would ask to come with me. I have been in here for some time now and you are the only person who's had my interest all night. I mean, usually I don't go places like this. Actually never, and you're the only reason why I didn't leave ten minutes after I got here. You actually made me stay here. I did spend quite a lot of time building up confidence to ask you, what I'm asking you now."

Thinking back, I don't think that I articulated myself very well that day. I'm also pretty sure that I spoke way too fast, but today it still feels like it took forever.

Valerie just stood there quiet and surprised. She had let go of the door handle and was now facing towards me. It felt really good to me being able to take her breath away like that.

"Wow, I don't know what to say. What exactly are you saying?" she kind of muttered out.

"Do you want to travel somewhere with me?" I said kind of eagerly. She definitely thought that I was too excited at one point. Her look wasn't as positive as mine.

"You want me to travel with you?"

"Yeah," I replied in a less happy voice.

"But take a look around, dude. Do you know where we are right now? I'm a dancer; you're a customer."

Some rational part of me under the alcohol and the big thoughts totally set off all the alarm clocks. It felt really crazy, and I just wished that I could take everything I said back. I tried to insist to myself.

"It's only fucked up if we say it is, Valerie." I couldn't think of a better answer.

"What? Fuck, creep, don't use my name like that. This is fucked up! It's not for us to decide, and even if it were, I would still think it."

It was kind of creepy and stupid using her name, but drunk me didn't think too fast, or too much for that matter.

"Okay, okay, sorry, calm down. I don't want to get you upset or anything, but see, the thing is that I have a decent amount of money, money that enables me to do what I want for some time. I don't want to be rational about it and throw it at some new computer or something."

A new computer, that was a clear nerd giveaway, but it didn't seem to bother her much. Then again, she wasn't a girl from school.

"I understand that, but you want us to travel together?" She almost sounded ironic now. Like she didn't really believe it but still fancied it in a way.

"Yes, exactly! Would it be possible for you to get off here at work?"

"No, well maybe, but fuck, I've got plans for the holidays. I have to see my family, friends, and so," she said. Actually, I did as well. It just hadn't been part of the drunken planning.

"Actually, I do too, but I was planning on making an exception." I couldn't really sense where this was going anymore, but I'm assuring you that I did my best.

"Yeah, I get you. You really practiced on being persuasive, huh?"

Actually, I had not. I don't know where my skills for that came from, and I had a hard time figuring out if she was being sarcastic. The fact that I couldn't tell if she was being ironic with me just made her more interesting.

"I'm not trying to persuade you into traveling with me. I'm just asking you if you want to. You're free to ask me any questions, as I would also like you to know that I'm not pulling any tricks on you. I'm really a straight up normal guy who for once in his life is doing something like this, spontaneously." Her facial expression was strange. What was she thinking?

"I don't know. You do seem like a straight up guy, but it's just crazy. Have you even got a plan? Where would you even want to travel to?" She was actually laughing as she said that. It was not because she wasn't serious about it. She just found it kind of unreal, I think.

"I know it doesn't sound like I've got a plan when I tell you that I have no place particular in mind. It's better if we decide together. After all, it's not even a real trip yet," I said.

"You're crazy," she said. She meant it, but she was still interested.

To this day I think that the only thing that kept me from running out off there was my willingness to make something happen when I decided that it should. It wasn't like me at all.

"You know what?" she said. My heart was beating with a million strokes a minute.

"I would like to go on the trip, but it doesn't fit my plans very well." Was she actually politely rejecting me? Out of the thousands of scenarios I had imagined, this was definitely not one of them.

"It's Christmas next week," she continued. Like I didn't know. Fucking Christmas.

"Maybe we will be home before that?"

It was starting to sound like I begged her, which I didn't want to at all. I kind of felt like the control wasn't within my grasp anymore. Whether the trip was going to happen or not.

"You're not missing Christmas. You'll just spend it somewhere else," I said in a way too desperate tone.

"I really don't know what to say." As she said that, someone knocked on the door. It was a dark voice on the other side of the door.

"Time's up, can't you count to five?" I hadn't heard the footsteps approaching, but I could hear them walk away.

Valerie seemed to have a short period of panic. She turned to me in what became some of the most awkward seconds of that night.

"I really don't know what to say. You seem like a nice guy, but I guess this won't work out," she told me that while she led me out the door.

"You can just go back to your seat and someone will come take your payment," she continued.

"Will it be you?" I asked.

"Maybe," she said in a slightly ashamed voice.

Maybe not, I thought. I was led out the door, and that's when I realized that what I'd just made myself go through might have been the most boundary-challenging experience I'd ever had. I was shivering but still felt glad that I did it.

Back then I didn't realize why I felt that way. To be fair, she did reject me pretty badly. Turning around the corner in the hallway, I was about to walk through the door that had captivated me so strangely earlier on. Suddenly it had become a very normal white painted door frame trying to hide that it was pretty worn down.

On the other side of it there was a bunch of bitches that would probably be talking like hell in a minute or two.

I remember holding my breath while walking past them. The walk this time didn't seem bad at all. It didn't feel bad, but it was pretty obvious why.

I got back to what had become my chair for the night. It felt good to be back in what now felt like secure surroundings. In that dark corner of the joint no one could see my face.

I had only been seated in my chair for a few minutes when I started analyzing which part of my persuasion speech went wrong. Sitting there I remember thinking of it as pretty solid. I'd prepared pretty well and it all went down quite all right, yet still she didn't say yes. It wasn't me, and that's how it is with something like that. You never nail it the first time, and that's why you better try two times.

Now you may think that it's squeezing the lemon a little too much. I'm not going to say what I think now, but in the moment it wasn't the case. I believed that if I evaluated and changed the approach, then the speech could work. I convinced myself that two tries weren't a shame. I had only taken a few glances around the room before a waitress contacted me. It was one of the girls over from the couch.

"Can I get you anything, sir, or are you done for the night?" I kind of had a feeling that someone would've clapped their small nasty hands if I had left the joint at that point, but I didn't.

"Actually, miss, I would like a single whiskey and Coke. Just put it on the tab."

"Sure," she said with an obviously fake smile. I didn't know whether I was being too sensitive or she really wanted me out of there.

Not a minute later she came back with the drink. It's a classic, I tell you. It tastes like Coke and you stay on about the same alcohol level when it's singles. Implied, of course, that you don't drink like a Welsh teenager. That drinking strategy seriously is picture perfect nine out of ten times.

This place was strange. Another dancer was on the stage giving it away in front of the still ever unappealing crowd.

Looking around the room, leaving became a serious part of my considerations. I really wanted to ask Valerie a second time, yet at the same time I really didn't want to be there anymore.

All of a sudden I began thinking about the trip home. It's a really long way that late at night. I shook my head forcefully, forcing the regular thoughts out. I had to give it another shot. She had showed a lot of interest when I asked, it was just the timing that was really bad.

It was still a crazy idea, but I couldn't get it out of my head. The trip wouldn't happen only with myself. She had to be there, and it had to be her. I was not going to ask anyone else in the whole world. When I think about that feeling today, it still seems kind of fucked up.

The trip could take a complete different shape if I had just tried to find someone else, but I didn't. Asking her and the softness of her voice declining my ideas still circulated in my auditory meatus. I didn't feel like I had any time to waste. I searched for eye contact and quickly caught one of the waitresses.

"I would like another private dance," I said. I sensed a small smile of enjoyment on her lips.

"Can you get Valerie for me?" I continued in a fast voice. It was easy to tell that she didn't like the fact that she had misinterpreted me.

"Of course. I will go get her right away," she said with the same superficial feeling.

Valerie was coming back in a minute. This was my last chance and I didn't even take time to practice. Now that I had done all this crap, exposed myself like this, I figured that I might as well just open up and talk from the heart. If she would reject me for that, then it would at least be honest and I could then leave and hopefully never meet her again.

Now was the time. Valerie came walking towards me. She had a very doubtful look on her face, yet still kept her cool.

"I would like another dance," I said, trying not to sound like a spoiled child.

"Another dance, as in I don't have to dance?" she asked in a low voice. It kind of seemed like a regular question, and it created a few seconds of awkward silence. I think my facial expression was golden if she just had been in the mood to appreciate it.

"I'm not gonna lie to you. I don't want you to dance, but I will pay so it doesn't look strange or anything." I could tell that she was intrigued in a skeptical way. I guess she was thinking that it was at least money if nothing else.

"All right, let's go," she said determinately while reaching out her one hand.

The second time walking wasn't as bad as the first. That is, in the manner of attention from the rest of the working force and rather nasty clients.

We were able to take a straight walk back to the exact same room as we were in before. I sat myself down on the same spot on the couch while she closed the door behind her. Everything went so fast compared to before. She leaned on the door and she didn't turn on music of any sort. She knew.

"I've been thinking a little these few minutes, and you don't seem like that bad of a guy," she began.

"But let me get this straight. What you're proposing is that we, the two of us, leave for a trip together. We leave as soon as possible to an unknown destination and you pay the entire thing with your money? Is that right, or am I mistaken?" she continued.

I was mute. Hearing the plan put out like that it really sounded like the dumbest thing I'd ever heard. We were looking at each other. Me being a little tenser than her. I even recall her smiling briefly. We both knew that what was being discussed sounded very peculiar. That's at least by the standard norms of society, which were the ones we were brought up under.

Despite that, I still sensed a feeling in both of us. The "fuck this godforsaken place" feeling, and of course accompanied by the "let's do something" feeling.

She was smiling.

"Yes," she said.

I wasn't able to muster any answer with the intensity there was at the time.

"Since we left the room before, I haven't been able to think of anything else. It's exactly what I want," Valerie said.

I smiled. I really didn't know how to react as it all seemed so unreal.

"For how long would we travel?" she asked.

"My money could take us pretty far," I answered.

"You're crazy," she said with a cautious smile on her face. It actually made me kind of glad that she said that. Crazy was something I had never been before.

"But I don't understand. I mean, how and when are we gonna do it?" she asked curiously. I was contemplating a little.

"We book last minute tickets and go to the airport. It's really easy nowadays," I said while trying to sound convincing.

"Would it just be vacation, or quitting my job if we did it?" she asked.

Quitting her job, she was actually thinking that? No matter what happens, quitting that job would never sound like a bad idea in my ears. That's, of course, what I thought, not what I said.

"Well, I don't know your boss, you know?" She became quiet. Judging by her reaction, it really didn't really seem like the answer she wanted. I figure I hit a soft spot, or maybe just sparked a thought. It was easy to tell that she was thinking. There was some kind of choice that had to be made. I felt that the plan and the entire thing could have fallen to the ground for a minute. Luckily it didn't.

"My boss is kind of a difficult man," she said.

He's a man who is selling women for money. How is a man like that not gonna be difficult? Again, that is what I was thinking, not what I was saying out loud.

"But would it be so bad to lose this job?" I asked curiously.

Having the guts to ask her something that really wasn't my business. I don't know where that came from.

She raised her voice a little bit.

"I know people in general don't like this job, but chill, you don't even know me," she said in a firm voice.

"I'm sorry," I actually was; it was going a little bit overboard.

I felt that I was being biased towards her. To be honest, I was probably judging her without knowing her story. Subconsciously, I will just assume that someone who works in a strip club has some kind of troubled past. I think it was her being able to see that I was really sorry that saved me.

"So what do we do?" she asked.

She was so gorgeous. It was like reality hit when she asked that, yet still it felt like a mad dream. A mad dream which I've had so many of, but they were never real until then. It was like it suddenly walked and danced out of my head and into reality. That doesn't happen, yet it did, and I didn't feel ready for it.

Typical to want something so bad and then not feel comfortable and ready when it comes.

"When does your shift end?" I asked.

"I could try to get off now," she said.

"Should I go grab a drink?"

"Yeah, or you could go wait on the street?"

"I would rather have a drink," I said.

"All right," she said with a smile.

"If you can't get off, I'll just wait around."

She nodded, smiled nervously, and walked out the door.

I exhaled, stood up, and looked myself in the mirror on the wall.

I leaned closer, staring myself dead in the eyes. It all seemed so unreal. I said my name four times. The whole thing seemed more unreal for every time I said it.

Looking at myself in the mirror like that is just something I do sometimes. I clapped my cheeks, smiled, turned, and went out the door.

Walking back into the room, I had the other girls looking at me in strange way. I felt a whole lot more confident walking past them now. So much that it didn't even seem awkward anymore. There was a new girl whom I hadn't seen before performing on stage.

It was at this point reality hit me. I didn't even wanna look. It seemed so disgusting all of a sudden. It's like you break this barrier and all of a sudden these sex symbols become humans again. What was Valerie actually to me? Was she just some sexy dream? Was that why she had caught my interest? I really didn't think so, but I wasn't sure.

I was getting drunk as well, which certainly didn't help. Valerie, I was thinking. Was that her real name? I had to ask her that. Being back and seated in the comfortable chair again felt really weird. It was like I had served my purpose there. Everything that was back in here was disgusting. The fact that I didn't feel like looking at anyone made it even worse.

I tried to peak at the door without catching eye contact with someone at the couches. It was funny. I had never felt so uncomfortable, then comfortable, only to feel uncomfortable again. It sure was weird.

A new girl came to me.

"Do you need anything?"

"Could I get a single whiskey and Coke, please?" I knew that it would be my last and that it wasn't a bad choice.

It was funny thinking about how Valerie was out there trying to get off of work. It made me feel less lonesome.

I'm not going to lie. I like being alone, but I don't like being alone in a room full of people. Actually, I don't like being alone that much, but I am alone quite a lot. It has made me pretty good at escaping inside myself.

The waitress brought me the whiskey and Coke. I thanked her, and I went back inside myself. Nothing in this room interested me. All I was waiting for was Valerie.

I began imagining where we would go. What it would be like, even who she was. What was she like? As soon as that thought hit me, I panicked. What if we didn't even like each other? Was this all going to be a nightmare? Was she going to work again tomorrow and I go to school on Monday?

I had to clear my head, but didn't have much time as Valerie came walking in. She came straight towards me. I felt petrified. It sounds dumb, but the looks of everyone on the couches turned me to stone for a moment. I guess I still did care about them.

Valerie leaned down and quietly spoke to me.

"Walk out in the hallway and pay at that bar. Then go out and wait on the stairway and I'll be there in a few minutes," she said.

"Okay," I responded. I barely looked at her, but it seemed like she had the plan locked down tight.

This was fucking madness.

She walked away and I felt how there were a lot of interested looks from the couch. Nothing could shake me now, as my confidence was back. I was going to meet with Valerie in the hall. It was such a relief and freaking exciting as well.

I took myself a good minute before I stood up. I tried to do it as quietly and unnoticeable as possible. I took my jacket, calmly swung it over my shoulder, and began walking. Passing the eyes on the couches felt like it lasted for eternities, but once I went through the door I got strangely calm. How could they be messing with me so much? I didn't care much as it was all over now. I walked straight to the small bar in the hallway.

"I would like to pay my bill," I said.

The girl behind the counter got up from a chair and prepared my bill. It was insanely expensive, like nothing I've ever seen.

I remember once when my family went out dining for my mom's birthday. It was a really nice restaurant and the food was fantastic. I remember having a look at the bill before my dad paid it, and the drinks there were not even as pricy as in here.

The counter girl handed me my credit card back. Thinking a little, it really was stupid. I know that these drinks were crazy expensive item wise, still I had just invited a stranger on a vacation on my tab. The funny thing is, though, that I won't feel bad about spending money. I only feel bad for misusing or paying over price. Of course, it was the girls that I had paid extra for in here, and that actually just disgusted me even more.

I finished the payment and told the girl good night. I got out into the hallway to find that one bouncer was gone. The other one stood with his arms crossed and looked at me. He greeted me good night without moving an inch.

I decided to walk down to the first floor and sit up against the wall. That way I wouldn't be in proximity of any of the two bouncers. As I sat down, I could feel how the red carpet was chilly and thin. It felt quite strange sitting there waiting. It was like waiting for one's turn at an oral exam. You know it's coming up and it's just a matter of minutes. There was no running away. You know the circumstances, but have absolutely no idea of how it's all going to go down. My patience when drunk isn't exactly noteworthy, but playing some good tunes is something that I find highly relaxing.

The second track had just started as she gently kicked me on my foot. I pulled out my earphones and got up. It was strange seeing her like that. She was wearing a grey fur-like coat and a red scarf.

"So what now?" she said with quite a positive smile.

I didn't know what to answer.

"What were you listening to?"

I looked down on my pocket not finding an answer.

"Ehmm …" There was a long silent break.

"Am I just going home feeling stupid now?" she said quite critically.

I just stood there.

"Ehh, no, no."

"So do you have a plan?" she asked more calmly.

"I kinda figured that we could go straight to the airport?"

"Straight to the airport? You're crazy." It sounds harsh, but she said it with a smile. I kept looking at her waiting for something more.

"Straight to the airport, really? Do you even have your passport, and shouldn't we go pack first?" she asked. My passport, my fucking passport. I didn't have it. It sounds like the stupidest thing ever. It basically implied that I hadn't thought anything through. I didn't even know how to dodge it.

"We do need to go get our passports, but if you want to we can just buy stuff there?"

"I would like to go pack," she said.

"All right."

"And where exactly is there?" she asked in a funny voice.

"That's what we figure out together," I said with a smile.

She wanted to go home to pack her stuff. I couldn't refuse. It is, after all, the most normal thing to do before traveling. I didn't want to pack anything. I also figured that it would make too much noise. I would just sneak into my room and get the passport and nothing else.

"So we go to my place so I can pack, then past your place, and then to the airport where we find a flight. Is that the plan?" she asked.

It sounded freaking crazy when said out loud like that.

"I guess it is," I said with a big drunk smile on my face. I mean, what we were doing right there was really funny to me. We turned and began walking down the stairs.

"What music did you just listen to?" Valerie asked.

"It was grunge right now, but I listen to a lot of different music."

"So do you like music a lot?"

"Yeah, I suppose I do," I replied.

As we exited the building, we both stayed quiet. It was no coincidence that I avoided all eye contact with the bouncer at the door. Not that we were in trouble, but I figured it was for the better.

We turned left as we exited the building. It was strange walking out into the night like this. It was cold and dark. I was thinking of how, if it had been a summer night, we would have seen the earliest rays from the rising sun. We didn't though. Instead we saw the dark blue sky with a horrendous white light to it. I'm glad I remember, as I didn't have too much energy to focus on my surroundings at the time.

Walking out the door into the fresh air together felt really special. It was like reality hit me, and I realized what I just had gotten myself, and most of all her, into. What were we about to do? That's what I asked myself.

"We can take a tram just a few blocks away," she said.

"Okay."

"My name is not Valerie, by the way," she said with a goofy smile. It really broke my panic and made me smile as well.

"What is it, then?" I asked curiously.

"Emma," she said confidently.

We smiled at each other while walking there. Her eyes were like nothing I had ever seen. The types of eyes that you get lost in, you drown in, and declare your love to until you're all out of words. That's what she did to me, and so we walked on in silence, strangers to each other calmly walking together. I bet we didn't, but I felt that we looked confident walking together. Not that there were many people around to look, yet it still felt good.

We had a good distance between us as we walked. It was kind of close, yet not intimate close. I felt it was a good beginning, but still the rational part of my brain was kicking the shit out of me. I don't remember how many times I was thinking of just making an excuse and leaving her.

Still, I kept telling myself that I would regret it and that I should keep my promises. I always told myself to keep the promises I made. If not, I shouldn't have made them. I grew up with a father that made tons of promises and only kept a few. It always pissed me off, or made me very sad. That's why I had sworn to myself never to be like that.

Till this day I actually think that it might have been the last stand that kept me in the deal. Of course, along with other things I had promised myself. Things like not being scared of opening myself to complete strangers, yet at that time they were still not strong enough.

We had only been on the sidewalk walking for a minute or two, yet in silence with a stranger that counts as months to me. I was fighting some inner demon that I just had the pleasure of meeting. It felt like all my cultural morals were sliding down my back. Like my entire family was whispering corruption in my ear. Corruption is a harsh word. They really only had good intentions, to be fair. It just doesn't always help. I ignored it; something different was filling up my mind.

This girl Emma, whom I barely knew, was already part of at least a hundred scenarios that I imagined. I gave myself a beating about it while we were walking there.

I didn't want to think like this, but my fantasy ran crazy on me. It was not that I even wanted any of the scenarios to really happen, well, maybe a few, but far from all of them. You can probably imagine what kind of stuff I was thinking about. Well, maybe not, as it was all so different. Some of it was pretty weird.

Leaving the comfort zone was already wearing on me. I couldn't figure out if my imagination acting like this was normal. I was trying to figure out if it was my nature and therefore a natural call in me. Maybe I had suppressed it for a long time?

I couldn't really figure it out. Maybe it was my socialization and the norms of my upbringing, or maybe it was something else? I did think it, yet I can't understand how I could picture myself having kids with Emma just after I'd gotten to know her. It's not that I really wanted to. It was just sort of fun thinking about how they might look and be.

Finally I could see the tram stop, and I felt thankful. My thoughts could go on rail instead of going somewhere completely crazy. Still, I wondered, nature, norms, or something else. I really couldn't tell.

We were standing at the tram stop. I didn't remember having been there before. Emma's face was lightly lit in yellow light from the lampposts. I looked at her and she at me. I felt so insecure, but I did my best not to show.

She smiled briefly and then I did the same. Then she smiled even more and we burst into a short laughter. It was magical. We both felt it and we didn't even need words to communicate it.

"So tell me. I got to know a little about you, now that I agreed on this quite stupid and crazy idea," she said. She was waiting for a reply, but I really didn't know what to answer.

"I'm not sure if I'm still gonna chicken out on you or what's going to happen. I know being a stripper is not exactly viewed as the nicest profession and that you can't be too sensitive, but that doesn't mean that you can try anything. I don't just go with strangers without any worries," she continued.

I was about to say something, but she just continued.

"It's only that you strike me like quite the transparent type. That's when it comes to evil, at least," she said with a smile.

I was glad she said that. I mean, about my exposed heart. It was something my friends and family always told me as well. Hearing it from a stranger was different, though. She just kept going.

"Are you sure you feel good about this? I've never heard about anyone doing silly shit like this. You have to promise me that you don't all of a sudden demand money from me, because I really haven't got any for that. Also, how can I know that you're not just drunk and making promises that you won't keep?" she asked.

It was a lot of questions, and even admitting that she might still bail out. I didn't know what to answer. It was like my IQ dropped to a third when we had left the gentlemen's club.

"You can't," I said.

Silence occurred. She was staring at me.

"I mean, you can never be sure of anything," I said.

She was still staring at me, waiting for me to explain. It's silly, but I basically took that statement out of this text that we once read in English class. I definitely wouldn't have said it if I hadn't been drunk. It was definitely a good reply between two fictional characters, but right there it was a shitty response. The only thing positive was that it was at least honest. She looked up at me completely misinterpreting me. Her doubtfulness transformed to anger.

"I can't? You know what, maybe this is a shitty idea," she said.

When I think about it, that moment was for sure the time where I was closest to blowing everything. I tried saving it by beginning to explain myself. My head suddenly felt clear again, and I began to explain. I'm sure that if it hadn't, and I had just stood there, then she would have left.

"I didn't mean it like that. I mean you have to trust me, because nobody ever can be sure. All we can do is trust," I said, trying to sound pseudo philosophical or something.

I could tell by the look on her face that she got my point.

"I don't trust you, though," she said with a smile that could have implied sarcasm. I still played it as cool as I could.

"Of course not, but maybe with time?" I said.

Of course she didn't trust me, but I could tell that her intuition told her that I wasn't the worst of persons.

I really sensed it, and as I looked at her, we had our first real intimate moment. It was about three seconds of raw eye contact. It may sound and seem like it wasn't much, but it was enough to send a crazy chill through every bone in my body. Maybe she felt it too.

At least the slightly disappointed and doubtful look on her face had disappeared. She had some of the most joyful eyes that I had ever seen. Even when they were in sad doubt like before they were still outstandingly beautiful.

"Traveling is a brilliant idea, if you ask me. Just imagine what we're gonna experience and see. Not to mention that we get to escape this," I said with a discrete smile.

"Escape from this, it would feel good," Emma said.

"I don't know if it's in the same sense as you, but trust me, I feel stuck. So, are we gonna travel together?" I asked.

"If you will you keep your promises?" Emma asked.

I took my time and mustered the most trustworthy, "Yes," that I could.

When I said that out loud, I actually realized why we were standing there. This shit hole of a city might actually be one of the major reasons why we would take off together. A mutual hate.

I couldn't figure out if that was a good or bad platform for a friendship. Thinking back on what I know about history, I remembered a lot of people who based their entire life and work on mutual hate. It can't be the worst place to start, but surely not the best either.

Being honest, I did lie when I said brilliant idea, but I sensed a need for it. Time was going to move on and something was going to happen. You never know what, but making the history worth remembering is a goal in itself.

There wasn't time for more, as the sounds of riding and rumbling on tracks were closing in. The hiss from the streetcar slowing down cut an open wound in the silent night. We both briefly covered an ear, looked at each other, and got on the tram.

Chapter 3: Tram rides and taxi drives

The tram on this line was old yet still very neat. It reminded me of an old film that I once watched. It was called something like *Taking Pelham*. I watched it when I was younger and remember liking it a lot. That's probably also why I remembered it and how the tram in it looked.

Emma and I had found seats opposite of each other. There was a sufficient number of drunken people on the tram enough to excuse not talking to each other. Of course, that's also the norm on the tube and trams. It's definitely different at night.

We just sat there and looked at each other and around us. It was almost like we didn't know each other. Technically we didn't, but we did a little now. Most of the people in the wagon were small groups of friends or couples in their twenties; it was the usual people out at this hour all except for one.

He was an old guy in a group of younger people. That's not so unusual, if not for the fact that he was dressed like them. It interested me. Emma leaned forward towards me.

"It's only an eight-minute ride," she said.

"All right," I replied with a smile. I don't know if she sensed that that I looked at him, but I couldn't resist.

The noise from the tram made it difficult to hear what they were talking about, but I could follow their gestures. They were what I would call hipsters, yet they seemed more confident than the usual. They definitely had something to drink, but they weren't annoying, just outgoing.

They pulled small gimmicks and jokes on each other and laughed together. For what they were they seemed like a really nice little group.

It felt so natural, but I could see the wrinkles on his face from over here. It was like I was the only one that saw him for what he was, an old man in disguise. I believe he even wore makeup to make his skin look youthful. Didn't they know? Did they ignore it? Him acting like them, dressing like them, and smiling like them? They acted like he was one of their own, how could it be? How could a person be that old and want to act like he was in his twenties?

I felt weird watching them. The alcohol was making my head feel heavy. Like nothing felt normal anymore. It was as if the world was still more strange and distorted as in a dream. A dream that I couldn't figure out how to end. Could I stop looking? I don't know. I didn't try. It really didn't feel like a possibility in that unreal state of mind. Such a strange time.

I looked over at Emma. She was either more observant than I first assumed, or I was more obvious than I first assumed. Either way she was looking at me. It was kind of a skeptical look. I hope she didn't think of me as a stalker freak. She obviously saw me looking at them.

I smiled at her and with my eyes led her eyes towards the old man. Luckily she had seen him too and smiled back. It felt good not being the only one seeing something strange.

"We're getting off at the next stop," she said in a way that I almost had to lip-read.

I replied with a discrete smile. I don't remember the number of the tramline, but it drove into a lousy part of town. The architecture had changed to a lot of grey concrete buildings. That's only the architecture, though. The rest I didn't know about yet.

We had less than a minute left of the tram ride, and yet I couldn't resist peaking at the old man in disguise. He lifted his old weather-beaten wrinkled hands out of his pocket. On the fingers were several rings and a tattoo. I couldn't figure out his motive from over here, but it seemed disgusting.

With the tip of his tongue he slowly licked the commissure of his lips; it was vulgar. He was an old man lost in youth, barely standing from the alcohol in this late night hour. Trying to keep up with a youth that overtook him a long time ago.

He frightened me, gave me a dazed feeling, like nothing could change the world from getting more distorted and frayed.

"It's now," Emma got up and so did I. Luckily that was a feeling I never indulged in. The tram seems like a haze, but like exiting the gentlemen's club, exiting the tram really sparked the life in me.

The platform was grey and dull. The cold concrete was still moist from the morning dew. I had never been on this platform before. It had to be on the complete opposite side of town from where I lived.

Emma led the way, and we walked into a somewhat uninspiring neighborhood. It's not that it was bad or anything, just plain concrete. It made me wonder who really got the idea that they wanted to build housing like this. It's practical, I know, but I think architecture should be a joy to look at. Maybe I'm being too romantic, I don't know.

Emma began telling me about how we weren't very far from her home by now, and how she would like me to stay down on the parking lot while she went in and packed her things.

When she was talking like that, it suddenly felt like we had known each other forever. Everything just seemed so regular and normal. It wasn't. I was getting very tired. The cold morning air only keeps you fresh for that long. I tried concentrating my energy on answering Emma clearly.

She didn't want me to know how she lived, and I actually didn't have a big problem with it. I didn't know if she lived with anyone, maybe even her parents. With that thought in mind, I found it perfectly fine waiting in the parking lot.

We got to the parking lot outside of the apartment buildings. There were apartment blocks all around it. Beside the parking lot was a little park. It had swings and plants that were covered in a thin layer of icy morning dew. The moon made it sort of light grey, like all the colors had disappeared for a while. This is where she wanted me to wait.

"You can just wait around here, it won't be long," she said.

I agreed and told her that I would order a cab to be here in twenty minutes. She didn't think that it was a lot of time, but she too felt the cold and wouldn't let me be out there for so long. She starting walking, but turned around and looked at me.

"Are we seriously doing this?" she asked from the distance. I already had my phone in my hand while feeling partly hungover and partly drunk.

"Yeah," I said. It made her laugh, but thinking back I must have looked really hilarious. It wasn't something that I paid much attention to at first, but the girl had humor.

She turned around and went inside a building. Suddenly I just found myself standing there in the parking lot freezing. Calling a taxi only took thirty seconds, and so there was a lot of time to kill. I took a deep breath and exhaled. The air looked like smoke in the cold air. The moon was illuminating it in the dark night.

It was dark around here. There were a few lampposts lighting the lonely park and parking lot. I looked around, only a few out of a hundred apartments had light in them. I turned on the spot to look around; what else could I do?

The cold crept up on me from below. It was cold. Walking around getting the muscles to work a little kept a little warmth in me.

Slowly I just escaped inside my mind. I imagined how it would be. That came first. How was the trip going to be? Would it be like an adventure? It wasn't long before other thoughts and fantasies began streaming through my head.

Who was she? Who did she live with? What was she really like? Why did she work as a stripper? Was I even awake?

I was.

I tried to clear my head. Just focusing on thinking on nothing. That's something I taught myself to do. I usually do it at times when my thoughts begin flowing rapidly and way too freely. I found it seemingly hard though.

Her name was Emma, she lived in an apartment building, supposedly alone. She was beautiful and worked as a dancer in a strip club, yet not being promiscuous. Also, she obviously felt enough desire to leave this place that she would go with a pretty average-looking young man like me.

Who was she? Why the fuck did she work that job?

Maybe she did it to feed her sisters, or maybe she liked it and used all the money on herself and nice things? Maybe she lived with her parents, maybe she didn't.

My thoughts were broken in two by two eyes in a not so distant window. It was on the first floor in one of the apartment buildings. They looked at me from what I suppose was the kitchen window of the apartment. I looked back and we just stood there looking at each other. I suppose that they were the only two eyes awake, except of course for Emma and me. I bet he slept in the kitchen as his owners had left the light on. He probably never slept for that long, and so I imagined how he crawled on the kitchen table by the window, so that he could look out at the world every early morning when he woke up. Few eyes contain less evil than the ones of such a creature.

Suddenly this feeling of the supernatural descended upon me again; it was the same as on the tram. The eyes led me to the same place as the elderly teenage-like man.

It felt so surreal, and suddenly I couldn't really handle all the consequences, as I began thinking about them. What should I tell my parents, what would they do when I didn't come home? I really had to make some sort of plan. I had to tell them that I went somewhere where they could trust I would be safe.

Still they would be mad at me for skipping school the last five days. Really it was only four days, but still. I also had to do it all without Emma knowing.

It all overwhelmed me. I took out my headset and began to untangle the cable, as always. I always wondered how it was able to tangle so bad every goddamn time.

Finally, the music began playing. I chose Mellon Collie and the Infinite Sadness. That record always had something on me, it was like a soundtrack to real life. You can probably guess who showed it to me. Hair or no hair, Corgan would have been freezing to death out here as well. Though he would at least have had his angel voice going down with us.

I didn't remember thinking anything else before the taxi driver was calling me.

"I will be there in five minutes." Hearing his dark masculine voice somehow threw me out of imagination and back into the cold reality.

I was alone. Only thing I knew was that I was standing right there, and Emma was inside that grey building. Maybe the greyest of buildings in all of human history. I felt weird. What if I walked away now? Everything could go back to normal in a split second. I could probably avoid ever meeting her again. She would be sad, but understand.

These things really ran down my spine, and I had to tell myself, no. You made a promise, you've made a plan, and now you're going to stick to it and keep your promises. I had never felt inner torture, but this must be what it is like. I was so goddam terrible, what was going to happen now? I couldn't handle any of these thoughts, all those potential consequences.

I don't remember thinking anything in particular as the taxi rolled in on the ice-covered road towards the parking lot. The silent humming from the engine reminded me of how nice and warm it can be inside a car. I looked towards the apartment building that Emma had entered. I couldn't see anything.

I made myself visible to the taxi, and it pulled up next to me. I couldn't resist getting in the nice and heated car, even though it meant that the meter would be running. The contrast of the taxi and the park was like nothing I had ever experienced. The cozy backseat combined with my fatigued body was not the best thing possible at the time. Though I did at least manage to tell the driver my name, and that we were waiting for a girl named Emma before I tugged in.

I woke as Emma opened the door. She looked at me like I can't describe. I can't imagine how miserable and tattered I must've looked. Luckily for me, adrenaline kicked in. I exited the car promptly. Emma had the front door open and was looking over it at me standing there.

"I'm sorry. I'm just really exhausted, to be honest."

Luckily she wasn't mad and she just smiled.

"It's almost dawn, and you've been drinking. Of course you're tired."

I smiled since I didn't really know what to expect, but she was so cool. I walked around the door and helped her with her luggage. As we closed the trunk, we just awkwardly stood there in front of each other.

She was thinking something.

"Hug?" Emma asked.

I didn't react until she just hugged me.

It felt fantastic. I could smell her scent even though I didn't turn my nose towards her head. It gave me that extra portion of energy that can suddenly appear. I didn't feel that tired anymore. We stepped away from each other, and all I could think was how weird and surreal this really was.

"That was nice," Emma said with a smile.

"Yeah—" I mumbled out in a low voice.

"How do you feel?" Emma asked. How was I feeling? I hadn't run away yet. I couldn't really think of much else.

"Good," I said with a smile.

The meter was rolling and the yellow lights ran quickly through the car, one after another. This situation would have been the most awkward if I had looked at it from an outside perspective.

The driver was quiet as he drove. He was probably tired from a long night of drunks and douche bags. Emma and I sat on the backseat and were both quiet as well, yet it wasn't awkward.

I don't know if it was the hug from before, or if it was something else. I was looking at the road disappearing under the car and wasn't sweating, panicking inside, or anything that I expected. At least not right now. I turned my body and looked at Emma instead. I had a feeling that she was already looking at me.

"So where should we go?"

She looked like she just now realized that we didn't plan anything. The way she looked, she was so beautiful, but it seemed unreal. Was I on drugs, was she? How can things get this sensual?

She just started laughing, and I followed with a quiet laugh and a smile. I was thinking of possibilities, as nothing sadly happens by itself. The driver looked over his shoulder. I reckon he found us to be really weird. Emma had stopped laughing, but she still kept her hand in front of her mouth as she had a hard time stopping.

Suddenly we were the pupils in the classroom that couldn't stop laughing, and the taxi driver with his strained rearview mirror look was the teacher. We sat there for a while before the mood eased out.

"What about we just go on Google maps and just look at the maps, and then we decide where we wanna go. Or we check for the cheapest tickets departing within a few hours and pick one? What do you think?"

"That sounds reasonable," Emma replied.

So now we had some kind of plan, but we were still strangers to each other. I kept thinking about how it would be safest to open up to her, get to know her. I wasn't really afraid of it anymore as she seemed pretty cool, but deep inside I still was.

Luckily my place wasn't too big of a de-route driving to the airport. I was tired but kept awake, as I had given the driver my real address. I didn't want him to pull up right in front of my house. Just an idle engine can seem strange around there at that time of night. I wanted him to stop on the main road and then I would run to the house, sneak in and get the passport.

The driver pulled over as I told him to. Emma was being a little curious, as we weren't exactly in front on any house. I felt really drunk when I got out, but concentrated on walking normally.

When I turned around the corner onto my street, I was getting nervous. What if I met someone in the hallway, if someone was going to the kitchen or toilet? It would ruin everything.

The street was quiet and cold. A couple of streetlights and the regular Christmas lights from the houses were lighting it. The Farrell's house was always the most decorated. They really had a thing for Christmas lights. Wonder what Jesus would say if he saw what had come of it.

My room was on the first floor. It meant that I had to go in through the house, up some rather creaking stairs, and into my room. I opened the door as slowly as possible and even that felt like it made way too much noise. As silently as possible I got rid of my shoes and walked inside.

Light was coming through the windows into the house. It looked kind of scary. I didn't feel welcome; it was a strange feeling. It didn't quite feel like the home it really was to me. I really felt attached to that house. I think it's quite a normal thing. A house is not just an inanimate object.

As I walked up the stairs, I concentrated my best not to make noises. It was impossible, but when you know them you can minimize the noise quite a lot.

I got to the first floor and began walking towards my room. I constantly peaked over my shoulder towards my parents' bedroom at the other end. I got to my room and opened the door. It was one of the better and less creaky doors in the house.

I got in and closed the door behind me; it was a relief. I used my phone as a flashlight, as I didn't want to turn on any light. I knew exactly where my passport was, and I went straight for it. Just for second I was thinking about packing some clothes, but I decided not to. It simply wasn't worth the risk. The only other thing I grabbed was my cell phone charger. Now it was just about getting out again.

Slowly and silently I exited the room. I walked down the stairs into the living room area that I had to pass through. I still remember the light freaking me out. It was like I didn't feel welcome, like the walls knew that I was up to something.

At the end of the stairway all our family pictures were hanging on the wall. I looked at some of the family pictures. I looked around at the whole family. I loved them so much, and still something just alienated me. I was looking at a portrait of myself. It wasn't like looking in a mirror.

I stood there for a while looking at these pictures. It felt rather unreal, my sister and brother, mother and father. They were all there. What was the deal?

I couldn't stay there any longer. I turned around and began sneaking out. The house was silent like a monastery. With the long casts of light, it even looked a little like it. I turned my back on it all, put on my shoes, and exited the house.

My heart was beating like a horse in full gallop. I'd managed without panicking, and I still felt like going back to Emma. The adrenaline pumping kind of repressed the alcohol, but still my heart beating fast made me feel even drunker. I turned around the corner and got into the cab. It was reality.

The ride from my house was calmer. The sun was slowly rising, and we didn't have any big obstacles to face.

We pulled up in front of the airport and asked the driver to just let us out at the main entrance. Emma sat in the car while I paid the bill. She could have gone out and gotten the luggage, but yet again, we weren't busy. I figured that she might also want to see me actually pay something. After all, it was what I had promised to do, and this was the first time I had to. As far as she knew my credit card could be false or nonexistent. I guess it gave her some kind of calmness when I paid.

We grabbed the bag in the trunk. I, of course, helped Emma with her big one. It was a quiet morning in the airport, or as quiet as it gets in a big international airport, of course. I closed the trunk carefully. The sky was pink and yellow from the sunrise.

"That's some sunrise," I said. Emma looked at it as well.

"It's beautiful," she replied. We stood for a moment enjoying it before we turned around and walked out of the cold morning air and into the seemingly warm airport terminal.

We looked around. Emma looked at me, probably wondering what I was thinking or something. I let her lead the way.

First we were just looking for a departure overview. It was our only possibility, after all. I've heard about the last minute deals in airports, but I don't think it really exists anymore.

As we walked, I was thinking of how strange a place an airport is. There are always people on the move, they never stop moving, and still no one seems to attach anything to the place. That's even for the people working there, and that is a lot. It is essentially a non-place with all its weird unnatural-looking food wrapped in plastic, loads of billboards, and the weird woman voice in the speakers.

It kind of fitted our peculiar situation pretty well. I was still deadly tired, and I think that the lack of sleep was what kept my other senses down. If I'd been wide-awake and sober, I would probably have panicked.

We were standing in front of the departure screen. We were looking at names, and we decided to sit down and check for some available tickets online.

Emma picked a spot to sit and I followed.

"God, it's gonna be so good to get away," I said.

Emma agreed with a very determined look.

Suddenly I remembered how I had to write my mom an excuse, but I had to do that later.

I took out my phone and downloaded an application for flight tickets. Emma did the same, and we started browsing tickets. For a second, I just realized, even more than usual, how awesome smartphones are.

From where we were sitting we could still see the scheduled departure screen. We both began checking tickets for them online. It was a big airport and there were basically flights going everywhere.

We kind of discussed where we wanted to go, but there were so many possibilities. We wanted to go as soon as possible, but it seemed that we had to wait at least a couple of hours. Emma had found some reasonably priced tickets that would take us far away to a place neither of us had been before, basically tickets to a new world. The world seemed so blissful, like a hazy dream. There was no deceit, nothing bad in the world at that very moment.

Emma had chosen three flights that she thought we should choose from. I had chosen one, but looking at Emma's, we discarded mine pretty quickly. We discussed the pros, cons, and prices.

The cheapest would take us far away, but to a country that reminded us of our own. The middle priced would take us far away to a culture we didn't know, as would the most expensive. The big difference, though, was that if we picked the middle-priced flight, our destination would be cheaper because of the exchange rate. At least that's what we thought, but we had never been there before.

It was kind of a silly way to pick destinations, and I think we also got a good laugh out of it. We booked the tickets and began to find out how to get our luggage checked in and boarding passes done.

It was quite easy considering that we already were in the airport. We went to the airline's information counter and figured it all out. That meant that we could go through security and probably even get a couple of hours sleep on the other side, which we were pretty satisfied with.

We got into quite a calm security area. The guys working there also looked tired, but compared to us it was in the "had to get up early" kind of way.

It was nice not having to rush in the security check. Usually this airport is really busy. The four other times I had been on flights, security had always been rushed. We took our time and got through. By then it was like we were just doing it.

We didn't even know each other, but it didn't seem to matter much at the time. It was strange, but we had given ourselves a purpose, a goal of getting somewhere, and now we were just doing it. That's really how it was, without it having to sound like a Nike slogan.

Airport waiting seats really aren't made for comfortable sleep, that's one thing I can tell you. We had found two empty rows that we could rest on. Given our situation, we both tugged in really quickly.

I opened my eyes, sat up, and looked over at Emma. She seemed to still be asleep. I felt relaxed but also very unkempt and a little hungover. That combined with the lack of sleep didn't make a good combo.

I had fallen asleep with in-ears in and Chet Baker was still playing. God, it is such good sleeping music. I tried to get my head straight and look around. We were sleeping just outside our gate and it was starting to a get a little crowded. Once again that surreal feeling was coming up in me. The same feeling that I had while being drunk and dreamy. I'd arranged a trip with a stripper, and in drunkenness I had decided to leave without any luggage, not even a handbag.

I was totally screwed in my head, at least it sounded like that. I mean, if you were to tell the story, then that would pretty much be the story. Of course, you can romanticize it, but people would put it like that. It sounded crazy. I didn't think of myself as crazy, and I didn't feel crazy. Was I crazy?

I was thinking about that for a while, but suddenly I realized that I had to text my mom, and that it had to be a good one. What was I going to write? I had to excuse my absence for an unknown amount of the days at the time.

I was contemplating for a while and then the idea came to me. I would say I was sleeping over at Calvin's. It wasn't something that I had done too much, but that was exactly why my mom would be happy about it. It meant that she wouldn't ask too many questions, or at least I hoped so.

As I was getting towards the end of the text, I realized that it was a little weird to send a text like this in the morning, but it was getting to nine o'clock, so I guess it wasn't as bad as seven. I mean, I was a teenager, after all. I ended up sending the text and turning my phone to flight mode. Not long after, the gate opened and they began boarding the flight. I walked around to wake Emma up, but she was just snoozing and perfectly aware of what was going on.

"Good morning, slept well?" I said in the best sarcastic voice I could produce.

Emma also looked unkempt, but in a beautiful way.

She sat herself up.

"I hate life. What are we doing here?" she said in a rigid voice.

I looked at her and she was looking at me. It was a dreadful kind of look. My stomach almost felt like it was on a roller coaster ride. It was a harsh thing to say; it didn't seem like her at all. Finally, I sensed the thick sarcasm. Emma smiled and so did I. God, I was slow that morning.

I picked up her bag and put it on one of the seats. We were hanging back, no need for waiting in line. We didn't speak much. I guess we were both very tired. I was thirsty, and Emma was as well. I walked to the closest shop to get some water. I bought some gum as well. I couldn't exactly taste my own breath, but I supposed that it wasn't that good.

When I got back, Emma had gotten up and walked to the back of the line. The line was moving pretty fast, and people seemed so eager. I didn't and still don't understand why people are so eager to get on the plane. You already know which seat you're going to get, it's so fucking crowded, and they sure won't fly without you.

I didn't understand, but we had water and gum, so I was satisfied.

The line was gone and we could calmly, in our own tempo, walk onto the airplane bridge kind of thing. The stewardess was smiling at us. I think she enjoyed seeing someone not being in a hurry. I told Emma how we really had to do some shopping for me, as soon as we got out of the plane. She laughed and just found it very funny. I guess it reminded her that I had left completely without luggage. Man, what was this plan, even?

Chapter 4: Metal Bird and a reasonably priced dream.

I leaned my head back while contemplating and scrolling through the music library on my good old iPod Classic. What music fitted the world in that moment? That is what I asked myself.

It had to be soft, tender, and relaxing. I was going through a lot of different stuff, mostly film soundtracks. I actually love listening to film soundtracks. There's that sense of completeness and story in many of them. It's that kind of common thread that is rarely found on a regular record. That's the positive side. There are also some huge downsides, but I won't talk about them now.

I had finally narrowed it down to four different choices. It was either going to be the *Twin Peaks* soundtrack, *In Bruges* soundtrack, the *Paris, Texas* soundtrack or *The Last of Us* soundtrack.

The Last of Us wasn't even a movie soundtrack, but I think it counts. Actually, these four were also some of my all-time favorites. Right when I was about to pick, I remembered another record that I thought might fit.

When I got to it, I was done scrolling. It was the perfect record. It would just totally fit sleeping in the air, in a relaxed and dreamy way. Once again it was a record that I had heard about from Calvin. It was an old jazz album by Stan Getz and a guy named Joγo Gilberto, whom I didn't know too well. I didn't understand the vocals, as they were in Portuguese. It didn't matter at all, though. It was such a calm and beautiful record.

The file on my iPod was one continues file, so I didn't know how many songs it was actually divided into. I probably could've counted by listening, but I didn't.

Taking off over a big city in the early morning is special. All the black spots looked like water. It looked like the city was floating. The airport terminal looked so small, yet I know it wasn't. We had just been down there, spending about twenty minutes just to walk to the gate. I felt small as my eyes fell upon all those yellow lights all connected and holding hands. It was as far as the eye could see.

I felt longing, and in some weird way I recognized how small I was. How small we all are, really. This time in space was all there was. All the memories I had had passed and they were no longer my life. This was.

There were so many flickering lights and I couldn't tell whether it was TVs and houses or lampposts. Given the early hour it probably wasn't TV's or houses as much as lampposts.

I kept looking at the massive city even though my view wasn't that good anymore. There were a few thin, black clouds looking very ghostly in the yellow light cast from underneath. The moon was crawling back on the other side, and sunlight felt like it had come to stay.

Insignificance is a feeling that hits hard. I tried really hard to tell myself that I wasn't. As I leaned towards the window and looked down, I really felt longing. I knew that someone down there in the flickering lights was looking at this plane and longing. Someone down there wanted to be here. In the early morning light, headed into the rising sun still with yesterday's blue hour in fresh memory.

God, I wish that I knew that person. At least we did share thoughts for a second, and that can be enough, I guess. With the perfect jazz playing, I slowly tugged in and escaped into the world of dreams. I felt hazy like in a dream. My anxiety was gone at least for that time.

As I opened my eyes, I felt nicely rested. I had never slept on an airplane before. I mean, literally slept without waking up once in a while. Emma was already awake and looking out of the window.

"Good morning," she said.

"Good morning. How long have you been awake?"

"Oh, not for too long. Look, we're almost already there," she pointed at the screen in the seat in front of her. It's the screen where you can watch movies and stuff, the one that also shows the flight route. We were actually almost there, as the screen said eighty-five minutes until arrival, which would make this one of the most convenient flights ever.

Soon the world was going to be different; of course, also the same, but everything would be kind of new, I supposed. As I was sitting there trying to look out the window, it struck me. How weird it is that you can get inside a box of metal and sit more or less comfortable for a given amount of hours and then get out of it and experience a whole new world.

From where we were sitting we could see the wing out the window. All the small metal rivets. I couldn't comprehend how that piece of metal was holding us all in the air. I know that some remarkable engineers had calculated everything, but the flight was really just a collection of metal plates, wires, computers, engines, etcetera. It was all just things put together, but together it was magic.

Thinking about it, it really amazed me how it worked. I actually really admire the people who can build such stuff for the rest of us. It was poetic and magical. Usually I would just love the concept. Maybe get amazed by ideas and stories about flights.

The true reason, though, for me to really understand, love, and worship handcraft like this that was my father.

He taught me to look at things for what they are in a technical manner. There's always a reason why different metal parts work together and are able to fly, for example. It was like that with everything. He didn't care much for the magical and poetic way of looking at things. He just cared about how and why they worked.

I actually think that it's kind of a blessing for me to have something from both sides. I mean, I can always look at stuff for what it is and how it works, yet still also let myself fall into the feeling it creates in me. The only disadvantage is not knowing which foot to stand on sometimes. That's what I thought until I learned that there's always a way of finding balance.

One thing I know for sure is that when you first start to think about balance and then take a look around, that's when a lot of things become interesting. Smartphones, TV screens, I knew how to use them, but who didn't? What I didn't know was how they worked; it was literally like magic to me. It may sound stupid, I don't know. Of course, I know that there are some kind of wires and electronics connected to a motherboard, but how that can show a movie or a flight position was still a mystery to me.

I decided to think a little out loud and told Emma how technology amazes me. She actually followed more than I would have thought, and we got into talking a little about how everything is like that. How in modern society we don't create things ourselves and, therefore, we won't know how they are produced, and then we won't have a healthy relationship with the product.

It became quite an interesting conversation, but that wasn't even the most important part. The most important part was that I now knew that we would be able to talk about something.

It felt good, but I still wasn't sure. After I'd woken up, I felt completely out of the bliss, to be honest. I wasn't drunk, the dreamy feeling was gone, and concerns actually really began stacking up.

My anxiety when drunk was nothing compared to this. I mean, I never really considered abandoning the trip because I had made that promise, but I kind of did anyway. What if we couldn't talk about anything? I mean, we just did, but what if it all turned awkward?

Thoughts like that rose quickly in me, but it was still a spell, as I was still madly attracted to her appearance and aura. I don't know if that's something that you can say about a real person. Honestly, I think it entered my vocabulary through playing Diablo, but aura was a good word, I think.

It wasn't just her appearance, but the way she went about everyone and everything and the way she looked when she did it. I haven't mentioned this yet, but it was everything from the taxi diver, people at the airport to the stewardesses. Of course, she was just being normal, but it was like she did it with a certain energy and tone. It wasn't many people to tell from, but I could.

I don't remember meeting other people who were like her. After a second thought, I believed that it was what got me attracted to her in the first place. I mean, out of all the girls in that club and all the other possibilities in the world, I winded up asking her.

All that, though, was still just inside my head. How she would really be, that is what scared me. Before we knew it, the seat belt sign had come on and the pilot had put us all safely on the ground. We had trusted him with our lives, and he had proved our trust right.

Now I felt weird again. We had reached the point where people could exit the airplane. People were really rushing and squeezing just like when they were entering the airplane.

I had gotten up in the rush and noticed that Emma was still sitting down. When I had gotten her bag from the overhead compartment, I sat down again.

"Is something wrong?" I asked.

"No, everything is all right. People just always rush like crazy when they're leaving airplanes. I mean, we're not in a hurry, why bother?"

She really did think like me. People really were rushing like crazy. We were on vacation, and that should equal no worries and no hurries.

"God, I really need a shower," Emma said.

"I can't even imagine how much," I answered.

"I mean, I don't mean it like that," I continued.

Emma laughed. Probably because I looked silly and she knew I didn't mean it in a bad way.

"I mean soon, soon we'll have a place to stay and shower."

We both craved that idea so much. We decided to go to a McDonald's in the airport, as we knew they would have decent Wi-Fi. I guess it's an old trick, just buying a small Coke to get the password.

Nonetheless, it's still a good trick and we quickly began searching for hotels. Once again it was Emma who found a nice-looking place at a decent rate. It didn't seem to be too far out of the city center. It was an old but neat hotel built entirely out of black painted wood. It had outdoor stairways and was completely surrounded by tennis courts.

It seemed to be some kind of tennis-oriented hotel, if such a thing exists. It was placed in the hills outside of the city, and at night one could see the flickering lights of the city in the distance. It looked and sounded like a dream at a reasonable rate.

"We could just stay there for the night and then make a plan for what to do?" Emma said.

I agreed, and so Emma booked it for one night. We figured that we could always extend if need be.

We checked the transport possibilities and quickly figured out that the easiest way of getting there was the tram. From the tram stop it would be a ten- to fifteen-minute walk.

We looked up the tram network of the city and quickly learned that trams apparently were quite a big thing in this city. Being in the airport, we would have to catch a train to the city center and from there transfer to a tramline.

Boy, the Internet really made it easy to travel.

We picked up our stuff and left the McDonald's. Getting to the train station and platform was pretty easy. It was basically part of the airport and we were just walking through the crowd. It was like we both really just wanted to get there. We both felt pretty unkempt, but it didn't even matter anymore.

The crowd was pretty busy, and I realized how many people we actually are. I mean, not really, but there were so many. Everybody tending to their own business and barely noticing each other. Then again, I had a feeling that people noticed each other in some way. That's Emma and I included.

I wondered how we looked next to each other. I didn't feel like it was like back home on the street walking together for the first time. That time I felt that we felt really cool, it wasn't like Mickey and Mallory cool, but still. When you're out of your own town, people just seem different, or maybe it's me who seems different to people. It's like you know that you will probably never see them again, and that makes you wanna leave a really good impression with them.

We got onto the train and everything went pretty smooth. We couldn't talk on the train, as we were standing just too far from each other.

Emma was looking out of the window. She had a beautiful, longing look on her face. The sunlight was flashing by and gently lighting her face. I wondered what she was thinking about? I couldn't know.

Then I started wondering who might be thinking about her. I didn't know yet, but everybody has someone in their lives. Who Emma had in hers and what troubled her mind was something I didn't know anything about yet. Was she even troubled? It was hard to tell if something was hidden under her skin.

I looked around the train but didn't get a vibe. It was like the surroundings didn't matter much compared to last night. Last night was also a little extraordinary.

Generally, I think it's something that I'm pretty good at. Many people tend to not appreciate where they are just now. It sounds very cheesy, but every day can't be the shit. Life is pretty ordinary. You can at least try to enjoy the little things in the moment. This is actually almost entirely my grandmother's words. It's stuff like this she would be telling me.

I think it's a virtue our generation is forgetting. The smell of green grass, flowers, when the light falls in the perfect angle, small human gestures, it's all overlooked most of the time. I remember how she used to read out loud from old poetry collections. It wasn't anything pretentious, just really simple and great poetry. It was about everything and often made small things feel significant.

It was our stop. The train door opened and we got off. I was reminding myself to enjoy and experience my surroundings, but it seemed like it didn't work when forcing it. It has to come from some poetic place in the heart. It takes practice.

We minded the gap between the train and the platform and suddenly we were on this quite empty platform. We could finally talk a little and discussed the way of getting there while looking at the boards.

I wanted to ask her about her family, but I held it back; it had to be at the right moment.

We walked through the station and got to an escalator. It was a quite new but really classically designed station. I've always liked underground architecture, and this was no different.

On top of the escalator we found the tram stop. The tram didn't leave as often as the underground, but we got lucky and almost directly got on one. Emma got to sit at the window this time as well. In a tram it doesn't really matter though. It was really nice because you could see the city and everything while being transported. In that way it was so much better than the underground.

"How do you feel?" I asked.

"What?" She got it. She was just surprised by the question.

"How do you feel, are you still happy about being here?"

"Yeah, I mean, being honest, then it's quite surreal in a way." We were talking in low voices given all the strangers that were around.

"Surreal is a good word for it, I think." She looked glad when I said that.

"I don't know if you want to answer this or if it's a good idea asking it, but how is your life back home? Who did you leave behind?" Emma looked at me and then out of the window.

"I'm sorry," I said.

"No, it's all right, but it's not something that we need to talk about right now. I mean, I don't want to talk about it right now." The tone she said it in made me sure not to try to ask the same in any different way.

"I'm sorry," I said.

"No, don't be. It's all right," she said in a soft but very determined voice. I was waiting for the right time, and this surely wasn't it. It became the end of that conversation, at least for the time being.

We had reached our tram stop and got off in a very cozy suburban area. It had small shops here and there, beautiful brick buildings, and a bunch of other good stuff which just gave it charm.

We had turned network roaming on our phones off. It was simply just too expensive. What it meant, though, was that we had to ask directions. Emma had been clever enough to screenshot a map, but it turned out to be a real struggle.

The first person we asked was a young student. Her English was decent, so it wasn't that, but she sent us in the complete opposite direction of what we needed. We only realized that after asking three other people.

The guy who saved us was in a suit dealing cars. Not exactly the type of guy I would normally ask directions, but he had time and a smartphone. He showed us the route on a map and we finally got it right.

I was carrying Emma's bag and it was actually pretty heavy. We got back to where we had initially gotten off the tram and were now walking to the other side.

The thing about this place was that on this side of the tramline there were hills and they were pretty steep. We walked up some stairs and got into a park. In the park there was a twisted path, which we followed to the top. The park was beautiful; there's nothing like a park when it's summer.

A cool breeze came through the heat, it smelled of vegetation and helped clear the mind. Both Emma and I agreed that the area was fantastic. We had been pretty lucky with choosing our destination considering the time zones. Us staying up late and sleeping on the plane fitted the time difference almost perfectly.

When we got to the top of the park we came into a very nice neighborhood. It was all big, white houses and a lot of trees and grass. On both sides of the road there were big beautiful trees. It seemed like it had given the roads a right to be there. Like nature invited it to be there and not the other way around.

We kept on walking and slowly began to doubt about the last few directions we had gotten. There was a women walking with a pram coming towards us. She walked slowly as she had a small boy walking on the side of the pram. We stopped her and

Emma began talking to her. Her English wasn't very good, but she was doing her very best.

She was tall, had lively eyes and long black hair. She looked like a nice mom and she was a very beautiful woman for her age. I peaked in the pram where this small little creature was just sleeping so peacefully. Her bigger brother standing on the side of the pram was all ears. He seemed really fascinated by Emma. I guess he didn't really know about different languages. I don't know if you do at the age of three or four.

He just had these big, beautiful, brown eyes. He noticed that I was looking at him and he got a little shy. Shy in the way kids do when they notice that you notice them. It's like they think it's embarrassing that they subconsciously are working full speed to observe and adapt to you. His mom noticed too, and she smiled at him and then me. I smiled back and thanked her for the directions. She wished us a happy holiday and we both smiled and walked on.

We talked a little about her, her kids, and how nice they were. It kind of saddened me knowing that we would probably never see them again. It is like that with some people, strangers that you wish you could spend more time with, but life just isn't like that. People are at different places in their lives, and you have to meet the right ones at the right time.

We got around a corner and then we could see this lousy hotel sign. It didn't look like much, but we didn't care. We were exhausted and had reached a bed. It felt like a relief, but really wasn't, as the steepest of all the hills was the last one.

It was so hot, and the sweat began to flow rather freely. That's even just from carrying one bag. There was a fair bit of bloodthirsty mosquitos having a go at us.

It felt really funny coming from home and the cold winter into this mosquito-filled heat wave. The temperature combined with the moist air and my winter clothes made it terrible. The mosquitoes kept flying in both our faces, and we kept using one of our hands to wipe them away. I, however, still managed to swallow one. I couldn't stop wondering whose blood it had inside when it went down my throat.

"A taxi might have been a better choice," Emma said.

She really made me smile. Her timing was just the greatest thing. Just when we were about there she mentioned a taxi.

That in itself was pretty banal, but in the tone and with the cheekiness she had, it was perfect.

Finally we arrived at driveway at the top. The smell of red clay and flowers filled our nostrils. It was such a relaxing smell. We were both pretty satisfied with being there as everything was going so smooth. I was pretty nervous about how it would turn out with the room, if it would be awkward when we weren't occupied anymore.

The hotel was pretty beautiful in real life as well. Emma thought it looked neat, too. I mean, it wasn't fantastic like the pictures and description, but I just think it kind of was. I had a weakness for buildings like this. Especially with it being surrounded by tennis courts.

I'm sure most people would have thought of it as quite lousy, or kind of mediocre or something, but I didn't. It might also have something to do with the inner feeling I had at the time. I don't know.

There were a few guys going at it on the first tennis court we had to pass. Looking at them made me miss playing. I had been playing myself for three years when I was younger. I wasn't good or anything. I just reckoned it was a really fun sport.

We came walking in through the empty restaurant area which looked like something from a late 1980s' commercial for charter-vacations.

As we walked inside the lobby, a thicker and crumbier air filled our nostrils. A tender, old woman's voice welcomed us.

You could tell that she had greeted a decent amount of people throughout the years. The reception was small and old, just like her. It was true and faithful to the wooden outside, but had the interior classics, like the watches on the wall. If I'm not mistaken, they still had a 1998 Windows model running. That killed me. I had one of those back then. I remember playing Age of Empires and Diablo on it. God, it was good times.

It was a family-owned hotel, the kind of family that work and live together. I've always respected that, but I could never do that. I guess I'm just different, and if you've never tried anything else, it might just seem natural.

Together with the old lady, who seemed to be the grandmother, were two grandkids. One wasn't that much younger than me, and the other was around six. Emma was already talking to him while the grandmother and bigger brother were checking our passports for check-in.

He couldn't speak English, but Emma still made him laugh. Everything went quite smooth in the reception, and it seemed that we made ourselves some new friends quite quickly.

We left the reception smiling and amazed that they were so welcoming. I don't know if it was just happy summer, but whatever it was, I definitely liked it.

Walking up to the third floor on the outside stairway was gorgeous. It was a really good sale text online, and it was pretty honest too.

The third floor wasn't as good looking as the rest of the hotel, though. It was one night, so for us it didn't matter. We found our room and opened the door slowly.

Twin beds. I was relieved.

"This is quite all right," Emma agreed, and we were chatting a little.

We both needed a shower, and I needed everything else as well. I needed underwear, T-shirts, a toothbrush, shorts, and even a travelling bag. I didn't have anything, but it actually felt quite good. I felt so unkempt, but not having any stuff was kind of liberating in a weird way.

We realized that we didn't have a bathroom in the room. It kind of sucked, but there was one just down the corridor. Emma was preparing to take a shower, and I reckoned that I had a possibility of calling my mom without Emma knowing during that.

I told Emma that I would take a walk and see her after the shower. I walked onto the top deck, which pretty much worked as a terrace.

Standing there, I was contemplating lies and overlooking the beautiful city. I felt pretty happy. I was anxious, but also satisfied with myself. I was here, and that meant that I'd already overcome the greatest fear.

What was getting clear to me, though, was that just because you overcome the supposedly greatest fear, then it's just proof that you weren't thinking about all the other ones and their consequences. Looking at the cityscape view and realizing that definitely both scared and helped me. Always ask yourself what you feel and why. Always think of the potential consequences. If you can, it's a huge strength.

I had gotten Emma and myself here, but really being around her was the real fear. I hadn't really been thinking about that. I mean, I had, but it was a dream, a drunken dream.

I began giving myself a beating. I should have thought the consequences through. Actually, I often had this quote playing inside my head. It was my grandmother who'd said it to me. I'm not quite sure if she invented it or not. It goes "People always know what they are doing, most of the time also why they are doing it, but rarely which consequences that will come of it."

It's one of my favorite quotes. I really think there are so many interesting aspects personally and for humans as groups. Imagine if we were all focusing way more on the consequences than our motivations. Utopia, I know, but just imagine it.

Right at that time, I was the perfect example of someone who didn't think the consequences through. I couldn't do anything about it now. I wasn't going to break my promises. My mind step-danced back into contemplating lies. I had gotten an idea for a lie, and it was a solid and plausible one.

I would excuse my absence by saying that I was staying at Calvin's for a sleepover. My mom would definitely believe me. It hadn't happened too many times in the past, so I guess she would be happy about it.

It felt pretty sad, though. I didn't like lying to my mom, but I really didn't feel like I had a choice. She would go crazy, or actually, I don't even know what she would do if I told her the truth. What she really would have done is something I'll never know, as I decided not to.

It was pretty uncool of me to include Calvin in my lie like that, but it wasn't like it made him look bad. It's not like I said he did anything, and again, what other choice did I have?

I felt it was worth it nonetheless. I don't know if I should feel bad, but I figured that he really didn't do anything wrong, so how could someone possibly blame him?

I dialed in and called her. I knew that it would probably cost me a shitload, but I had to call from my own number, otherwise the cover would be blown right away.

It rang a few times before my mother picked up. It was just when she picked up I remember that there was a difference in time between us now. That meant that I would be calling like afternoon or evening there on a Saturday. It's a bit late, but not totally out of order.

"Honey, where are you, why weren't you home last night?" my mother asked way too quickly. I really didn't feel like twenty questions with my mom right then.

"I called you five times, why haven't you picked up?" she continued.

"Mom, I'm at Calvin's. I slept here last night and I might stay here tonight as well. I just called so you wouldn't worry," I said, trying to sound sorry, yet still integrative.

"It's all right. I know you're an adult, but please respect the house rules. You live here and part of that is us knowing you're all right."

"I'm sorry, Mom. I thought I would be home late, but then I decided to stay."

"It's all right, honey. Is you staying all right with Calvin's folks?"

"Yeah, yeah, they're all cool."

"It's all right, honey. Do you want me to pick you up tomorrow?"

"Maybe, Mom. I'll just call you tomorrow and we can talk again."

"All right, have a good one and say hello to Calvin."

"Thanks, Mom." I took a deep breath and looked at the view.

She believed me. I guess mothers always believe the word of their own son. I loved her and I felt really bad for lying straight in her face. This meant business, though. I was in it for good. No way I could back out now.

I didn't stand there for too long before I walked back inside the corridor and to our room. Emma was already dressed and drying her hair. I guess that's why the door was unlocked.

"How was your walk?" Emma asked.

"Oh, eh, it was all right. It's really a beautiful area."

"Cool, did you see anything special around?" she asked curiously.

"No, no, just houses and stuff," I said, trying to sound casual.

"Really, which way did you go?"

"Hmm, just around the neighborhood, same streets we walked."

You could just tell that she was skeptical. I think she could sense that I hadn't taken a real walk. She wasn't nervous or anything. She just sensed that I was hiding something, being a little mysterious.

"I guess we will have to get closer to the city to see something special," I said.

"Probably," Emma answered in a vaguely skeptical voice.

After that, I quickly prepared myself for a shower. It was the best shower that I'd had in years. It was like everything bad just washed off with the smell. The bathroom was old, but in a cool retro kind of way. Actually, it was just really tasteless, but it was almost like it became a style because of that. I like it when things are so weird and ugly that they get cool and beautiful.

I jumped out of the shower and walked to the room. It was empty; Emma had left. I figured that she was waiting for me in the reception, so I just began getting dressed.

It sucked getting in my old clothes from yesterday. That's when you really learn to distinguish a dream from reality. Leaving without anything may seem liberating, but it also sucks and you just need to buy new stuff. Luckily we had more than enough shopping hours left. I walked out and down to the lobby. Emma was there talking to the family. The little guy seemed to like Emma a lot. Not to mention the old lady managing the place.

I just stood and observed them from outside the door like a little creepy fly on the wall. That's something I really like. Just looking at people's body language when you can't hear their voices. It shows communication in another way.

I walked in there and got welcomed with smiles and laughs. Emma brought me into the conversation.

"I have told them that you left with no luggage at all." I was a little surprised by how they all looked at me.

"Ha ha, yeah. You wouldn't happen to know a place where we could go shopping?" I said with a smile.

It made them laugh, but also a little curious, and they ended up telling us about a place.

We had to go back to the same tram station that we got off at in the first place. Then get on the tram and only three stops down towards town there would be a mall.

We thanked them and walked out. Emma was pretty happy from the conversation, and the walk down the hill in the shade in the midday sun was lovely. The mosquitoes were still looking for a feast, but it was more bearable now. It was actually crazy that the walk uphill had been so tough compared to this.

There was an awkward silence until I said something about traveling without anything. It was kind of crazy, but it made us laugh. We literally had to go buy everything for me.

We decided to walk down the roads instead of through the park. The walk was a little longer, but it was all good. This area was truly beautiful, a little weird, but really beautiful. In a way it was the place that I wanted to live most in the whole world.

On the other hand, it was the place that I was most afraid of. It seemed so calm and happy, but unreal as well. There were few people on the street, yet still these big beautiful houses all surrounded by big beautiful trees. It might be the biggest illusion, but I just felt they had happy people living in them.

Though I couldn't really tell if it was just me or if the world really was like that. I wouldn't know, so I just tried to relax and enjoy Emma's company.

It actually surprised me how well everything was going. We got to tram station and checked the schedule; eight minutes was the time we had to wait. We stood there for a while before entering a convenience shop. It was just next to the station and we figured that we might find something that we'd need.

We came out of the shop with two packs of chewing gum. Emma had paid, and I was surprised. She said that it was money she would have used anyway, and that she would pay for herself in that way.

I could understand, and I actually liked the principle of it. It also made me think twice, though. All this money I was using, which I hadn't earned myself, it really wasn't good. I accept being dependent on the money system even though I don't always like it, but using money that I hadn't earned myself, I at least had to think about it.

The way I justified it was thinking back on that feeling that I had last night when I was far away from all this. The feeling of a need to escape far away. When thinking of that and the regret I would have felt if I had been lying at home in my bed right now, it really justified it all. The regret probably wouldn't have been that bad. I would've nagged myself for a day or two, but it would have stopped. I think it says a lot about wasted opportunities.

I would have been lying in my bed looking at the ceiling right now. I wouldn't have known what I had missed, but that's just life as a coincidence, I guess. I would have been home now probably looking out the window watching the snow tangle it's way to the ground. I would have dined with my family, watched TV, read my homework. It was crazy to think about. Especially considering what I was doing instead.

I was standing there in my smelly clothes on a tram, accompanied by a stripper that I had just gotten to know, and together we were going to travel for an unknown amount of time. That was fucking crazy.

I can tell you that I was afraid. It was mad when thinking about it like that. Like should I blow it all, be normal, or go back and not spend the money? I didn't want to; even though some part of me wanted to feel that security, I didn't.

If people at school found out what I was doing, then I would probably get bullied for the rest of the time there. Not that I would mind much, but stuff like that gets to you. There's not space for things like this.

People are too damn busy throwing mud without cleaning their own fucking doormat. Fuck high school and its lack of self-esteem. I don't care if people will think of me as a maniac or lunatic. I really didn't want something like that to hold me back, but it had its hooks in me.

Luckily, I had put myself in such deep water that the hooks weren't strong enough. I had done it. I had really done something spontaneous straight from my heart.

We got off the tram after three stops just as we had been instructed. We could see the mall instantly, and we just walked across the road to enter. It was a relatively big mall building and it had a nice air conditioner going on.

We discussed what kind of clothing I needed, and to be honest, I just wanted something plain and cheap. We found the right shop for it and began to pick away.

Emma began by taking something off a stand and I laughed. I had never been shopping like this before, but it was ridiculously fun. I guess we were still both kind of tired, and that it influenced our humor a little.

We kept finding ridiculously ugly shirts and trying them on until it finally got old. Until we walked around pretty done from laughing.

We had found some neat clothes. My new wardrobe consisted of six boxer-shorts, three packs of socks, one pair of light denim shorts, one pair of swimwear shorts, four T-shirts, one sweatshirt, one hoodie, and three shirts with different prints. My favorite was a red and black lumberjack shirt. I really liked that. The best part was that it all added up to be really cheap.

I thought about the expenses, but told myself not to care. I needed it, and so there was no choice. I had fallen in love with about half of it. I guess it's like that when you buy clothing. Some things you like more than others, and those are what you buy. It's plain and simple. I just had to buy so much stuff that I didn't love half of it.

I had finally tried all the clothes on and could now go buy it. Emma didn't want to, but she did have quite a big influence. I asked her if she liked it and if she didn't then I would consider not buying it. I winded up buying a couple of things she didn't like, I reckon, but it wasn't a problem.

I asked the girl at the counter for a pair of scissors so that I could remove all the price tags, and so I did. When I was done, I walked into the dressing room again and changed everything on me except for my shoes. I put all the dirty clothes in one of the two plastic bags I'd gotten and walked out.

When I came out, Emma was standing there in the middle of that brightly lit room just looking at me. She thought I looked really different. I don't blame her. She had only seen me in my cool going out at night clothes. Now I was in a brand-new selection of cheap warehouse clothes and I felt fantastic.

With smiles on our faces we began walking out of the shop. On the way out, Emma said something to the cashier that I didn't understand, but I could tell it was in the local language.

"What did you just say?" I asked.

"Thank you, in their language," Emma replied.

"What, how did you learn that?"

"From the lady at the hotel."

"Are you starting to learn?" I asked, a bit confused.

"No, I just want to know a few important words."

I didn't understand. Why bother to learn a few words if you could never reply with an answer anyways? Or even just understanding what the other person said? I thought it was kind of stupid, but I didn't say it out loud. English was her language; she could just say thank you and they would understand—whatever.

We got out of the shop and were ready to do anything. We were both hungry, so we decided to go for a late lunch, early dinner kind of thing.

We discussed it a little and we wanted to get closer to the city center. We had already done three stops on the tram, but there were still around eight to go. Well, not really, because then we would be on the other side of the city center.

It was quite a big city and it had a lot of beautiful historical buildings. Luckily, we had seen a lot on our tram ride from the airport and knew that we, in reality, only had one stop until we got to an interesting area.

We decided to walk there. It was a quiet area and still had a nice combination of 19th century architecture and medieval times in it. There was a very old and beautiful bridge that was all lit in yellow lighting. The view of the canal, cityscape, and the other bridges was amazing, Emma was loving it as well.

We decided to go back on the side of the bridge that we came from and then go under it. Down there the sun had already set and it had gotten dark.

There was a quiet chat going on all around the cafés and restaurants. We decided to pick a table at one of the cafés and it was just plain authentic.

We had only been seated for a brief second before a neat waiter in a white shirt welcomed us. The vibe there was good, and the menu was as well. Emma and I both decided to go for red wine, which was bold considering our sleep, or lack of, last night.

They served a whole lot of Italian and French inspired food, and we decided to go mainly for that. The waiter was really cool. I mean, sometimes you just get dudes that are so cool as waiters. He might still be serving you, but he didn't lose any dignity with that. He was one of those guys.

Emma and I began talking a little about all my new clothes. Everything was still so playful with her. We both thought that the whole concept of us being there was hilarious, and I guess it kind of was. There was a little silence, and then Emma asked.

"Why did you ask me and not any of the girls in the club last night?"

I couldn't answer right away. Saying that it was just pure intuition sounded pretty lame and cheesy, but really I didn't know what else it could be. I sensed her from the start, but saying that doesn't cut it. The standardized answers are so overused nowadays that they are not accepted, but really sometimes feelings are that simple. The problem is that a lot of the time the standardized answers are being killed. I have heard countless couples tell each other that they love each other, when everybody could see that it wasn't the case.

"It was just my intuition, you caught my attention, and then this crazy idea sprung from my head," I said.

"Really?" Emma said.

"Yeah, I mean, I'd had a wanderlust all night, but I told you that last night as well," I said.

"That's true. I would like to believe you, but I don't really know you yet." Emma was that kind of girl. You could just tell that she was streetwise, like, you know, good with people and stuff. She knew that she could never know if I told the truth, but she understood how to excavate my feelings to at least create some kind of impression.

We had our starters and the first glass of wine. It was pretty delicious and we ate away like we hadn't eaten for days. When the starter was gone we could start talking again. Now we both had a sufficient amount of food in our stomachs for us to concentrate on something else.

Emma wanted to know how my life was, and I decided to try being honest with her. I didn't feel totally comfortable about her yet, but I just figured that it would create some kind of trust with her.

My paranoia about opening up feelings and being vulnerable was actually not that strong here. It was like being so far away from home kind of killed it. I wasn't afraid that Emma would rat on me and tell anyone about the things I was telling her, and that was really important. She didn't know me at all. She was a fresh start; maybe that was why it felt so good.

Speaking my life story out loud was really special. It was like I even experienced some things in it myself despite me being the narrator. I didn't really know what she expected, but I told her all I could.

I told her about my early childhood, about moving, Calvin, my family, school, meaninglessness and longing after so many things. From my story it kind of emerged into my feelings and dreams all before I knew it.

Suddenly I stopped and realized that I had never ever opened up to a human like this before. We hadn't even reached the main course and I was all out of words.

It must have been like tipping over a glass for Emma. I literally just poured all my feelings and thoughts out in a few minutes. Not all, of course. There are things I kept back. Things I will tell you about later. Things that have been going on for the last couple of years.

Emma was pretty cool, though. She recognized my problems as real. She didn't neglect them like others would have. She told me that I was a good guy and that my problems were real. She also explained how many others had similar problems and how she thought that a lot of people stare out the window longing. Longing but not doing anything, and that's why she really admired me.

Not that I had the courage, but I kind of found the courage to be spontaneous. I liked that, but if she really knew how I had gathered myself to ask her. I mean, I did it and that's what counts, but it's not like I'm not a pussy because of that.

She was telling me what she was thinking. I don't think calling it a small thesis is too far off.

She said that she thought that a lot of people were longing. Looking at the stars, having a tune or color inside them. All something that wants out, but gets trapped because of so many different things in life. I liked that thesis. It was very broad, but I think it had some truth to it. She was quite poetic for a stripper.

We got our main courses, and once again it was just delicious. The waiter refilled our wine, but I could feel that one glass of wine in my stomach was quite a lot.

I told Emma, and she was following. We began to talk about what we wanted to do in this city and realized that it wasn't much. There were some beautiful architecture, churches, and bridges, but we were already dining under the most beautiful of them.

We agreed to just take a long evening walk after the dinner. I figured it was a good idea, even though my mind still wondered like crazy about how a girl like Emma even winded up a stripper.

We had both finished our main courses and were pretty happy with it. The waiter offered us dessert, but it would have been too much, so we declined. Then we just sat there slowly working on the red wine.

It was very magical under that bridge; it was like it was stuck in another time. It reminded me of that Woody Allen movie that takes place in Paris, though we weren't in Paris.

"Do you realize that I don't even know how old you are?" Emma said. It just came out of the blue, and it really made me smile.

"Yeah, it's crazy, but does it matter? I mean, as long as we're on the same page?"

"No, no, it doesn't, but it's just funny, right?" I couldn't disagree with her on that.

"But can I know?" she asked with a cheeky smile.

"Of course," I said and told her. She was surprised, but only a little. We were a little under two years apart.

I could feel that she wanted to go a little my way as well. She wanted me to know about her. Maybe because I had been so honest with her about myself and my story. She really wanted to be, but she couldn't. Luckily I was clever enough to notice.

We bottomed up the wine and asked for the bill. The waiter brought it, and we thanked him for great service and some astonishing food. He seemed glad and wished us a good night. I bet he thought we were a couple.

We got up and left the café. When looking back at it, I realize how many interesting people were actually sitting there in that restaurant. Being in my own little world I just hadn't noticed at all. I wondered how many of them actually spoke English. How many had been listening to me talking? Overhearing conversations. I do that myself all the time. That means that I can't really blame anyone, still, I was just wondering.

Having people in a contained space is always special. We've gotten really used to it, but sharing a location with strangers for a certain amount of time is a possibility and experience every fucking time. Restaurants are like that, except if you go to the same one way too often. A specific amount of strangers will by more or less pure coincidence be in that place at that time.

It's all coincidences, and that kills me. Emma's, mine, everybody's lives are just coincidences. How many small possibilities don't we miss every day? I know it couldn't be any other way. Life is definitely meant to be a coincidence, but isn't it depressing nonetheless?

I was contemplating a little and couldn't really get to agree with myself. The question was soon to be forgotten as the dimmed yellow lights flushed my mind. We just walked by the river without going anywhere specific. I think both of us really didn't care much at the time. It seemed like Emma was forgetting some worries as well.

Moments like these were what my life had lacked so much. Having one really made me wonder how you can have as many of these moments as possible.

One thing I liked to believe was that you cannot force them, but then again, everything happens for a reason, right?

I can't speak for Emma, but the wine had me good. We had been walking on some quite empty streets until now, but the area we were entering seemed a little busier. It was kind of a shopping area, but of course all the shops were closed by now.

If it hadn't been for a few restaurants, it would have been quite spooky with all the jailed mannequins.

I told Emma how I've always felt freaked out about mannequins, and she agreed that they were a little creepy. Even though I think that she thought I was being a little childish. I had to avoid being that.

Slowly a soundtrack was creeping up on us. We were walking towards music. It wasn't long until I could see a guy who was playing piano on the street.

I don't know a whole lot about playing piano, but it was beautiful to my ears.

Without even talking we just slowly walked towards him and stopped. He was young and very skilled, but didn't look like a piano player at all. We weren't the only ones, and I think people really enjoyed his playing a lot.

It isn't like that with all street musicians, but this guy was different. He wasn't playing the regular covers just to earn money. No, it seemed like he was actually playing something he cared for. You could just tell that it mattered to him. I don't know if he wrote it himself, but it had soul nonetheless.

Many of the people who walked by seemed to stop and listen at least just for a short while. It seemed like a night where people had time for music. Emma and I did as well.

I felt a little anxious next to Emma. The mood was getting pretty tender, and I couldn't tell what she was feeling. She seemed pretty happy, but how was she feeling about me? I promised myself that I wouldn't kiss her, or take any initiative to do so for that matter. It wasn't the reason that I had invited her.

She was marvelously attractive, and that, of course, had something to do with my interest in her. Her looks and aura were what got me interested in her, but my spiritual loneliness had far outrun my physical desire by now.

She was smoking hot, but being her friend was all good. I couldn't really comprehend how a stripper could be like her, or how Emma could be a stripper, for that matter.

Every time I thought this, it always led back to her past. I was curious and always kept wondering what her parents were like. I mean, do they know that she winded up here? Did they care, were they even alive?

My mother always wants to know what I'm doing, which usually sucks, but I'd rather have that than nothing. Did Emma have nothing? Did she want me to kiss her? What was she thinking? I just imagined something, which is what I do if I don't know the real story. I shouldn't, but basically I'm just curious about her past.

The piano player finished a song and the music was replaced by a temporary subdued applause from the audience. He looked around and thanked us in a mellow voice. He had eye contact with most of us. I really liked that. He seemed like a really humble and genuine guy.

Emma and I were standing close now, and it wasn't because of the temperature. I could feel my skin cripple like my blood was just under it. I was nervous.

"Should we walk on, or do you wanna stay?" Emma asked.

"What do you think?" I replied quickly.

"It was me who asked you," she laughed out.

"All right, let's walk on then," I said.

"Cool." She was smiling. I liked that she did that because of me. I took out my wallet, gave the guy some money, and then we went. He actually got quite a lot for a street musician, but he was special so it was justified.

We decided to walk back to the riverside to have a cigarette there. We began talking about the piano player, and I began telling Emma about Calvin and how practically everything I knew about music had sparked from that friendship.

Emma began telling me that she had played a little herself, but that it was back in primary school. Nowadays she mainly just listened to music, just like me.

It turned out that we had pretty different tastes in music. Emma's was really different, and it bothered me a little. What helped was that it meant a lot to her, and as long as people don't take things for granted, then I don't think you can blame taste. Music is mood, and it's very different.

Emma loved Beyoncé, Rhye, Lana Del Ray, and other girly pop music. It's actually not the worst kind of music. I could definitely listen and enjoy it. It's just that it's not my favorite. I would have loved to see Calvin witnessing me liking these bands. He would have been furious, but hey, honestly, he really is too religious about his own taste.

The streets we were walking on were completely new, but they were so beautiful. I usually have a pretty good sense of direction, and this time was right as well.

We got out and crossed the main road running parallel to the canal. On the other side there was a path that we walked onto. It was calm and cozy, and once again we felt a little like a movie.

We decided to sit on one of the wooden benches along the path. It was magnificent. I took out my cigarettes and we both lighted one. We talked a little about smoking and it turned out that we both smoked occasionally, Emma a little more than I.

The city was buzzing like a humming bee in the distance, quiet but constant. I could hear Emma's breath, the tobacco burning, and the water flowing. We were there, just there.

I couldn't think of something to say, but really didn't feel it was the worst time. Emma didn't seem to either, and so we just sat there. We turned a little towards each other and just enjoyed the time passing by.

I was thinking about asking her how she felt about me. Just straight up. The mood seemed quite good for it, but it didn't happen. We were interrupted before I could prepare for any of it.

Two guys in black clothes had walked up to us. They came on the path just from the other direction. They literally came out of the blue, but then again, we were in our own world and not vigilant at all.

It was hard seeing their faces because of the hooded jackets. It only took me so long to figure out what was going on.

One guy said something that I didn't understand, the second after he said money. I couldn't think much, and I felt so vulnerable sitting on my ass. I felt like I had to protect Emma, or at least show her I could.

That's really the only thing I remember. Things like that happen pretty fast, and I just stood up with a quote I once read on my mind. I don't remember it precisely, but it was something like this: "You should always feel fear when you stand face to face with your enemy, but you must always be so terrifying that he feels fear the most."

It didn't quite work, you know. I got hit. I had never been punched before. I've always hated fighting, even in early primary school. I don't know what was on my mind when he got me right on the cheekbone, but I tried to punch him back. I know I hit him once, and after that everything went black.

I slowly opened my eyes and felt blurry. I could hear a strong hissing sound, my head throbbed like a hundred horses were running around. Emma was over me and got me up from the cold pavement. She was horrified, upset, and distressed at the same time.

"Are you okay? Are you okay?!" Emma kept asking.

I finally mustered energy to mumble out, "Yes."

She was crying now. I was getting my head back, but I still felt pretty hit. I guess the shock was hard on her, but she wasn't all panicked or anything.

She got me up and sat me on the bench. I had never been in such pain before. It was mostly my head that was hurting. It was the stupidest thing I'd done in a long time. I mean, they got my money anyway.

"How are you feeling?" she asked again. I tried looking at her and answering.

"I'm all right, but it really hurts."

"Come on, let's go to the road. We have to get you to the hospital."

I didn't think that was necessary, but I couldn't argue against the pain, though. Emma got me up, and that's when I realized how much I actually just wanted to sit there with her. It was over.

We walked to the road just behind the pedestrian area, and it wasn't long before a taxi came by. The taxi driver was pretty skeptical about me. He probably thought I was pissed drunk, but when Emma said hospital, he agreed on taking us.

Emma was asking me how she could withdraw money, as we didn't have any. I could barely concentrate, but told her my pin-code and just hoped that there would be an ATM at the hospital.

We were in the backseat and I was just looking up at the grey ceiling inside of the car. It felt kind of hypnotizing looking at it. It made me want to close my eyes, and so I did. I got a little shock as Emma briefly put her hand on my forehead.

I guess she was just feeling my temperature or something. She gently lifted her hand again and then took my hand. It was so nice that it even made me want to open my eyes. I didn't, but it still took my mind off my head feeling like it was galloping.

Emma and I were holding hands. I couldn't believe it. I wanted to know how she looked; if she held my hand out of pity or empathy. I opened my eyes and turned my head a little. She was looking at me with sad eyes.

"Are you okay?" she asked.

"Yes," I answered in a low voice. It made her squeeze my hand. That's the last thing I remember until the taxi driver opened my door and Emma helped me out. I wasn't dizzy anymore, but my head still did hurt like hell.

Luckily, Emma could pay by card in the taxi, so that was one less thing to worry about. We came walking side by side up the small staircase to the emergency department and got welcomed by a nurse.

The light in there was horribly light and white. I kept squeezing my eyes together, as I couldn't bear the bright light. Emma was telling the nurse what happened, and she was writing it down.

She said that a doctor would be with us shortly and pointed out that we had to involve police. Luckily, my dizziness had disappeared and clear thinking had come back to me.

I didn't want to involve police. It would be a big hassle and not worth anything. I mean, would they ever catch them? I hardly think so. I told Emma that I just wanted to see a doctor and that was it.

She disagreed, but I think she could hear that I wasn't at sixes and sevens anymore. It was plain talking. I just wanted to go home and sleep. Interacting with police in a foreign country. How could I know that they wouldn't contact my parents? It couldn't happen. Of course, I was also at my legal age here, so it probably wouldn't, but still I didn't feel like it.

I didn't get to think more about it before a young male doctor was in front of me. His English was quite good compared to the other people we had met and talked to. His accent was a little funny, but that wasn't a concern right now.

He pressed on different spots on my head, lighted my eyes with a small flashlight, and other stuff. He asked me questions and I answered to the best of my ability. It only took three minutes before he concluded that I didn't have a concussion and that I was fine.

He did want to do some X-rays, though, just to be sure about fractures. He said that I had been hit quite hard. I couldn't disagree with him on that. I agreed to the X-rays, but other that that, rest, painkillers, and putting on ice were the only things that would help. We sat down in the waiting room and got something to drink.

Emma told me that she'd been pushed over by one of the guys. Something I hadn't even noticed. I asked if she was all right, but she refused to have any pity on her. I suppose even cowardly thieves don't hit girls.

"Fighting them was stupid. I should probably just have given them the money," I said.

"Yeah, it was a little stupid, but putting up a fight for your own belongings isn't that bad," Emma replied.

"Probably not, but it hurts a little though."

"Honor can't always be kept without getting hurt," Emma said.

I became silent.

"It's something my father used to say. I don't really know if I believe it," she continued.

I was a little surprised. Not only was it the first time I heard her say the word father, it was also painting quite a picture of who he could be.

"I don't know. I guess I didn't lose any honor if he's right," I said.

Emma laughed a little.

"No honor, only a couple hundred bucks," Emma laughed.

I don't know how she had done it, but Emma had managed to keep my wallet, only giving them the cash inside. It was bearable to live without, but still around two hundred dollars. I had withdrawn around three hundred at the airport, but did spend around a hundred today.

We waited for another ten minutes before a nurse came and took me into the X-ray room. X-ray machinery is actually quite crazy. I always wonder who invents and builds machines like that when I see one.

The nurse put on the protection gear for the scan. She was really nice, but you could just tell how routine-like it was for her. X-rays are pretty harmless and it was all over pretty quickly.

The young doctor with the accent came in and checked them against the light screen. It was pretty creepy standing there beside him looking at my own skeleton.

"Everything is fine, you don't have any fractures. Just get a good night's sleep and keep something cool on the cheek if possible," he said and handed me some prescription painkillers.

"Whom do I talk to about insurance and stuff?" I asked him in a low voice. He looked at me with a smile.

"Just get out of here."

I looked at him curiously, trying to figure him out. He could tell.

"It's all right, just go," he said again. I thanked him and walked back out to Emma in the waiting room. She eagerly got up as soon as she saw me.

"Is everything all right?"

"Yes, it still hurts, but I just need to sleep. Let's get out of here before they come and ramble on about the police."

"What about insurance and everything?" Emma asked.

"Everything's good. Let's just get out of here," I said.

We walked out and got ourselves a taxi right away. I actually wanted to sit out in the open to have some fresh air, but we needed to get home.

There was a weird silence in the car. It lasted a few minutes until Emma suddenly began talking about the hospital and how they didn't charge me anything. I don't know if it was solely out of goodwill, but it was a very nice thing to do given the situation.

I'm not sure that I have any travel insurance. I could have been in trouble. Usually they ask for ID and stuff, but that didn't happen. It was really nice. I mean, ideally stuff should be like this, but the world is never ideal, is it?

The taxi driver was a cozy old man, and he had some very nice music on. He didn't speak a word of English, but Emma had the address on her phone, and it was enough.

The music he was playing was a kind of dark folk music, or at least that would be my closest to a label. We didn't understand a word of the lyrics, but sometimes you don't need to. I've always been a lot for lyrics, as I think writing and poesy matter a lot, but I had learned to appreciate music just for what it is.

It also has a lot to do with Calvin and the Stan Getz record that I listened to on the plane. I don't even know if it's Spanish or Portuguese, but I know that I love it.

Nobody in the car talked, we just drove and enjoyed music. I was looking out the left window, Emma out of the right, and the driver through the windshield.

This city was truly beautiful. I loved driving through it. We'd quickly gotten out of the city center. Less people in eyesight tends to clear my head, but I still felt like a techno-rave was taking place on my top shelf.

We drove off the main road and into the hills. The angle made me lean even farther back. I felt like sleeping. Apparently that's what getting your ass kicked feels like.

We got into the hotel driveway, and I realized just how easy it is with a car. We struggled so much when we first walked here, and this is how easy it can be.

Emma paid with my credit card again. Looking at the bill made me think twice. Walking was better anytime but now.

I walked straight up the outside stairs while Emma went into the lobby to get the key. I didn't feel that I was that slow, but she still managed to catch up to me before I got to the room.

I was trying not to be pathetic, but my head just couldn't concentrate on much else than the pumping pain.

The lock made a small click, like we unlocked a treasure chest and it sure felt like the satisfaction.

"What a fucking night," Emma said as she sat down on the bed.

"Indeed," I said while already lying on my bed.

"Thank you for helping me," I said. Emma looked at me with a dormant look.

"Don't thank me, stupid. You did well, but acted a little stupid, if you know what I mean," she was being cheeky. I could barely squeeze out a smile, but of course I did.

Chapter 5: The Coincidence of Identity

I was on an island. It was summer; I could smell it. The mild breeze was carrying the testimonies of the flowers and vegetation. It was so green and full of colors, all around me these beautiful summer colors.

It seemed that the people here lived with nature in the traditional sense. I couldn't really tell if it was an island, but it seemed like it was in the middle of a very big lake.

I walked into the city which consisted of beautiful black and white and red and yellow half-timbering houses. It had small discrete shops, but they didn't advertise, nor wanted to sell anything unnecessary. They were just there.

It was a calm city. I didn't see any people, but the town still felt full of life and soul. I felt happy there. I had walked to the end of the main street, and from there I could see the hills surrounding the town.

It had large hills with agriculture and vegetation on three of the sides. On the fourth there was a field leading to the water. I felt bewildered and just observed it.

The tense smell of flowers and plants overtook all my senses. I felt an unreal lightness as I turned my back on the countless flowers and walked towards the water. I could see the water behind a straight line of gigantically tall and beautiful trees. I wouldn't know what type of tree they were, but they were all tall and alike.

Behind them lay a small house, also a half-timbering one. It was where I was going. I don't know why, but it was where I was going.

The birds were singing and it seemed like it was their time as well. I got to the house and realized that my grandmother lived there. I could hear her humming and smell her cooking as I got closer to the door.

I saw her from the back. She didn't notice me at first. I walked closer. She was wearing her neat red apron and was still humming the melody of the past. I never knew the songs, but it seemed like it was always old songs of love, life, belief, family, happiness, and an occasional melancholy.

She turned around, though I didn't even say hey, but she did, and she was happy to see me. We hugged and I could smell her special scent when we did. It reminded me of being a child, cuddling at sleepovers and watching cartoons. That made me happy too.

She began telling me about the cooking and asked about my day, but I still wasn't talking yet and it didn't seem to matter.

I told her that I would just quickly go to the lake before dinner. It was fine by her. I went to my room and took a small black book and a pink pen off the night table.

I walked out and said a temporary good-bye to my grandmother. I drank a nice, cold glass of milk and then I went. I don't think I'd realized it before, but I really love my grandmother. She was so happy, and I admired that. She had been a widow for so many years, but she still made the best of it.

I got out of the house and walked towards the water. There were a few other houses lying around, but no people in them. It felt like people were in the gardens, waving as I walked past, but they weren't. There was no one. The wind softly cooled the warm bodies, but I couldn't see them.

The breeze on my cheek felt like a hand of silk, a mother's hand. I got through the last grass and trees and into the sand. It was warm, but the sun was setting so it wasn't getting hotter.

A guitar was leaning against one of the trees bordering the sand. It was my guitar and I picked it up. I didn't play well, but I liked playing.

I sat down in the sand and overlooked the water. I could see other land all around the horizon, but it was mostly the fluids that had my attention.

I began touching the strings. Being gentle, I made them murmur like a cat getting petted. Then I just sat there practicing my guitar to the sound of nature.

I was playing this song called "Adult Boy Thoughts" which I had written myself. I didn't know how to write music, but I liked writing feelings. Whenever I felt like it, I would take the pen and write in the small black book.

Occasionally I would draw as well, mostly things of woodwork that I wanted to build. I wasn't in a hurry for anything. I had all the time in the world.

Light slowly emerged into my eyes as I opened them. I looked around and everything was gone. The island, summer smells, and my grandmother.

My grandmother had never lived on an island, but I understood and remembered everything. I slowly turned in the bed. Emma was looking at me, and she asked me what I was dreaming. I froze. How did she know?

"I don't remember," I said.

"I was watching your hands. They move when you're asleep."

I looked at my hands and began turning them around.

"Maybe that's what they do when you don't realize what you're dreaming about," she said.

My head was clearing up, and I decided to tell her.

"I was dreaming about my grandmother."

"Really?"

"Yes, and playing guitar on a very dreamy island." Sometimes dreams sound so weird when you say them out loud.

Emma smiled and it really kind of proved to me that I shouldn't be so afraid of her thinking that I'm weird. When I thought about it, it really bothered me. Why did I care if Emma or anyone thought I was weird because of a dream I had?

A dream is in the subconscious, and you don't control it, right? It was stupid, and I decided that I would try my best to just be honest. That's despite the fact that it might seem strange or weird to someone.

My head was hurting and suddenly I remembered what happened last night.

"Last night was really fucked up, huh?" I said.

"Yeah it was, how are you feeling?" Emma asked.

"I'm all right, but I need a few more painkillers."

I reached for them, but Emma was quicker. She grabbed them and gave them to me.

"Out of all places, this was really the last I ever expected bad things to happen," Emma said.

I was thinking about that statement for as long as you can in the middle of a conversation.

"Yeah. I could imagine that you've had a couple of bad experiences. I mean, no disrespect, but with work and everything."

"It's all right. I know what you mean. Actually, work has never really been that bad. We do have bouncers, you know?"

"That is true. What do I know?" I said with a smile.

"Come on, you saw them," Emma said.

"That's true. I get what you're saying, I wouldn't fuck around with them." Emma smiled and we both started laughing for a bit.

"You know what?" I said.

"No," Emma said with slow anticipation.

"I don't feel like being in this city anymore."

"What?" She heard what I said, but I didn't think she was sure what I meant.

"What do you mean?" Emma continued curiously.

"I don't think we did right by choosing a big city," I said.

Emma looked funny.

"And? What do you propose?"

"I propose that we go somewhere else."

Emma smiled and slowly started laughing.

"Really? We have been here for like one day!" she kept laughing.

"I'm serious. The ocean is not that far away." I was serious and Emma couldn't stop laughing.

"That's really one of stupidest things I've heard in a long time." Emma giggled throughout her laughing. Now she got me to laugh as well.

"Come on," I said with a big smile on my face.

"All right, all right." She had a hard time being serious.

"So what do we do?" she was a bit calmer now.

"We pack our stuff, check out, Google a place, and then we find a bus or something."

"What about finding a place and a bus and then checking out? Then we can go tomorrow morning. There are still things that we haven't seen here," Emma said.

It seemed pretty reasonable, and I agreed with her. It also gave me another day to rest my head before having any big activity going on. Suddenly I remembered that I had to call my mom. I really needed to make a plan for an excuse.

"You're crazy." She said it with a smile. I was just sitting there contemplating how to fool my mom. I guess I might have looked a little fucking crazy.

My mind was just going at it, and it made me feel bad that I hadn't even asked Emma what she wanted to do. She might rather want to stay in the big city.

"How do you feel about the ocean?" I asked.

"I love the ocean, but I love it here too. Except for the ending of last night, of course."

"I love it here as well."

"So why do you think we should go?"

"I'm quite sure that I'm a city person, but a big city is what we came from. A swim in the ocean can't hurt."

"You're right, good passive persuasive skills you've got there." She said it in a soft tone, but you could hear that she still meant every word. I couldn't really tell if that was true. I guess you just can't with yourself sometimes.

"It's a deal," Emma said, and we concluded that it was how it was going to be.

It only took a few minutes on Google, and then we had found what seemed to be the place. Then we went on to discussing the possibilities for the day.

We decided that we wanted to go to the city hill. It was a beautiful old castle on a hill. It was a big perimeter and inside it were different churches and religious buildings. It was all in an old quarter, which meant that the general architecture in the area also had its charm.

Actually, it was on our side of the river. The river that split the city in half, like with any major city, I suppose. Really it was only around two kilometers from where we dined last night, so it was really easy to go there.

My head was still hurting, even through the painkillers, so I decided to lie down again. I didn't want to, but Emma insisted, and actually, she was right.

Emma went down to the reception to see how we could get the bus tickets. We had to decide between an early or late departure. We agreed that an early one was preferable, as it was around eight hours, and sleeping in a bus is never good. I put my head on the pillow again. It was still tense and hot, but it didn't keep me from sleeping.

I opened my eyes to look at Emma lying on her bed scrolling through her phone. I picked up mine from the bed table, and she instantly noticed that I was awake.

"Feeling better?" she asked in an almost mother caring kind of voice. I loved that.

"Actually I do." I picked up my phone from the bed table and looked at the time.

"That's strange, the horse tranquilizer should have stopped working now." I smiled. It made Emma laugh a little.

"You're silly." I got out of my bed blanket and sat up.

"So how did things go with the bus tickets?"

"Easy, receptionist helped me book them."

"Nice! That's good service," I said.

"Yeah, but really I just think it was just plain help," Emma said.

It made me think a little.

"God, people post pathetic stuff on Facebook," Emma continued and sat herself up on the bed.

"That much is true," I said.

"Literally, I really used Facebook a lot until not so long ago, but now it's like my way of looking at it changed," I continued.

"Changed how?" Emma asked curiously.

"Like it's just all self-centered bullshit. I mean, all people know it, but it's like our profiles matter for our personality now." I think she could see what I meant.

"Still we love to nag in other peoples' lives. We love reading shit, but why can something online make us feel better in real life?"

"I don't know, but it seems that it does," I replied.

"Yes, it does, but why?"

"I don't know. It's funny, because since I stopped being the 'all over Facebook guy,' I'm just the loser who doesn't even have shit to post. That's at least how people at school see it."

"School? What school are you in?"

"A regular public high school, sort of on the southeast side of town."

We talked a little about it, and Emma agreed. She said something like this.

"Of course you do. You could easily take filtered photos of some hipster shit and post it on a blog, but you don't. And don't call yourself a loser for that. It really doesn't suit you."

It made me stop. The way she was talking to me just felt so good. It made me realize why I felt sexually attracted to her. It was because she made me feel so much better.

My attraction to her had actually declined a lot from when I first saw her, but this just sparked the ember once again. She was a weird girl in many ways. She seemed so independent and intelligent at times, but she was also so ordinary and traditional in others ways.

"All right, but yeah, Facebook is Facebook. I don't think it'll change; we just have to conform with it. I've done it for a long time. I don't really get why people complain about false expectations in life, because the online people look better than the real you. Come on, everybody knows that." I could see that it hit Emma a little.

"Yes, but you know people shouldn't make themselves look better online. It's just fucking bullshit." Now she was getting a little aggravated.

She just told me she knew, but it looked like she didn't. How could she say she knew, which obviously meant she had to, and then still get hurt by the bullshit?

"I know what you mean, but they do and they will keep doing it. My best bet is just not to give it any attention whatsoever."

"Maybe you're right, but it's not as easy as you make it sound." I wanted to wrap up the discussion and make a loophole so I could talk to my mom, but what was I going to tell Emma?

I thought about telling her, but reckoned that it seemed too childlike. I really couldn't, not now. Even though she would probably tell me it was cool and everything, she would still judge me. She was more grown up than me like that. That I'll admit, but getting nagged by Facebook is way more childish in my point of view.

What was she really, though?

"Should we get going? To the hill, you know? It'll give us a few good hours of daylight if we are lucky," I asked.

"If you are fit for it, then I think we should," Emma said.

"Can I ask you something personal?" I said. Emma looked curious, but a little skeptical.

"Yes," she said very carefully.

"Where do you come from, and what brought you to where I met you?" I asked. Given what I was asking, I think that I phrased it very well. I'd thought about it for hours, but still.

"There's things I don't wanna talk about, but I understand that you're curious."

She was being reasonable, knowing that being a stripper isn't the most understandable profession. I was all ears.

"Let me just say that it was good, then it turned bad for a short while. I didn't see either of my parents for a little more than four years, but I don't blame them. I know that they had their troubles and dealt with them the best way they could. My aunt and uncle took care of me during that time. I enjoyed staying with them. We were a family and everything. One day my dad showed up and everything went weird again. I don't want to get more into it, but let me just say that things went weird. I still love them all, but I'm doing my own thing and being myself for some time." She looked exhausted as she finished.

""All right. I'm sorry, but it sounds like you've come to terms with it.""

"I have. I took time and sometimes it backlashes, but yes I have." Her look revealed how much it meant to her. I really like the way she told me. It wasn't in depth, but I kind of sensed what it was all about.

"I didn't think it would, but it actually feels good that you know," Emma said.

I was a little surprised.

"That's good. I really appreciate you telling and me knowing," I said. Emma smiled.

"If you ever want to talk about it, you can seriously just start the conversation. I don't care what date, place, or time it is." Now she smiled even more. She also wept a small tear from her eye. She wasn't sad, just a little sensitive.

"Now go get a shower so we can get going," she said in a voice that reflected her sensitiveness. I got up and took what I needed for the shower, including my cell phone. Emma didn't notice, and it would only be a minute or two calling my mom anyways.

The bathroom floor was wet from the guy before. It really sucks when people don't clean up after themselves.

I opened the old wood-framed window in the inclined walls and squeezed myself in the opening. It was an awesome view from there. Big trees from the forest made up the background, and at the same time they shaded the three tennis courts on this side. Tennis players often prefer the shade, and this time was no different.

I could just stand there and watch tennis, which really might be my favorite spectator sport. I called up my mom, and as always she answered the phone.

"Hello," she said in a happy but rushed voice.

"Hey, Mom." I was trying so hard to sound excited, as I reckon I had to.

"When are you coming home?"

"I don't know. I was thinking about staying here at Calvin's, we're having such a good time. His family is going on a Christmas trip and I'm going with."

"A Christmas trip?"

"Yeah, a Sunday trip. Just today, and then we get home, sleep, and go to school tomorrow morning."

"Going to school from there?"

"Yes," I replied.

"Are you sure it's all right with Alice and Matt?" Alice and Matt are Calvin's parents.

"Yes, yes, everything is cool."

"All right, honey, so should I count you in for dinner tomorrow?"

"Yeah, but let's talk again tomorrow."

I felt like a psychopath lying to my mom like this. I love her so much and she trusts me, and I just abused it like that. It really felt terrible, but I didn't feel like I had a choice. My lie was even so bad that I would probably blow it anyways. I blamed myself for not having thought more long term, but even in retrospect I couldn't.

I took all my guilt in the shower, but didn't manage to wash off any of it. I was trying to be quick, and it wasn't long before we were handing in the key at the reception desk and were on our way.

They were all there in the reception. It really was a family hotel. Emma once again had a little chat going with the small kid. They were all smiling, and we were as well.

While we walked out I was thinking of how different they might have looked at us if they knew that Emma was a stripper and that we met just two nights ago. I couldn't really believe it myself. Emma interrupted my thoughts.

"It's his birthday tomorrow."

"What, who?" I answered, a little confused.

"The small one," Emma said.

"The boy?"

"Yes. I think I'll buy him a present," she said.

"Yeah, why not? He is so cute."

"Yeah, all right." I was thinking a little, and after all, it was a nice thing to do. He would probably appreciate it a lot. Once again we took the walk down through the hills, and I enjoyed it just as much as last time.

Some places look beautiful in the morning, others in the afternoon, but this place had something any time of the day. I felt that I could spend the rest of my live here, just because of the way it all looked.

We took the tram all the way over the river and into the city center. Once again, by asking around, we were led to a mall. There were quite a lot of shops on the streets, but it seemed that they really conjured shopping malls here. Not that it's really bad. You can get a lot of things in one place, but it's like they still don't belong inside a big city. We got into the mall and were of course looking for a toy store.

"How old is he?"

"Turning six tomorrow."

So yeah, the boy was turning six. A toy would totally be the right choice. As we walked there, I felt like it was a little waste of time, just spending so much time to buy something. I felt like Emma and I could do so much other stuff. I really wanted to get under her skin again. I tried to tell myself that it would make the boy happy, and of course that justified it a little.

Still, I just wanted Emma and I spending the time doing something more important. I don't think that enough time is spent on important stuff. People spend their time on things that don't matter at all. Like buying random stuff that they don't need, or spending time on brainless entertainment.

It's basically what they say in that movie *Fight Club*. I remember watching it and really condoning the message, but really it wasn't there that I got those ideas.

"Got those ideas." I don't really think you can say that. Those ideas had already been had. Somebody thought them before me. I merely just read or heard about them.

I remember the first time those thoughts entered my head it was like they really fell in place. It was a history class with my history teacher John. I would go so far as to call him one of the most important people in my life. Simply because he connected all those loose feelings I had to something. I remember that day; it was almost two years ago at the time. It was one of the first real summer days. The air was moist and hot. We were in the last lesson of the day and concentration usually is long gone by then.

This day John had me locked tight, though. We were discussing life in the retrospect of history. That is really what I liked about him. We didn't have to learn history a lot. We had to learn about life looking at things in history. It may sound stupid to some, but it really came to mean the world to me. I would go so far to say that because of his teachings my way of looking at life changed that day forward. All because of something John told me. I'll try to quote him to the best of my ability.

"Panem et Circences, bread and circus. What does that mean? Anyone?" Nobody answered.

"All right. Bread and circus has it roots in the Roman era and empire. A poet and author by the name Juvenal put into words what he saw going on. The Roman Empire was big and politically fragile at times. It was expanding and the demographics were also changing. There was an emperor, senate, and aristocracy. People at the top, like in any other society. Like in any other society, there were the people, all the ones that weren't at the top. What did they care about? Bread and circus. What do we understand by bread? It is the need for something in the stomach, it is the need for food and drinks. What do we understand by circus? It is entertainment in any form, something that we can make people care about and that they will spend endless time on, maybe even their entire life. Usually that would be gladiator fights and horse racing. It was the football of the first century. So tell me, is it really any different from how it is today? What is the difference between Premier League and gladiator battles? What is the difference between the corn they ate and the processed food people eat nowadays? We know from Juvenal that people slowly gave away their political voice and freedom because they would rather spend time on circus than politics. Is it different today?"

Then he just stopped his speech and wanted the class to answer and discuss the question. That's why he was important, that's why I loved him. What really shocked me, though, was the amount of people that the message got through to. I mean really through. I would say that it was only around six to eight people in the entire classroom. I guess that even those six to eight people interpreted it differently. That was what I had been doing.

The way I saw it, was that I wanted to put everything into boxes. What was mindless entertainment and what really mattered in life? Here, a couple years after, I have learned that entertainment also has its place in life.

It's really boring to be human without some form of entertainment. What I still see and believe, though, is that way too many people live for the circus entertainment and not fighting for a better life. There could be a battle for better lives generally throughout society, but still too many people are busy doing something else. Something that isn't worthwhile.

Change must come from the bottom and go through the middle to the top. The problem is that the middle is so busy watching the game that they don't even have time to answer the door.

To me bread and circus really had ties to a lot of things in society. Consumerism was also a part of the circus to me. Spending time and caring for things that did not serve a real purpose.

Nobody was idealistic anymore; it was what saddened me. No one was really fighting for a better world, and that's really where *Fight Club* entered the picture. Putting that consumerism part onto the hook of circus. I like how different things in culture can tie like that, and I guess that ability to tie them was enabled by John. I don't really think that he knows how thankful I am.

I guess the ability was always within me, he just sort of started the avalanche. It's really since then that I've felt like a different person. I haven't been living strictly by it all the time, but it's like I'm out of the cave, over the cliff. There's no way back to a life of bread and circus, yet I still haven't found my way of purpose.

I turned around a pink corner to see Emma standing in the blue aisle. She was holding different toys in both her hands. I walked up to her and she looked at me.

"What do you think?" she said.

"Honestly, I don't really know," I said with a smile.

"Really, what did you want for your birthday when you were five?" Emma asked. I liked the question and contemplated a little, but I really couldn't remember.

"I don't know," I said with a smile.

"Really? Come on."

"I really don't remember. Maybe something related to Pokémon," I said.

"What type of boy is he?" I continued.

"What kind of boy? I don't know." Emma laughed out loud.

"Yeah, you talked to him, what does he like?"

"I'll have to think about that," Emma said with a big cheeky smile on her face.

We separated and began looking again. It was a massive toy store, and I realized how many new franchises had started since I stopped buying toys. There were still many old ones around, but the amount of different toys was ridiculous.

I tried to remember what I wanted and got when I was six, but I really couldn't. The earliest Christmas I remember was one where I would have been around eight or nine.

While I looked at all the toys, the thought of bread and circus kept going through my mind. It was a constant battle because of the contradictions. Of course children should have toys and play, that's how they learn, but really they should also learn about the world, economy, philosophy, and politics. I know kids and young people also do that, but I just think that the balance between circus and purpose is out of the healthy balance.

Nostalgia grabbed me as I saw some Pokémon linens. They had a big, beautiful Charizard on them. I thought that it would be a pretty good and useful gift, so I took down a package.

I began walking around looking for Emma, but she found me first. She had also picked a gift for him. It was pretty different from mine, to say the least. It was a big plastic gun, kind of looked like something Rambo would use in the 90s.

"What do you think?" Emma asked. She seemed pretty energetic, and I couldn't believe it. Was she really serious? Did she think that a toy gun, which really is the worst kind of toy, was better than Pokémon bed linens? I know it's just a toy, but I really don't think that guns should be made toys. It's like simplifying and making fun of their purpose.

"Do you really think he will like a gun?" I could see that it made Emma a little uncomfortable.

"Yes, why wouldn't he?" she asked curiously.

"Oh, I don't know," I said. Emma seemed a little skeptical about me.

You get kids in Africa who get recruited as child soldiers, and then kids who play around with guns. It may seem harmless, but I think it's wrong. Really, I enjoyed a lot of FPS and RPG involving guns as a child. So I'm not quite holy myself, but still, at the time, a toy gun didn't seem right.

Actually, when I think about it, the games I used to play were something I grew up with. I loved those games. To me games are a whole new brand of Circences, circus. It's a massive industry that keeps thousands of young people at bay, but it's also something else.

Really, when I think back, playing those games was something I enjoyed. I had a great time playing those games by myself and with friends. I know that I did not gain much as a human from them, but they entertained me. It's really one of the things that helped me balance my view on Panem et Circences.

When I first got into that way of thinking, I wanted to abandon everything that wasn't development. I wanted to abandon everything that I didn't learn from as a human. What those memories taught me, though, fitted perfectly to the feelings I had when I abandoned entertainment.

It was a dull time, nothing seemed to amuse me, and everything made me feel down. I read a lot of philosophy, psychology, history, and some of it felt really good and enriching.

What happened was that I felt even greater distance to other people, as if it wasn't big enough already. Life wasn't so happy, to be honest.

It was only when I gave way to entertainment and amusement that I learned that it also has its place, and it's a big and rightful place. It wasn't like John had put it, and I realized that I had always known.

John just wanted me and the others to find it within ourselves. Once again life showed that there was a balance and that finding the right one is gosh darn hard.

The thing about balances was something I had thought about for a while. It was something that began a few months after I first started thinking about stuff like bread and circus. I kind of got around the topic with Calvin one day, and I guess that's why you can call him my only true friend.

We were talking about it, and I was trying to explain some of the things I was thinking, partly about entertainment and partly about balance.

I don't exactly remember how we got there, but all of a sudden we were discussing the balance between enjoying and understanding. We talked about it in relation to music, but it's really not only music, it's everything in the world that can be understood or experienced.

Music is poetic. It's feelings and much more. Almost all people listen to it and enjoy different kinds of it. I myself am one of them. Calvin, on the other hand, is speaking the language of music and can play, which means he understands it.

What we then talked about was that understanding must give a different perception of music. What really brought me there was the fact that I often felt that I enjoyed music more than Calvin.

It was strange because he was the one who understood it, right? Of course, I didn't tell him that, but we kept discussing it. What we kind of concluded was that the closer you could get to balancing the understanding and the pure enjoyment of something the better.

My theory was that I was too far to the pure enjoyment side of music, while Calvin was too far to the understanding side. I reckon that balancing the two sides in any case is really hard, if not impossible. Still, we agreed that the closer one could get to the middle the better.

Of course, it ended up with Calvin believing that he was closer to balancing his perception than me, but I really didn't think he was. He really didn't know how to close his eyes and let his soul crumble from instruments and human voices; I did.

Coming back to the toy gun and having contemplated a little, it really didn't seem that bad. I myself went through just fine, and that's why I questioned my current belief. If I'm a product of violent games, why would it then be bad to own a toy gun? It probably wasn't, and does it really have any connection to real guns? I didn't know the answer.

I was waiting outside the shop and Emma finally came out of after buying and getting the gun wrapped. I concentrated not to think about all the stuff that I wanted to think about. I knew I had to be in the moment.

Really that had been my biggest problem the last few years. Ever since that history lesson, I had become less and less good at being in the moment. My thoughts would always wander off to somewhere else, somewhere they found more important.

It could be in school, with friends or family, it really didn't matter. It wasn't something I did on purpose, just something that happened. Sometimes I could be in social relations or conversations and my mind would just suddenly slip out. Slowly I would listen less and less to what was being said. I couldn't let that happen with Emma, and I did my best on concentrating not to. All despite the fact that something inside kept telling me that thinking about it was better than thinking about toys, a mall, and a girl. I'm telling you, sometimes my head is crazy.

We had done our errand and were now on our way to the old city hill. We did a little planning and the walk there was spectacular.

We came down by the water and soon began walking into a majestic area. It was a medieval area and it really had a feeling to it.

It had gotten expensive and was packed with expensive cars, but it was still charming. It was a contradiction, but really didn't ruin anything.

The streets were steep like nothing I had ever seen. Some of the older tourists had a proper battle going on. There were still a lot of tourists there, but we agreed that it was probably still one of the better times to arrive.

We would not be able to sightsee so much, but we would have the sunset from up there. I think until this day it must be the most beautiful view I have ever seen.

We tangled ourselves through the small streets with brightly colored town houses on both sides and had now come to a long stairway. The pavement was all cobbles, and with the authentic shops surrounding the staircase it was a heavenly place.

I was trying to stay out of all the thoughts that I wanted to dig into. It became a little easier with all the beautiful architecture and history surrounding us. Way more people were going down the stairway than up.

When we finally got to the top, that's when I couldn't understand that at all. There was a massive castle and several churches. The walls were massive, almost unreal, and it was all surrounded by a garden that could have been Eden.

The sunset was slowly working its way, making the sky look like a psychedelic liquid. All the benches were occupied, but Emma and I found a stone ledge where we could sit. There was a five-meter drop from the wall, but it felt safe sitting there.

The view was out of this world, and we just sat there and enjoyed it. We talked a little about how crazy humans are and what they can build if they really want something. How much humans can achieve if willing.

We didn't know how old the castle was, a lot of people probably died making it, but there was nothing we could do about it. We were just sitting there absorbing the liquid sky.

"Thank you," Emma said. It broke the silence and was pretty out of context, to be honest. I looked at her, and it was quite intense.

"Seriously, thank you for being so crazy."

"Thanks," I said with a smile on my face.

Being crazy had never seemed like a compliment to me, but it definitely was now. Now we were sitting here overlooking this beautiful city and just enjoying ourselves.

I think I understood what Emma meant: if I hadn't been crazy we wouldn't have been here. We would probably both be home or doing our daily stuff under the frozen sky. Nothing noticeable would have happened. Just another few days of life would have passed. They would be forgotten and probably spent thinking of something in the future or past. I wouldn't have spent the money that I've inherited. Hell, I would probably even have saved it for buying something like real estate. Now I spent some of it here, and it felt totally right.

I felt pretty confident that I would have a home in the future as well. It wasn't even that expensive, but I agreed to pay for Emma, and paying for two is, of course, twice as expensive as paying for one.

I realized that I didn't know how long we would be going for. Sitting here it all felt right, but sometimes I just felt that I couldn't relate to her. As much as I was mad about her, just as much didn't I relate to her. It was small things that we hadn't talked about, but I could just sense it. Again, it's got something to do with that underlying gut feeling.

Sitting here enjoying this sunset I knew she liked me, but what if she knew of all the things I was thinking. Would she like me still? I knew I could probably never tell her about bread and circus. I really don't think that she would relate to me. I fear that most people won't, as most people are under the influence.

If my biggest concern was which football team was going to win, and I then learned that football is a big mass hypnosis and that whoever won was totally indifferent, then I probably wouldn't like that thought, and it would probably also take some sense out of my life.

I know that a lot of people have football as their hobby and not their life purpose, but still, learning that all those hours, all that energy and feelings that you put into it was indifferent. That it all didn't matter and that while you and all the others were occupied with wasting time on football, a few other people were busy benefiting the masses through other parts of society.

Of course, that's only the political side of bread and circus. Bread and circus is actually originally only a political term, but I think the burden of it in life philosophy is even heavier. At least it was to me. Because maybe people only care about bread and circus, but what else should they care about?

I learned that we need entertainment, otherwise it simply isn't fun to be human, but we need to find the balance. I had an example that I always liked to think about. I really think it's a good one. It goes, what if all the hours in the world that were spent on watching football were spent reading and studying psychology or philosophy. How would the world look? Would we treat each other better? What if they were spent studying history or finance. Would we build a better system?

One mind is only so much. Humans that work together achieve so much more. I think that's what good progress comes from. The problem nowadays is that humans only work together in smaller groups.

There are other aspects about that that also interest me, but we can talk about that later. I mean mobilizing people to gain political control through general strikes and so. We've forgotten. I think maybe our generation never knew. Even though we live as a society, people always work against each other. We disagree so much, but most people don't spend time getting smarter. I don't know how these thoughts came to me and I often contemplate it. I know they changed my life, but I also know that I still want to play on the computer sometimes. Because to be fairly honest, it's a lot easier and way more fun than reading economical finance. So now my thoughts had once again tricked me on a detour.

The sun was setting pretty fast. Obviously not faster than usual, but I'd never seen the sun actually move. Of course, you see the sun move every day, but it's just an explicit action. It's not something you pay close attention to.

I looked over at Emma and words really didn't seem to be needed. She was happy, and that made me happy.

We were sitting pretty close, not intimate close, but close. I don't know if it was just me, but I seemed to sense a sensual tension from her. It was weird because I didn't really felt like moving closer to her.

If this had been the first night in the strip club or maybe even yesterday at the riverside, I think that I would have. I felt less attached to her now, and it seemed that it was quite the opposite with her.

It's weird, but I think it's because I cared more about her as a person. Well, I didn't even know what she was thinking; after all, it was a magic sunset and everybody knows what kind of magic they can work.

Suddenly Emma moved closer to me and it immediately gave me a lump in my throat. She just leaned her head on my shoulder and relaxed. It felt a little awkward at first, but it only took a few seconds for me to start enjoying it.

I couldn't think of the last time that I had sensual body contact like this. It confused me quite a lot, and I couldn't figure out if she was moving for a next step.

All of a sudden, the sunset was completely out of my mind. Now all that I was thinking about was how to react if she tried to kiss me. I really wanted to kiss her, but

I could just feel that now wasn't right. I'm not sure that you can refuse something like that politely.

That memory is something to me. It was like Emma and the whole scenery got me in a mood. I was enjoying being there so much, a lot more than I had enjoyed being any other place before. Every little detail was beautiful to me. I realized that it was because I was aware of them. I saw details in the sunset that I had never seen before.

Emma raised her head from my shoulder, and it made me relieved and sad at the same time. The constant humming of humans and birds relaxed me. Looking down the castle walls, human ingenuity amazed me quite a bit, and when overlooking the city I lost words.

That different mood version of me, it was like it was a slightly different person. I felt normal, but more sensitive, not only to my surroundings, but also the inner state. It was a fragile, yet blessed state.

We had decided to jump off the wall to begin our descent. There was still quite a walk. We still walked on the main platform of the castle with the garden surrounding it. Seeing such big constructions and so many small humans beside it frightened me a little.

Suddenly I understood why people in the medieval times believed in God. It wasn't strange to me anymore. A building like this must have broken any human perception of possibility at that place and time.

I began to think about all the lives that had passed these very bricks. History could be repeating itself, someone may have been here like Emma and me, doing the same thing two hundred years ago.

It was a nice thought. I hoped someone else felt just as happy here. It also saddened me, though; it made me think of my mortality. This wall had been here all while great men had stood and fallen by its side. It was the silent, living survivor, and it had seen stuff.

I think everybody knows that they have to die, but few think of it very often, and even if they do, they really don't. Perceiving that uncertainty, accepting that unknown experience.

I think it's kind of exciting. I mean, you get all the final answers about human existence when it happens. Getting all the answers, it's like finishing the game, yet we are all afraid to do it, me probably most of all.

I think it's the biggest tragedy, and that is why we want to forget about it. To me it's something about enduring the tragedy step by step. In that way it may not be a tragedy after all. Really it's guessing, maybe there isn't really an answer to the fear of death. We are all going to die one day, but we are, after all, going to live and wake up all the other days.

Passing the castle gate, we saw a small but very cool poster. It was a historical overview of people who had been affected or connected to the castle in any way. There were a few people that I knew on there, and I thought it was very cool that they had been here.

Once again all they were to me were memories on a piece of paper. They were all too old and famous to have vocal stories going about them. It's funny how they were still like real living people to me. Actually, they were way more important to me than a lot of living people, yet their skeletons had been eaten and absorbed by the mud and grass long before I even breathed.

To be honest, I had never read about these guys anywhere but online. All the things I knew were things that I read online. I still think it was real knowledge, but it seems a little superficial that people think they can know about philosophy from Wikipedia.

I myself was one of them. I felt that I knew these guys' works and their thoughts, but I actually was so lazy that I only read secondhand recaps.

As we walked down, yesterday began to feel tepid compared to this. It was a happy walk and it was like the world was waiting for us, humming and watching as we strolled by.

We talked a little about the people mentioned on the poster, but it was quite clear that Emma neither knew nor cared about any of them. I don't think she was into books. I don't mean to make this sound like I am reading a lot, but as I told you, I still read a lot online.

Emma didn't seem to have the interest. I don't understand how you can't want to hear and learn from the guys in the past. The past is basically everything, and that's why you should know it well. Emma didn't, and I don't think she ever would.

The conversation just died out, but because of the mood it didn't seem awkward. It was to me, though. It was awkward that she didn't care. Of course, I couldn't force her, but it irked me a lot.

When the weather is hot, the breezes are cool, and you're off to dine by a river, all that can wait, but it was inevitable that it would irritate me in the future. Whether or not Emma and I had a future was still a question, but one is allowed to hope. If then the hope vanishes over time, that's when I'm really afraid.

Deciding where to go and what to eat wasn't hard, yet there was another feeling erupting in my guts. I think I needed to be alone quite soon.

While we were walking looking at restaurants and shops, I realized that I hadn't been alone since I met Emma. I think that is very healthy and it felt good, but I could feel that I had to take some alone time soon.

I wouldn't say that I'm an introvert. I guess I'm actually more of an extrovert. I always was like that as a kid, all outgoing and playing with everyone. I think that the recent realizations about the world, meaning over the course of the last two years, had changed me.

The ideas that arose from the bread and circus made me more of an introvert. Still I think that whatever you are, it's in your nature and you can't truly change that. I think that I would be very outgoing if I felt that I could relate to people. The problem is that I just don't meet anyone who thinks like me.

The big problem is that I wouldn't even know. Someone may think like me but never speak of it. This kind of encouraged me to speak my mind, but how?

Emma had spotted a restaurant that she vouched for, and I did agree. It almost felt marriage-like, even though I don't know what a marriage feels like. She picked places, I paid, and we were never ever out of each other's eyesight. I guess that's a pretty square perception of marriage, but it felt like it nonetheless.

We got a table and everything on there was pretty fancy. It was quite the modern restaurant, yet they had still managed to keep some kind of ambience. The menu was quite fancy as well, but it tasted great, so you couldn't really complain.

It was a romantic dinner, but the conversations bored me. It felt like I was talking to someone superficial. My mind had wandered off and I knew it, yet I still couldn't help it. I think Emma sensed some kind of absence, but she didn't ask me about it.

The dinner went quite smooth and my head wasn't giving me any trouble whatsoever. I think taking a beating over materialistic things was quite a wake-up call. It's one of those things that everybody knows happens, but it really doesn't seem like it does.

I had spent a long time blaming the state of the world on all humans, and it was like that assaulted me. I know that there are millions of different persons, but I bet that that guy probably also suffers under bread and circus, being one of many. It had been a personal development, as much as it had been wanting the world to just change.

Basically there had only been change inside me, so I don't really think that I can say I've ever changed anything. Emma broke my thinking, as I apparently had wandered off.

"What are you thinking about?"

I hate questions like that. It's like it's never convenient to get it. If it was something I wanted to talk about I would already be speaking about it.

Still, I found that it wasn't impossible to talk about this to Emma. She would probably enjoy talking about a million other things first, but, after all, everything I've learned boils down to one thing. Be honest and always strive to have the most purposeful conversation possible.

I know that many conversations will be about ordinary events and people, but striving to talk about the important stuff is my main rule. I think it came out of being driven crazy by thinking and never talking about the thoughts, and of course a thought from the past. More specifically a quote I once read.

"I was thinking about last night … Getting my ass kicked."

"Yeah? It's—" She stopped.

"It's really horrific, but—"

I interrupted her, and I couldn't help it.

"I think it was really good for me." She looked surprised.

"Seriously, it's a long story."

She didn't look like she cared about me interrupting.

"Yeah? I've got plenty of time," she said in a slow voice.

"I'll have to think about how to tell it right."

"You can try."

"I'd rather wait. I'll have to think about it a little. What I can say is that it showed me that there are a million other problems than the ones on my mind."

Emma was kind of silent. I was about to go on, but then she asked.

"What problems do you have on your mind?"

"I'll explain, but not right now. Basically I'm thinking about some things about the way this whole world is and I've been doing so for some time now."

"Yeah, like what?"

"Like a lot of things. How and why we spend our time, what our lives really consist of. I was very different a few years ago. I guess maybe it's just maturing, but I see so many other people at my age go in different directions."

"That sounds interesting."

"I think it is, but you know what a punch to the face can tell you?"

"No."

"It can tell you that there might be a thousand things on your mind and a thousand problems in the world through your eyes, yet still another person would hurt you for a smartphone."

"That's true, but people have always been hurting each other for money. We do everything for money. Trust me, I know." She said it kind of cheeky, but she was dead serious.

The picture I got in my head disgusted me. It reminded me of the things Emma had gone through. I met her while she was literally selling her body. The most sacred thing we have, and she was selling it for money.

That thought led me to another idea. Had I been more drunk or just a different kind of guy, I would probably have had Emma's naked body on me two nights ago. After all, that's why people come to the gentlemen's place. I would have left and felt more or less guilty, all depending on my moral and BTC.

Now that I knew Emma, the worst thing I could imagine was her selling herself again. I had never told her, but it would. I don't think she knew, but I actually cared a lot about her already.

I've never been able to determine if starting caring for people quickly is an advantage or disadvantage. It's a fun thing, but imagine if everybody could care for a stranger just a little bit more. Just like I did for Emma.

I know this is probably what every religion and a lot of other texts have been telling us for a thousand years, and we still haven't learned. What I think is that if people are just aware of the distance to a stranger, then that would mean a great deal. It's like bread and circus; you can't kill it completely, but awareness is what we lack.

Of course, there's also the fear most people carry. Believing that there isn't enough and being afraid of losing what they have.

Emma was quite understanding, and it was like we found some angle to talk about what happened. We didn't quite get to where my mind was, but we got closer. There was depth and she had perspective; actually she was very streetwise. I guess that's everything that I'm not, but we still connected on that.

We finished up at the restaurant, and even though my head felt good, we both felt like a cab home. Thinking of the expenses, we should've maybe gone for the tram.

It's funny with the money. I guess everybody in my whole family would consider this wasting the money, but right there in the moment it felt like I couldn't put it to better use in any way. That's a good feeling, even though your responsible voice will be in the back of your head whispering.

That night was a good night. The irresponsible had become the responsible, the skies were clear, and the streetlights as yellow as ever. It felt different being there in the backseat and walking through the lobby, different in a good way.

Walking through the lobby there was no need to hide the present, as it was already too late at night for the little man.

Before I knew it, my teeth were brushed and I had squeezed myself under the blankets. Emma was sitting in the windowsill smoking a cigarette.

The slanting window was wide open and the distant city and birds were quietly flowing together with the cool night breeze. The lights from the terrace down under cast long yellow beams on Emma's face.

I was just lying there completely still while observing her. It was so silent. All I heard was my breath then hers, the cigarette whistling quietly, and then my heart beating. She was so many things, and then just a girl smoking a cigarette.

Some time passed before she looked at me. Normally I would look away quickly if I was staring at someone, but I didn't that time. She knew I was looking at her, and there was nothing wrong with it. She looked me in the eyes while she exhaled the smoke.

The smoke was like a lazy haze moving through the thin morning air. It felt like she had a word on her lips, but nothing was said. I felt like finding a word, but nothing came to my mind.

She slowly turned, leaned, and put the cigarette out outside the window. She then jumped down into the room and put it in the bin. She sat down on her bed and looked at me. Silent and beautiful, she was.

"Do you mind if I come and lie next to you?" she said in the most tender voice.

I had no chance of answering her comfortably, and I didn't know if I wanted to. I know I was sexually attracted to her. I wanted her, but it was like there was too much at stake. Yet nothing was really at stake, but sometimes things just aren't as easy as they seem.

Before I knew it, she was next to me. It felt pretty awkward, and I didn't know whether to turn myself completely to her or not. It was awkward, I was awkward, but she did have some kind of calming skill.

She began stroking my hair and moving her hands slowly around my arms and head. It was the best thing I had ever felt in my life. The worst part about it was that I didn't know what to do. I was afraid that this could fuck everything up between us. I think that's why I decided to stay still. It was magical being touched by her. I had never known of such body contact, but it remained that. Emma was talking in the softest voice. The mellowness of the voice is a strange thing.

"I'm so glad I met you." I didn't know what that was supposed to mean, but it made me glad. Emma was now sitting up in the bed and still stroking my head, which I had put on her thigh. I did start touching her skin a bit, but she removed my hand signaling that she was nursing me.

Chapter 6: Living eyes and morning light

The cover fell off my leg as I turned over in the bed. The sudden chills on my leg made me open my eyes. It took me a few seconds to realize that I had slept an entire night's sleep.

Last thing I remembered was Emma stroking my hair and talking to me in her wonderful voice. She wasn't next to me anymore. I looked to her bed and saw her lying there sleeping peacefully. She was so calm in her sleep, not like me with my snoring and rapid movements. She was a pretty, little, peaceful sleeper.

I picked up my phone from the bed table and looked at the time. It was quite early, and the bus wasn't leaving for another three hours.

I sat myself up in the bed, a big yawn came out of nowhere, and I felt rested. I reckoned that I had fallen asleep on Emma's thigh and that she had then crept back into her own bed. She was fantastic, yet still the urge for a little time by myself was there.

I didn't care for it last night, but that wasn't bad at all. Now was the time, and I sneaked out of bed as quietly as possible. It was quiet enough, as I didn't happen to wake her.

Quietly I dressed in the clothes that were lying on the floor. I picked up the room key and exited the room silently.

I got onto the outside deck and overlooked the tennis courts. They were all still moist from the morning dew. The sun was pulling itself up once again. This was a good day. I felt good. Rarely do I feel so alive in the morning time.

I avoided walking through the reception on purpose. I needed a quiet morning, as if I needed a break from everything that was taking place right now. The big concern that I kept repressing was my mother and family.

Ultimately my cover would be blown within thirty hours. I had reached my legal age, but stuff like that doesn't concern my mother. She cares about my well-being and whereabouts, and I don't blame her. I blame my parents for some things, but I knew that they never had bad intentions.

What worried me, as I walked under those beautiful trees on that random road, was which easily could have belonged in paradise, was serious. What would her reaction be?

On one hand she would know that I was well. On the other she would go mad for me lying to her. I had never done anything like this, neither had I never heard of anyone doing something like this. Would she go to the police? She very well could, but I don't know what it takes to get reported missing.

If she was in contact with me, it technically couldn't count as me missing, and she probably couldn't force anything from police, as I'm over eighteen. That was from my rational assumption, but I don't know if that is how it works.

Even if I managed not to get into trouble like that, I would still be in a shit storm whenever I got home. I still lived under their roof, and I lied straight to my mother's face.

Suddenly the weight of my morals even managed to tear down some of the beautiful trees along the boulevard. My sorrows weren't strong enough, and the birds in the falling trees soon found other branches to rest upon.

I dragged myself and my conscience through a long, hard walk. The walk was exactly what I needed. I felt sentient again, as I returned to the hotel. It really doesn't take much to recharge my battery. I felt the liveliness to walk into the reception and say good morning.

"Good morning," the old lady responded. She was a cool old lady, working early until late. I have a lot of respect for that.

"Happy birthday to the little man," I said.

"Thank you!" She smiled out, like it was a sensation that I remembered it.

"Where is he, though?" she continued while looking around for him.

"Don't worry, I'll catch him later," I said.

"Yes, yes. You have a bus today, right?" she asked.

"Yes, we do," I answered like it was almost a question.

"I'll arrange some transport for you. To the bus station, I mean."

"Thank you, that would be great," I said with a large smile. She nodded her head with a smile.

I walked to the room to find that Emma was already wide awake. I didn't know if we were to speak about last night, but there was nothing awkward going on. Emma just seemed happy and excited about going.

We were both efficient in packing, showering, and getting dressed. Within half an hour we were eating breakfast with the bags packed. With my new clothes, it was quite heavily packed, but it was still all right.

Emma had put the neatly wrapped present on our table. Now we were all waiting for the boy.

I could see that the reception lady was truly moved, it really mattered to her. I had never imagined what happiness such a little present could bring. It's not about what's inside the box, but everything evolving around the thought behind.

We had just finished our eggs when he walked in. He was a perfectly happy kid, and it reminded me how much joy a birthday can bring.

Emma stood up and took the present to him. I turned around and got up as well. He was pretty surprised, as I definitely didn't think he expected a present from us. He unwrapped it calm and nicely for a kid his age, and when the gun showed, he smiled.

It seemed that I was the only one who had ever thought skeptically of the toy gun. With a little help from his grandmother, he said, "Thank you," and now the room was truly filled with joy.

The grandmother went to get a pair of scissors to unpack the gun. We finished up at the table and pretty much felt ready to leave.

Out of the back room came a smiling young man followed by his grandmother. He seemed quite satisfied with his new gun and ran straight onto the terrace playing with it.

We checked out with the smiling grandmother, and I must say it was quite efficient for Windows 98. She then revealed to us that she had arranged her son to drive us to the bus station. I remember her mentioning arranging transport before, but I naturally assumed it was a taxi. We both told her how she didn't have to, and that we could easily take a cab, but she insisted.

Five minutes later we were in the back of their family car driving towards the bus station. We hadn't seen the guy driving us ever before, so it was pretty much like a taxi, except for the fact that it was free.

The bus station was a little while out of town, and it enabled us to see a part of the city that we would have never seen otherwise. It was a lot of large, dull condominium spaces. It was real brutalism architecture. I only know that term because I actually looked the style up on the Internet.

I've always despised that kind of architecture, and that's how I initially got into looking at it. That's a few years back, and since then I've actually grown to kind of like brutalism. When at home, I would often take a bus somewhere around town, all just to take a walk and look at this kind of architecture, as it's literally everywhere. Not only everywhere around my town, but everywhere around the world.

Where I'm from there's also a great amount of abandoned ones, only if you get to the outskirts of town, of course. Abandoned buildings were actually what caught my attention first.

First, I got into it by looking up urban exploring sites, photo-blogs, etcetera. Over time I gained courage to explore myself. It's a hobby that I've actually found quite easy to share. We were a few guys from school who used to do it back then. It's technically illegal, and I think that's why most of the guys back then wanted to go. The adolescent borderline criminal offenses that many boys need. Not saying that I didn't need it myself, but there's a reason why I still do it.

I enjoy the walk, the architecture, and most of all sensing the life that once was inside a now abandoned building. People can abandon a building, but when you enter it you still feel the soul of it. It really doesn't matter if it's a factory or apartment, once there was life there, but it's all vanished.

Last Friday, the night that I ended up meeting Emma, could very well have been a night like that. I would go home and drop my stuff after school and probably grab a bite of food. Then I would go out and explore. Probably to someplace I had already planned. It wouldn't take longer than I could be home for dinner and meet up with Calvin afterwards.

Last Friday was completely different, and that still seems like a coincidence to me. I could have had a normal weekend and been in school today. Instead, I'm absent from school, lying to my mom, and traveling with a stripper. That really logical part of my brain drags me down every time I put the situation like this.

I'm growing afraid of that side, though. It's like my parents come out from hiding inside my head. They tell me how wrong everything that I'm doing right now is. It's all inside my head. It's scary and it scares me. Still, I tell myself that it's all a coincidence, but why did I end up in that club and with Emma?

I can't help but try to figure out if it was a choice or something that just happened to me. What are the statistical chances of me encountering Emma? Couldn't it have been another thousand women and not Emma? I know that the world is full of possibilities; everybody tells you that all the time. What they don't tell you is that for every possibility you grab, you miss a thousand, but hey, that's just the way it is. The beauty is that you never know about all the other things that might've happened. All you can know is what is.

I liked that, and I liked Emma. I also liked abandoned buildings and exploring them, so now that's off my chest.

We sat down in the bus, which actually was pretty comfortable. I always ride public transport busses, and I guess that's why I never knew that they make busses like this. This bus even had Wi-Fi, and soon I was connected.

Being a child of the Internet, I couldn't help but to Google "coincidences." I guess it's just a habit. When my thoughts dwell on something, I naturally want to know what other people know and think about it. With coincidences, I found something quite interesting. I was reading about something called Apophenia and got really immersed.

I think Emma was all right with not talking, but I think she did think I was being a little weird reading my smartphone like a madman.

So basically not any of the people who ever asked this question answered it. Some people, like me, like to think that with a massive world there is endless possibilities to talk to anyone and do anything, if, of course, you do it right. Some guys say that we like to think that there is a pattern and that we can explain coincidences. What I was thinking at first was that it was humans not being able to accept that their lives are coincidental, but reading some arguments they really made sense.

One guy that I was reading about calls it seriality and tried to prove that coincidences are calculated. I wouldn't follow him totally, but he argues that because we all have certain social norms and mindsets, we will subconsciously seek and meet more people that are like ourselves. That's all because we want to feel accepted and stuff.

I think it is very true, but I think my encounter with Emma didn't come from anywhere inside me, yet I still can't know for sure. He would say that we ended up in the strip club for different reasons. It's not coincidences, nothing is. There is a reason why it happens, and therefore it can't be called coincidence.

Like if you travel to the other side of the world and meet someone you know. You hear stories like that, and that they are all coincidences. What the guy then argues is that people would wind up the same place because of similar interests. I heard a story like this from a guy once. I don't remember where, but it is quite a good example.

From what I remember it was in the world's largest city where neither of those two guys were from. They were in a club or bar, and were the only Caucasians in the joint. They knew each other from home, but why did they coincidentally meet in Tokyo? Coincidence?

What the theory said is that there is a reason they both chose that club, and digging into it, there was. The guy told me that they both found the party listed on a website. Was it a coincidence that they browsed the same website?

Barely, as they are both mad about a certain type of electronic music. Because of that musical preference, they would both use that site frequently. Strange? Yes. Coincidental? No. That was basically how I came to my understanding of it. We do tend to affect our life patterns, but the people you encounter and life in general is pretty coincidental.

So they had found their reason for the coincidence, but now what bothered me was, can this happen every time? I was trying so hard to figure it out with Emma and me, but I realized that I had to involve her; otherwise, we would never know. I looked up from my phone and asked her.

"Do you think that it's a coincidence that we met?"

Emma looked up at me, all while staying silent. She really had to think about the question.

"I don't know," she said, but she was curious. She wanted to know what I thought.

"Do you think so?" she asked.

"I don't know," I said.

"I've just been reading about coincidences and if they exist at all," I continued.

"And, do they?" Emma asked curiously.

I began explaining to her what I had just read, and she actually followed me. It was quite a palpable topic. She did take my side, though. I thought that I might have been a little too subjective while describing it.

While I still had my doubt whether or not coincidences could all be explained, Emma claimed my first assumption. Simply that some things just are coincidences. She agreed to and understood my example and story, but she still argued that some things are just coincidences.

That's when I realized that coincidences might exist, but they are not coincidental. There is a pattern in everything, seriality, which means that everything is linked, but that it's just too complex to ever know.

Coincidences are the word for the things that are too complex to figure out. They are coincidences, but they are not coincidental. Coincidence is the word for such an event taking place which has such a complex backstory that it is untraceable.

Emma kind of agreed, but it didn't seem that the idea of it concerned her too much. She was more interested in what I thought about our particular encounter, and I couldn't answer her.

The idea merged from that event, but I hadn't thought more about it, probably because it was a case of coincidence. The background for us being there was too complex to trace and figure out. That is what I told her. She understood and agreed.

The next long while consisted of no talking at all. After a while of looking out the window, Emma's hands caught my attention. She was sleeping with her hands gently folded on her lap. They was the most neat and calm hands in the world.

I backed up against the window and began observing her. There was definitely something about her. It didn't take long before my mind started asking why I was doing all this?

I remembered something my father once told me. He wasn't exactly the sensitive type, but when he was telling bedtime stories, he got into a mood. Bedtime reading and stories were really the best interactions I ever had with him. Sadly, that ends when you are quite young.

What he once told me was in relation to something going on in primary school. It was in relation to something about competing, something that we all do.

He told me that I would never be able to not compete, and it's a natural thing in life. What I just had to remember and tell myself was that reaching a goal, no matter what kind of goal, only feels good under certain circumstances.

"If you are fighting to achieve something to impress others or feel superior, it will never feel true. Even if you were to achieve it, you won't feel good because you didn't do it for yourself."

I think those words will stick with me through eternity. I'm still not free of it, as I constantly discover things I do because of others. It's called influence, and I've come to learn that I can't avoid it.

The awareness that came from those words helped me a lot. I remember that we were reading Harry Potter at the time, reading meaning my father reading it out loud and me just chilling. I think that's another reason those books are so beloved by me and everyone else. It's because they were enjoyed like that, and they had the ability to beget such thinking and advice.

Emma's hands suddenly moved, and it gave me a little shock. I looked at her and she looked at me with that look you have when you've just snoozed sitting upright in a bus.

"Sleep well?" I said with a cheeky smile on my face.

"Best sleep ever," Emma smiled out in a sleepy voice.

"I'm freezing," she continued. The bus was being cooled heavily with air-conditioning, so it made sense.

I was all right and took off my shirt for her to have. She refused, but I didn't ask before taking it off. That way we avoided the "you don't have to," "I don't want it," part.

Emma smiled and put her head back to rest again. The bus was constantly filled with a subdued chatter, but the film that they had put on took up a big part of the sound picture. Fighting sounds and badly delivered lines.

I couldn't resist looking at the screen once again. Actually, it's really tough to avoid looking at a TV in one's proximity. Throughout the entire trip, they showed two and a half movies. The last one that they put on didn't have time to finish, but I don't think they cared.

I hate not finishing a film when I've started watching it, but in this case the films were actually so bad that it was kind of a blessing. I know that people say that you can just ignore a TV, but I find it really hard when the TV is right in front of me. That's why I hate restaurants and bars with TVs; they are always distracting. TVs should not be as widespread as they are. It's also a lot of Panem, but that is another matter.

The first film they showed was based on an old fairy tale, at least judging by the character names. It was the lamest crossover story with medieval characters and witches coming into modern-age Los Angeles. It was all to fight a bad guy named Rumpelstiltskin or something. It was ridiculously bad and pathetic, but amazingly a lot of people were still watching it.

The second film contained even more lame fight scenes and irritating violence.

Samuel L. Jackson played some villain trying to conquer the world with sim-cards. I don't know who makes these kinds of films, but it came out of Hollywood without doubt. I can't imagine a person that would truly appreciate a film like that. It's really just dumb, brainless entertainment.

Once again, the thesis about bread and circus seemed true.

The last film, the one we didn't get to finish, was Asian. It had a title in a language that I couldn't identify. Under that it had the English title. I only captured the word "vengeance," which essentially means violence. It was pretty spot-on.

The opening shot was a close-up of a football and guys playing with it all while fighting. Fighting, killing, and football; that was all they put in there. It's the most banal and simple things in the world, really pure fucking Panem, if you ask me.

I woke up after falling asleep for a while. It was quite convenient as I spotted a road sign revealing that we had gotten quite close to our destination. Emma was awake and looking out the window.

"Look how different this is. It's so beautiful." I looked out the window at an amazing landscape. I couldn't really believe that this was in the same world as the city we had just left. It was so different.

It was rural, but not in a bad way. There were houses all along the road, and in front of every house families were living. Like they all had moved their living rooms out under the liquid sky.

The liquid sky, it was the situation again. It was yellow, red, orange, and purple all fighting and liquefying into each other. That's while they were all fighting blue at the same time.

The sunsets here were truly something else. I don't think that anyone in the whole world could see this sight without being moved, one way or another. Emma agreed and so we enjoyed another sunset together.

The sunset melted time while the moon was rising. The bus stopped at a quiet suburban bus junction, and we got out. Yellow lights reflected on the white stripes and black pavement. It was a quiet place and we decided to sit down on a small bench just outside the bus.

A few taxi drivers were walking around waiting for us to contact them. It seemed that everybody but us had a pickup waiting there.

We both lit a cigarette, and it was my first in a while. It was delicious. It's funny with cigarettes. Sometimes I enjoy them so much, and then I'll smoke. At other times I'll find them disgusting and stop for a while. It varies from time to time. I was still going on the pack that I bought in the Indian convince store Friday night, so I really wouldn't consider myself a heavy smoker.

Emma and I were discussing where to go. We didn't have a hotel, but decided that we would just ask the taxi driver. I took a look around the dark parking area. Trash was randomly lying around, and nobody seemed to care. I don't really like when cities aren't clean. I think people forget how big of an effort it is with all the trash we are producing.

In primary school, we once had a school trip to a facility where they burn and demolish trash. We got to see the ovens and everything.

That's when I realized how much trash our species produces all together. It's crazy. What was lying around here wasn't really much, but still it just ruins a cityscape in some way.

Suddenly a dog came limping out of a bush. It was a three-legged dog missing a back leg. I felt really bad for it, as I could see how much it struggled to move. It reminded me of an album cover from a band I really like.

The cover has actually always seemed sad to me, but this was the first time I had seen a three-legged dog in real life. There was something really sad about it. For every step it took you could just see the pain in its face. It's nothing like a human, who would probably get a leg prosthesis or have crutches. This dog was clever enough to feel the pain, but couldn't help itself.

I pointed it out to Emma, and she felt bad about is as well. The dog lifted its snout out of some of the trash and looked around. It sensed that we looked at it and looked right back at us.

"He sees you," Emma said. I didn't answer but just looked at it. It was a creepy experience looking him in the eyes. We had finished up the cigarettes and turned around.

As soon as we looked at the cab drivers, one of them came to help with our luggage. Not that it was really needed, but it was a nice gesture.

We got into the backseat of a very old car of a brand that I couldn't recall having seen before. The driver didn't speak English too well, and when we asked for a hotel, he answered, "Which one?" Luckily, after repeating a few times, he understood that we just needed a random one.

"How do you like the weather here?" he asked.

"Oh, it's very nice, very nice," I replied. I didn't know how to continue the small talk. Talking about the weather is truly awkward sometimes. I know his English wasn't really good, so it kind of justified it, but even just for casual conversation the weather is boring. I mean, he is a taxi driver and it's my first time here. I would rather hear about the city and stuff.

Really, you could be discussing anything in the world, so why choose the weather? He was still a nice guy, though, probably had a lot of clients that day, so I didn't blame him.

We arrived on a street next to the ocean. It was the drop-off spot. A big area with loads of hotels. Right in the city center at water, it seemed like a really nice area.

We paid, got out, and began walking. We decided that we didn't want to stay dead center in the city, so we just started walking along the coastline.

People sitting at all the bars and restaurants filled my right ear while the ocean and Emma filled the other. The city seemed quite chilled and not too busy despite the beaches and ocean.

We walked on a pretty narrow sidewalk and had to move as there were two guys walking in the opposite direction. I walked behind Emma, so that we could pass each other nicely. One of the guys looked so strangely at me when we passed. I was looking at him as well. I really couldn't help it, as he really was staring at us.

They were both dressed in tank tops and looked like the casual douche bags. The other guy, the one that didn't stare, had a Chinese sign tattoo on his upper arm.

It's maybe the most hilarious tattoo of all time, especially when non-Chinese people get them. Honestly, I think that most tattoos are pretty lame. I still think there is a lot of beautiful tattoo artwork, but most of the people who get them and their reasons are what irritate me.

It's like they think they'll all be special because they get a tattoo. I don't understand their logic. I even knew a guy who had a tattoo covered up at the age of nineteen. It just says so much about a person. He was the kind of guy who was all about making everything look good. Facebook, Instagram, his appearance. It was like if he didn't have that, then he was a nobody. The worst part was that I don't think he himself could see that. He actually did some traveling, which I respect. The problem was that it seemed like it was more for the sake of imagery and uploading cool pictures to social media, than it was about actually traveling. Honestly, screaming out loud in despair sometimes seems like the best reaction to the way of our generation.

We got farther down the road until it led us under the crowns of beautiful summer trees. We had reached the end of the urban city, but there were still hotels all along the coast.

We walked onto a small pathway that was all covered by trees. It seemed like the perfect combination in comparison to the urban city behind us.

Here you had hotels that kind of lived with nature, instead of living within it. That is, of course, as much as you can within modern limits without being a hippie hotel.

Most of the hotels here had huts and small houses all around. It seemed more like motels, to be honest.

We were contemplating on which one to choose. We were close to picking one many times, but every time we kept walking on.

That's until we just found the place. It was just perfect and we both knew it when we saw it. I've never really paid so much attention to design. It's funny considering that it's architecture's little brother. My eye for it had evolved lately, though. There are endless possibilities in design, but many people who care about it are just being pretentious. That's at least how I see it.

This place was perfect, though. It's one of those places that is not too special at first, but then it gets someone with an eye for detail. When you have someone who pays attention to every little detail, then the big picture changes drastically.

So as all the other places, it was waterfront. Only separated from the beach by the trees with the pathway underneath. There was a main building with a pool in front of it. The entire middle area from the pool and down to the pathway was divided into different areas, most of them being under the treetops. There were a ping-pong table, pool table, hammocks, outdoor chairs and couches, and even a gym area.

The huts surrounding the area looked like something out of the desert scenes in Star Wars. They were round, white, and made out of some stone like material. There was one pathway on each side of the area, and the different pathways going into different areas.

In some of the trees they had put lightbulb fairy lights. On one special tree there were big wooden boards where people had drawn and written small messages. It wasn't like regular "thanks for a great stay" messages. No, it was poems and stuff. It reminded me of my experiences with poems. It's something I would like to tell you about later.

In the main room they had the coolest mix of design. The interior was really minimalistic, yet warm and chill. There were many different chairs, but one especially caught my attention. It was quite low and wide. It had a seat made of leather that was then stretched over a tree skeleton. It was cool.

There were cactuses and houseplants all around. In one corner on a pedestal was some kind of stuffed antelope, and there was one on the wall as well. On one of the walls there was a small bookshelf. It had quite a lot of popular yet also pretentious literature.

Emma walked to the reception desk while I was busy looking around. When I heard her begin talking, I found attention and walked up next to her.

Strangely enough, they had plenty of free rooms. Both of us wanted to stay in the huts, but unfortunately they were all designed and priced for four or more persons.

They had normal twin rooms on the second floor of the main building, and with the pricing it really didn't make sense to grab a hut. The receptionist was a girl in her early twenties, and she seemed really genuine.

We asked her about the lack of people, and she explained that it was quite usual. It's strange how hard it is to find paradise.

We booked us in for three days as a start and decided that we could always extend if need be. We got our key and walked to the room, which was no disappointment at all.

We had a big glass door that overlooked the entire area. The trees kind of blocked the view to the ocean, but it was still beautiful. There was a small ledge outside the door. It was pretty much designed for two people to sit and enjoy a cigarette opposite

of each other, and that's of course what we decided to do.

"I don't know what to think," Emma said. I looked at her and then back out at the

view.

"Nah, this is pretty perfect. I don't know how you feel, but I could stay here for a

long time." Emma smiled.

"I think I could as well."

"Do you know how to play ping pong?" I asked, and glanced at the ping-pong

table through the treetops.

"No," Emma laughed out loud.

"I'll teach you," I said.

She kept laughing.

"What? How is that so funny?" I continued.

"I don't know, but I'll give it try."

She made me smile with her silliness.

"All right, it's gonna be good. Trust me!"

"I do, I do!" she said with a nice smile on her face.

Actually, ping pong was one of my favorite sports to play. I played a lot when I

was younger. I even went to regular training sessions as a kid.

The way I looked at it, it had changed drastically with the awareness of bread and

circus. Sport as a spectator thing had always had my natural interest, as I was a

player. Watching the best ones at the craft you can learn a lot, pretty much like

everything else in the world.

Bread and circus made me see it as a mass hypnosis, which I still think it is in many ways. Ping pong maybe not so much, but if you look at Premier League, you'll see.

You have so many people who dedicate loads of their time and energy to it. The funny thing is that they just had a general election over there. I read how much they complain, even bitching about their society turning to shit.

The problem is they don't realize that they use their energy wrongly. I believe that if you turned the tides so that circus got 20 percent of the attention and energy, instead of the current 80 percent, then they could actually turn things around and make changes.

The problem is that people are too busy spending time on bullshit. By bullshit I also mean themselves. Self-centered bullshit that doesn't help the greater good in any way. There are loads of aspects to this problem. It's more than just hypnosis, but I believe it plays a vital role.

With that being said, I still rediscovered the positives in sports again. Like learning balancing competitiveness and cooperation, social bonding, motor skills, and much more. I mean, if we could get rid of the trend that sports can be a major life hobby, even a purpose, then I think it would be very positive.

You get small kids who are mad about football from age five. I don't think that kind of social heritage is a good thing. It's maybe not the worst, but definitely not the best either.

The problem is that most of the things that I find good in sports only apply if you're doing them yourself. That's why I still love playing sports myself.

It has always been a part of my life, but I'm glad that I didn't evolve into one of those beer drinking, football watching zombies. With that being said, there are still sports that I watch, but my consumption rate is maybe one-tenth of a regular sport watcher, and that is about a healthy level.

I almost forgot to tell you this. Really the best part of watching sports was watching them with my dad and occasionally my uncle. The reason for that was that when they were watching, they would always be totally devoted to one person or team; that, of course, depending on the sport.

Watching the sport wasn't the thing, no, I was watching them. They would swear and curse at the TV and it made it so hilarious to be around, especially if their guy or team was losing.

They were both mad about boxing and had been from a young age. My dad always told me that he improved his English by reading boxing magazines and writing fan letters to all the big fighters. He told stories about how he would actually write excessive fan letters with descriptions of how he specifically liked different fighters' styles and specific fights.

It's pretty crazy, but he actually got responses from guys like Holyfield, Frazier, and even Spinks, I think. Stories like this reminded me that kids find good things in sports, but it still doesn't change my opinion about the global, commercial, media sports.

My father didn't only like boxing. He had a big passion for tennis as well. Boxing and tennis were his sports. It's kind of a weird combination I guess, but that's what he loved watching.

My uncle disagreed as he thought that, in his own words, "It was the same morons weekend after weekend." I think he liked boxing because big fights were anticipated for so long. At the same time, they might be the only chance for that fighter.

The really funny thing was that he almost always vouched for the underdog and despised anyone who acted boldly. The rougher the background, the better he liked the fighter. That's why it was so hilarious when someone who, again in his words, "Didn't fight with blood and tears" won.

I remember my brother, who found watching sports with them just as hilarious as me, asking my uncle about David Haye. I don't know much about boxing, but apparently David Haye canceled a fight because of pains in his little toe.

First I thought it was a metaphor for being afraid, but he literally canceled because of his little toe. My uncle said that if he had been a real fighter, a Russian or Afro-American with a real heart, then he would have cut off the damn toe and boxed the fight. He then added that Haye was a chocolate marshmallow that was afraid that boxing a little would hurt.

I remember finding that so hilarious. I could barely stand it. So that was the way it went; they always cheered and shouted at the TV. They even gave directions to whomever they vouched for.

My father had these really marvelous fun expressions he threw out all the time. Expressions like maggot, work the body, what a fly fucker, tire him, beat him to hell, knock him the fuck out, he couldn't punch a fly off its course, he couldn't punch a dent in a soft hat.

They all made me cry with laughter. I would actually go so far as to say that it made me happy, and I know that my brother felt the same. I guess watching a seemingly meaningless boxing match with my dad, uncle, and brother gave meaning to it.

But that's all because of the circumstances. It's because that it was in those situations that we laughed hardest with our dad. My sister missed out on that a little. She didn't share the thrill. Because I know that sports actually can bring happiness, I've decided to embrace its existence, but I still despise what it is in so many ways. I felt bad for my sister, but she was special in her ways.

All of a sudden, another time in the living room came up on my mind. It was once pretty late at night and we had all stayed up to see this big boxing event.

The first was kind of a local showdown between two English boxers. One was white and orthodox, the other black and southpaw. My father vouched for the white dude, even though he hated his style, and my uncle did the same, but I think he was for the white dude because the other guy was being bold.

The most hilarious thing was once when they cut to the commercials during the eleventh round. Even though it wasn't the main event, they both swore like madmen.

Once it came back, they both cursed the commentator, whom they already hated in the first place. I never really liked the violence, but none of them saw boxing like that, and I think they had taught me to look at is as a craft as well.

Still, some part of me thought it was legalized violence, but with brutal stuff like UFC growing big, boxing almost seemed a nonviolent sport. The first match ended with a unanimous point victory for the white guy, and they were both pretty satisfied.

The second fight I don't remember too well, but I remember them both hating both boxers. My uncle refused to call them real boxers. My father responded by saying that the one guy was shitty and didn't have a punch to throw. The other really wanted to box, but didn't know how to.

The main event was coming up, and it was between what my father called "the freak of nature" and some skilled American fighter. My father was all for the American, while my uncle had bigger troubles picking sides.

The thing was that the American fighter was kind of fighting for money and not honor. In my uncle's book, that's a big minus, but then again he didn't like the big, slow guy. So yeah, he ended up being for the American as well. He was a good fighter, after all.

The first four rounds were pretty chilled. It was for the more calm things like "work that mutant belly," "look at the shots he throws," "there's no body behind them, God damn pretender," and "make the monster move, goddammit." In the fourth round, things started to heat up. There was a borderline punch from the American, and the big guy put his hands down, complaining to the judges.

"His shorts are right under his fucking mutant chest. Destroy him!" my father screamed. I remember looking at my brother trying so hard not to cry from laughter.

My uncle was just as big a boxing fanatic as he was an expert. While he was busy actually explaining to us technical stuff about the sport, my dad yelled again.

"Make him a fucking organ-grinder," and that's what hit the spot, even for my uncle. We were all laughing so hard.

The fight went on like that and ended with the American winning on points. There was plenty of fun that night, even despite the fact that none of their guys lost.

At this point, these stories and thoughts just overflowed my head. Either I wanted to tell Emma about them, or I simply didn't want to keep them inside anymore. I still don't know.

I decided to tell Emma the story about my dad and how I felt about sports. How I played so many and how I had grown to hate them because of the circumstances. It seemed like the perfect, most natural approach to me.

I think I explained it pretty well. Emma was mostly listening, but I think she could see my points. It felt like a big relief, like dropping twenty kilos off my back and another five off my heart. It was like some part of me thanked the rest of me. Thanked me for finally opening up to what it had been trying to tell me for a long time.

When I finished up, though, I learned that Emma appreciated the story, but that she didn't care, understand, or agree on the bread and circus part. It was like she just ignored that whole part, which was actually the most important.

I was glad that she liked the story about the good parts of a sometimes dysfunctional parent-child relationship and good family times, but that she just didn't care about ideas depressed me. We had finished the cigarettes a long time ago and decided to go downstairs to get something to eat.

I was thinking how it might have been my way of trying to explain it that was bad. To be honest, I really had tangled it in-between the story and not went full-blown on explaining it to her. I don't know why, but it was not that easy for me to just say what I think.

There was a decent amount of people in the hotel restaurant. The entire vibe was pretty chilled and the mood was good. This was the first time I began feeling bored by Emma. She kept talking about ordinary stuff and things that no matter how hard I tried couldn't care about.

I stayed in the conversation the same way I always do when I don't care. I guess I'm pretty well trained at that. I was looking around the restaurant, and it seemed like a generally happy crowd. Mostly consisting of couples and small families.

There was especially one family that caught my attention. They looked like the happy upper-middle class relatively chilled family. Where parents have a career, but it's not all that matters to them. Kind of like the family I'm dreaming about. They had three kids. There were two girls and a younger brother. I would have guessed the girls to be around fourteen and twelve, and then the brother around eight or nine.

The youngest of the girls was totally immersed in her smartphone. I know seeing people on phones during dinner is almost normal now, but it still annoyed me like hell.

We had ordered and gotten our dinner served. I looked at the girl from time to time, and all through the meal she had her phone in front of her face. It saddened me.

What also saddened me was that Emma began boring me so much, but my mind was much more interested in the girl. I was asking myself, why? Why do we let ourselves get lost to these devices? We don't have to be online and accessible all the time. I love being online. It's probably even one of my favorite things ever.

Still, there was something wrong about this. It was an addictiveness and also different from my usage. I couldn't see her screen, but I imagine she was on Facebook, Instagram, or something similar.

I use Facebook as well, but it's not my primary online activity. Searching for information, articles, interesting stuff that mainstream media doesn't cover, etcetera, is my main activity. It's the good part. In my world, nothing is better than discussing the state of the world with other people around the world. The problem was that it wasn't the agenda of Facebook or Instagram.

Even though Facebook is loaded with debate, it's still not in depth or progressive debates in any way. It creates an illusion and fuels the circus. That's all while Instagram fuels negative individualism, narcissism, and bad self-esteem.

The media should be there to serve the public and not enslave them. Facebook is such a contradiction as it actually has real value. Basically it's the ultimate communication network for a global world. The problem is all the other stuff that it is on top of that. Basically there were and are lot of communication platforms, but Facebook basically created a platform that could serve everyday communication needs all over the world.

The problem is that it's very addictive. I wish people were able to see this, by that I mean young people. How is media culture going to look when that smartphone-addicted girl across the room is raising her own children? Honestly, I don't want to know.

"Do you want to go for a swim?" Emma asked.

"Well, yeah. Maybe a little later?"

"Yeah, swimming after a meal is not good," she said and looked like it was supposed to be fun. I forced something close to a smile, but couldn't help to think how it's really not.

"It's probably a little chilly but really refreshing," I said. We finished up and billed the meal to the room. We went to the room to chill a little before going for the swim.

The really nice romantic mood had become pretty weird. All the magic I felt when she was stroking my hair the other day was declining. She was still beautiful to me, but it was like she took one step forward and two back when she opened her mouth.

We had a lot of interesting talks, and that's what I kept in mind. Still, her lack of seeing things my way, or actually seeing them at all, slowly made her fade. I wondered if I had picked and nurtured her only to see her fade. I never thought of her as the one, and maybe I really didn't let myself. Everything that was here and that she was to me didn't exactly feel right.

Suddenly I could see those red curtains, the stage and couches in the gentlemen's club. I remembered the faces of all the other people in there.

What if I had asked one of the other girls? Would she have gone with me, was Emma special? It was the eternal call of the void and possibilities tearing my heart apart.

What is perfect, what do I need to feel good? Were my expectations a crazy man's demands? All these questions were questions that I couldn't answer. It was painful, and that is when I realized that all the questions about everything going on outside my body were all I was able to answer.

I didn't know what to make of it. I was thinking and thinking about that limbo. I had all these things inside me, and I felt like they just wanted to yell really loud. It's like trying to fall asleep when you're drunk, all your feelings just want to yell out loud.

I miss being a kid. I didn't feel at home here. The sad thing is that I don't even want to be a kid.

A wave gently embraced my body as I dived into it. The water was black as the darkest night. The ocean felt so small, but watching the moonlight paint the pale waves reminded me how small we were.

"Is something wrong?" Emma asked.

I turned my body in the cool water. Being embraced by the water made me feel truthful.

"I don't know. It's just—" I stopped.

Emma was waiting for me to go on.

"I think about a bunch of stuff, and I've been trying to tell you about it, but I don't think that you care." Emma looked surprised. I don't know if it was a good thing to say, but I couldn't hold it in anymore.

"What kind of stuff?" She sounded aggravated. I felt like I had just put myself in purgatory. The water from hades was cooling me down all while the moon was casting its vague light so the death would be visible.

How could I tell her in a polite way? The cold was reaching my brain. I felt stunned. There was no other way than to just close my eyes and speak out loud.

"I like you, Emma. I think you're a very kindhearted person. I'm happy about being here, and when saying this out loud, it may seem lame to you, but it's actually a big deal inside me. I believe that I only have one life, and I want to live the most meaningful life that I can. I've slowly noticed how we, as a species, waste our time. We keep away from searching for truthful, ideal, and better lives. We stick to entertainment, and as long as we've got that and food, we go on. Most people live their whole lives for that, while only a few seek a complete ideal life. Some might work on human ingenuity progress and some on human spiritual progress, but rarely anyone works in both fields. I like playing sports and wasting time, but I think it's a waste of life. The problem is that filling life with all the things that is not entertainment is boring and hard. So basically this is on my mind all the time, and I can't answer it," I said.

Emma looked at my pale body shaking in the water. It felt really good to get rid of that weight, but Emma's reaction immediately put on new weight.

"I think about that as well, but I kind of think I know my answer." It was a relief to hear that she was interested.

"What do you think is the answer?" I asked, and so she answered.

"I think most people already found it. Life is not so fancy and not meant to be. We are enjoying ourselves, and that's what we're supposed to do. It's all the small things that make up the big picture. For me, I think having kids, buying a house, and decorating it is what I look forward to the most. I know that my current job is not the best, but I will move on and someday have a quiet and happy life somewhere. Hopefully I will be close to nature, and who knows if I will be close to you," she said.

Her heavy eyes were on me, and I could feel how she just passed the now even heavier ball back to me. All the small things, it's the kind of family I was brought up in. An ordinary and somewhat happy family, but that couldn't be the answer.

What was clear to me now was that you can come from anything and want to go anywhere. Your parents mean a great deal for your direction, but there is a world of information and some of it will change you.

I knew that I had changed. When I was thinking about a life in a brick house between all the others, I felt insignificant. It definitely didn't seem like my path, though it's was where I came from. I really endure and love kids, but having that square, planned-out life couldn't possibly mean happiness. I was confused, and Emma could tell.

"I just can't see the happiness in that." I was thinking really hard. "Or maybe I can. I mean, becoming a parent must be the greatest feeling, but it's the life that follows," I said.

"What life? You get to love and raise the kid, and hopefully with a wonderful companion. You can drink wine, laugh with friends, eat chocolate, and have sex. What's not to like?" she said.

She definitely had a point.

What she doesn't see is the *Groundhog Day*. I don't want to live the same day over and over again. Just be a tiny cogwheel running in a treadmill.

I know it's impossible, as we are all just small cogwheels and we should accept that. The problem with being a cogwheel to me is that it means being part of machine. Work, sleep, consume, and, of course also do the stuff that Emma mentioned.

The problem is not that any of it is particularly wrong. It's the underlying meaning for it all that is absent. I guess meaning is also motivation, and I guess I'm in kind of in motivation limbo. It's like I've dropped the ball and I'm still looking for it in the pitch-dark room that the world is.

Humans like Emma have a basic lust to move on, a motivation that shows and creates itself. It's kind of scary to lose that, but even scarier when both hands are looking for the ball, but all they feel is a cold concrete floor.

"I think it's about life motivation. I'm looking for mine." I sounded so depressingly pathetic.

"I don't think so. Look what you have done in the last few days. We didn't conquer the moon; it's not our call."

She didn't understand. It wasn't about conquering the moon or making a name for myself. It wasn't about being mentioned in the history books. It was simply trying to find a deeper core in life, something underneath the decadent and hedonistic human life.

I read about platonic love, and I guess it's kind of close, but still I haven't found anything like it. Emma is really a good girl, but there is something missing.

"I'll have to think more about it." Emma looked like she understood, and at least now she knew where my mind wandered to every now and then. It was a veiled open night with the ocean singing its lullabies. I felt unreal and honest. I felt good, and I felt bad.

Chapter 7: The Unforgiving Memories

The thick smell of books and teenage sweat, I remember it all too well. Longing looks out the window at the sunlit spring grass, birds flying around above it enjoying their nature in simplicity.

I remember that old, hard wooden chair and bitten nails. It was on that same chair that I changed without anyone ever noticing.

It wasn't like I was invisible before, but my opinion had always been my own. All twenty-eight pairs of eyes were barely looking beyond their own noses. How could you expect them to notice inner change? It takes a different approach to see inner feelings, and especially from a stranger.

It's funny how you can share an enclosed area like a classroom for years without ever feeling like anything but strangers to each other. They didn't know me at first, but I was there. When I changed, it was even worse to be there.

The entire circus that I had pretended to care about before straight up disgusted me. That fact made it kind of difficult to make friends in a school like mine.

The biggest problem was that they didn't notice the change. They presumed that I was myself. Humans are many things, children and men and we grow in-between them. The thing people don't realize is that a child can grow within a man and that a man can grow within a child. Both the man and the child can also resurrect inside their own flesh, which is what I believe I did.

I acquired new insights and ethics under the old skin, hair, and bones. Layne Staley could definitely have written a song about this. God, I love him! That's one thing I can't say enough. I don't think I've told you, but he is probably one of my all-time favorites. His take on suffering, life, and meaning naturally became meaning to me.

He said something like, "Whatever you think and feel when you hear the music, that's what it's about," and to me that gives feeling. Those were wise words. He was actually the voice that got me into my poetic mood for the first time. It's something that I told you that I would talk about, but I haven't done so yet.

Here it comes.

I write poems.

It had only been going on for a couple of months when the trip with Emma took place. It was something that came to me some dark and cold fall evening. Suddenly I just felt like expressing my thoughts in words and I discovered that I really liked expressing myself in them.

Actually, I was dreaming about making a collection of the poems. I felt that there was a really great opportunity in them. I don't know if I'm good at writing, but sometimes I get into this special mood, and then they just flow out of my hand.

I was actually up to thirty-four poems by that time. It's funny how I know now, but ever since I met Emma I haven't written any. It had been a few days, and the mood had disappeared.

When I think back, the time before Emma was a different time. Something had been adding up, and I needed relief from the chains.

It's funny how it was in that lonesome down period that I was writing poems. It was when I wanted to scream that my hand followed the ink stream. I've been thinking about that poetry collection. I think I'm ready to show it soon. Actually, as I'm writing this, the only person who's read it is Calvin.

I knew he would appreciate it, as poems are kind of lyrical as well. I felt really sore about it, and as much as I told myself that, it still was a weak spot. I just felt so naked through it. Even when showing it to a friend like Calvin. It felt like such a deep and hidden part of me, and therefore making it an open book didn't quite feel good.

It's funny, as it was meant for the world. If I were to just keep it unread, it couldn't ever help someone feeling like me. That's actually the only hope I had for it. That it could help some young person dealing with problems similar to mine. I'm sure that I'm not the first or the last young girl or guy to deal with these problems.

I'd been thinking for a while and really couldn't find a name, and then one day it just came to me. I don't know what you think, but the current title is *Adolescence in Orphalese*. I don't know if you know where Orphalese comes from, but I will tell you.

It's a fictional place from one of my favorite books. To me it's the world, everywhere. It's a world where people don't know everything about themselves, just like ours. They probably never will, but they can try.

Once again I was wondering whether or not I should show the collection to anyone. I didn't really like her much, but I could show it to my English teacher. She would probably have some kind of critique. Inviting her into my thoughts and problems was something I didn't feel like. At least I'd grown the courage to contemplate. It's a step closer. Well, back to Layne Staley.

I was listening to his voice while walking towards town. I was taking a break and looking for a place just to sit and think. It seemed like there was no suitable place in any of the streets.

That's until I came across this pretty steep street leading back into the land away from the sea. There were a few neon signs on both sides, and intuition just made me take the track.

I got into this really cool, modern styled coffee shop. Young people were chilling, doing homework assignments, all to chill music. It didn't exactly fit my mood, but there were three floors, and it was pretty empty.

On the top floor I found a nice table by a big open window. It enabled me to sit there and read and check things on my phone, just letting my mind slip off. I had my little black notebook with me.

Hours passed by and I began feeling better, yet still not in the mood to write a poem. I put on some Mad Season, which is by far the best record ever made, but still didn't get completely in the mood. It's funny, as Mad Season will always give me goose bumps, but only sometimes bring me in that mood.

It's funny how it ended up with me spending the time on Reddit, Facebook, and similar websites and that it kind of cleared my mind. Being a child of the computer age requires you to take a dose every now and then, I guess.

Suddenly my thoughts were interrupted by a raised voice. I looked out the window and quickly pinpointed the source.

There was a couple standing right at the entrance of an alley having an argument. The dude who had raised his voice was holding the girl by the arm. She was trying to get free, but he kept a firm grip.

Normally I would feel the urge to intervene, but this just made me sad. It would also seem like a little over the top running down from the third floor just to ask if they could figure it out themselves.

He finally let loose of her, and then she didn't actually leave. They began talking again until it got heated and then he would grab her again. She was trying to push him away but couldn't.

The street was far from empty, and I saw loads of couples walking past them. Many of them looked at it, even when he had her by the arm, and still they didn't do anything.

I realized that it was also why I wasn't supposed to run down onto the street. It wasn't my business and that seemed to be the culture here.

If it had been in my hometown, then I would at least have walked up and asked if they were okay. Also, if they would be able to figure it out themselves, and honestly, I think everybody should do the same.

Right now I know how feelings can twist you, but still I could never imagine laying a hand on Emma. The argument went on for a while until they finally walked off. I said a small prayer for them. I really hoped they would figure it out. Love can hurt, but it's not meant to.

When I got back to the hotel, I felt like sinking into a chair to enjoy a last cigarette before returning.

I came in through the same way Emma and I did the other day. At the furthermost table there was a man sitting, and strangely I just caught his eye contact. He had a cigarette in his mouth and a pack on the table.

"Young man, do you wanna sit around for a smoke?" he asked.

I looked at him, a tanned, clean-shaved, dark-haired stranger. His voice was wise and rusty from all the cigarettes. His eyes had a very special and rare glow. He had lived life, and he had something to tell. For some weird reason, I didn't feel uncomfortable with him wanting me to take a seat.

At the time I met him he was on a beach with a twenty-some-year-old girl while being in his fifties. People will have a lot against stuff like that, but you couldn't if you actually knew Harry.

We got into talking over a cigarette at the furthermost table of the hotel. His girl, who apparently was bisexual, had been taking care of herself all day. My companion had also largely been by herself today.

It felt weird, but I think Emma knew that I needed some solitude. Harry approached me, and I'm glad that he did. He had lived in most parts of the world and had three wives from three different countries throughout that time. Thinking back, having a stranger telling me that was amazing yet quite strange, but it didn't feel so at the time.

Harry had managed a lot of different nightclubs, restaurants, and bars. Fast-paced human activity seemed to be his thing. I think he was what you can call a street-psychologist. Street wise and very kindhearted, quite a strange and rare man.

He told me things that I don't even like to think about myself. It kind of made me happy that I was around today. It felt very different from last night's ocean nightmare.

Feeling alive is not the worst. Knowing how to is the hard part, but I was slowly experiencing it, and therefore coming to understand it.

We talked for a while. He was telling me about his story. I kept asking and he kept telling. He was very confident and calm. He calmed me as well and began asking about me and my story.

I was telling him and being extremely honest, maybe even more so than with Emma. It's strange, but he had some kind of effect on me.

That is basically how my soul opened to him. He looked me in the eyes and told me how me being, as how he felt I was, was good. That I should keep my empathy and kindheartedness, but that I should not let myself be fooled.

He told me that things could go very well for me, but that I had to build a facade.

"You're like me, you love people and want the best for them. I've always wanted that as well, but people don't always understand, and if you don't build a tougher outer, then you are gonna get hurt. Few people have empathy like you, at least around here. Don't let them get to you. A kind heart can easily be hurt and not restored, if it's not protected."

I don't think I am as good as he made me seem and sound.

It was weird. Nobody had ever told me anything like this, and why did he? I felt really flattered and didn't really know how to react. The shocking thing was that it actually felt kind of true when it came from his lips. Hearing other people say good things about you is, of course, always nice, but Harry was not saying things to flatter me.

I thanked him for saying it. It felt like something I had thought about myself, but really I hadn't.

My legs shivered as I got up. I had to pull myself together to tell him "thanks" in a way that he could tell that I meant what I was saying.

"Thank you, Harry. It's rare to hear something like this from a stranger." Harry smiled while he lit another cigarette.

"See you around," he said with an intense liveliness in his dark brown eyes.

As I walked away, he turned to overlook the pale sea. Wondering what he was thinking about. Those majestic mountainsides, that girls' eyes, the first ring on his finger, or was it just that summer? I will never know.

I realized how much I had been missing this. People who were thinking like me or actually just thinking in general.

Harry wasn't philosophical. It wasn't changing the way of life that interested him. No, he was interested in playing the current game as good as he could. It's something that I could learn from, but still I think I'll always think of change and not just optimization.

Still, people who had something to tell were something I'd missed. Telling me something that I didn't know or saw with my own eyes.

It reminded me of last summer. The hot air and smell of flowers. The slowed down city with happy people eating ice cream. I spent endless evenings and nights looking out the window. Longing in the blue hour. It was like I had been waiting for this. I had hit a point while walking in the snowy streets.

Now I was under the hot, blue sky again. Snow always makes summer feel so far away, and it sure also goes the other way around. Harry was important. My encounter with him was barely more than five minutes, but it felt more significant than several cold winter months.

The door creaked open in the silence. Emma was lying on the bed while using her phone.

"Hey," I said in a low voice.

"Hey." She sounded rather positive, which was quite uplifting. I had told her that I needed a day for myself this morning. She had actually been very understanding, even though this whole thing seemed like a big dreamy joke.

I looked at my phone, which I had turned off more than twenty-four hours ago. Wondering how many missed calls were on there, if my mom had me reported missing. Lying was irresponsible, but letting police officers waste energy on looking for me would be a whole new level.

I didn't feel like it, but I had to turn it on and make a call. Seeing the logo appear and the phone slowly warming up sure did send chills down my spine.

The phone finished loading, and I gently pressed my password combination, anticipating. One missed called ticked in, then another. In a few seconds I had sixteen missed calls, including a bunch of text messages.

I had fucked up. I began reading the text messages, which were actually going all the way from worried to anger to despair. That's when I realized how bad this actually was, and that I needed to sort out the mess.

I couldn't decide whether to call or text her. The good thing about a text is that it's one-way communication. It would kind of give me more time to think, so that's what I ended up doing.

I don't exactly remember what I wrote, but it was something like this: "Hey Mom, I'm sorry I lied to you. It wasn't the right thing to do. I'm perfectly fine and well so don't worry about me. Even though I know you do, just remember that I am good. I don't know when I will come home. Sorry! I didn't mean to make you worried. Hugs."

After I had written and sent the text, I turned the phone on silent and put it down. It was still a mad thing to do, but taking the conversation seemed like an even worse possibility. The whole situation was so lame that it actually put a smile on my lips. I had been away all day, and I actually felt like talking to Emma.

"You know what?" I said. Emma put the phone down and looked at me.

"What?"

"My mom has called sixteen times today."

Emma looked surprised.

"What, why? Have you talked to her?" Emma sounded worried, and it only made me smile even more. It was so tragicomic.

"She didn't know that I went on this trip. She thought I was in school until today."

Saying it out loud was weird. Like part of my body wanted to smile while the other part wanted to cry. Emma looked a little offended, like she was offended on behalf of my mother.

It made it even tougher until she cracked into a small laughter. I realized that my silly depressed look was what cracked her. I began to laugh as well. As I did, tears began squeezing out my eyes. I was crying and laughing all at the same time.

"Come get a hug," Emma said. She jumped up and sat on her knees in the bed. I walked towards her and got a big hug.

It felt so nice and actually made me feel attached to her again. The problem was that she was becoming my comfort zone. I wasn't leaving my existing one just to create a new one. Maybe it's a natural thing to do, replacing one comfort zone with another, but I would rather not.

The hug reminded me that I had to call my mom as well. I was being a rubbish excuse for a son.

We slowly broke up the hug and both sat down on our beds.

"How was your day?" Emma asked.

"It was relaxing. I went to a coffee shop and it was very chill all until I saw a couple fight. That kind of killed my mood."

"What? Fight how?" Emma sounded curious.

"I guess they were breaking up or something. It was very heated," I said.

It's funny with Emma as I could see how she actually felt bad for them. I was telling her a bit, but not too much time passed before we turned on the TV.

I know it's circus, but literally this day just had to be brain-dead. It's how it felt from the beginning and should until the end. I know that's why circus is even more popular. Because working people will feel like this most days a week.

We watched the only English language channel that was on. It was called More Movies or something like that. I'm in doubt whether they ever screened a good film, as the commercial breaks were full of terrible ads for movies and other bullshit.

The film that came on after the commercials was no exception, and that's when it made sense to me why they only showed shitty movies. Because good movies you don't interrupt.

I thought about all the shit that's on commercials and how if I ever got the money I would make my own commercial. It wouldn't be a commercial, but just me saying that I don't want to sell you anything. Just making awareness for the conscience and what people and firms are trying to make you buy.

Do you actually need it, or do you just buy it because they made you think so? What's your appearance towards the world? Do you need to consume, or have you been made a consumer? After a second thought, I don't think I would ever go on there myself, which is my problem, but there is always a solution.

So the film that was on must be the worst I've ever seen. Nicholas Cage was a NYPD cop living the ordinary life. He chills at American style diner, eats donuts, and solves crime. So he's got this terrible wife and one crazy hot flirt at the diner.

At some point he promises the waitress half of the money if he wins the lottery, and of course he does.

Other than that I don't remember much except for an action scene where, instead of using his gun, he throws a can of baked beans at the suspect and of course it knocked the suspect out.

Most pathetic shit ever. It even made the film on the bus look good. I don't know what's wrong with movie culture in this country. Really, you can't blame them as they are still American movies, but they could at least not watch them.

It's a funny thing with movies. It is such a poetic and informative media. You can seriously fit a lot of information and soul into a hundred minutes of film, not to talk about the discussions, feelings, and thoughts it can spark. The problem is that while still idealistic some places, it has largely become a circuslike industry.

Most of the movies that are coming out are part of the hypnosis. It's a tough thing with movies, as good drama can still have something to say, and a lot of times they do. The blurred lines make it kind of the difficult to actually distinguish between good and bad.

It's not always possible, but again, the awareness is good. I love some of the big epic stories, but as long as I remember and regard them for what they are, then everything is good.

There is one experience that I had with film that actually put this into a good perspective.

It might actually be one of the best experiences I have ever had back home. Maybe I should have told you about it earlier. It really was an important night. The reason for that was that it created a feeling in me. It fueled the void feeling. The feeling of a lack of meaning in everyday life.

It was a normal night, but it ended up feeling so good, and therefore going back to normal life felt so ordinary and meaningless. The night was far from all about the film, but it opened some interesting doors. It hit the feeling and sparked discussion.

It was Friday, and I had been talking to Calvin about hanging out after school. Calvin was game, but he had also agreed to hang out with another friend of his. She was a Russian exchange student and had her own flat. He had gotten to know her through music class. She was playing sax, and he had been telling me about her from time to time. I don't know if she played other instruments, but it really doesn't matter, as the sax is the coolest instrument.

The thing was that Calvin and she were hanging out and practicing music. There was nothing sexual between them. I knew Calvin and that he was being honest with me about stuff like that.

Her name was Aly. It wasn't really Aly, but it was an easy abbreviation for her real name. Calvin was over at her place since she lived on her own, and apparently it was quite the cool apartment.

We were texting back and forth and agreed that I could come over there, and then we could leave together.

School had ended, and it was actually one of those Fridays where I had energy and didn't just feel like going home. Aly's apartment was in a big building complex that had everything inside the complex.

The bus drive there was about thirty minutes, so it wasn't that bad. I got off in front of one of the entrances to the complex. It was a big and quite famous complex. I hadn't been down in this part of town in years, and that explained why it seemed like a totally new experience to me.

It was a classical brutalism complex and really had the sixties' functionalism feeling. The complex was like an organism, it seemed like the entire world, scaled down into a single complex. Beautiful and scary at the same time.

I was walking around looking up on identical terraces and apartments. The only way they differed was by the different color match and flowers on each terrace.

There weren't many people around, but I managed to find an old lady that I could ask directions. The complex was very logically designed, but just hearing an old lady voice felt good. I could have avoided her and found map overview, but it's not always the right way.

I got into the right building and entered a small, cute elevator. The door was made of stainless steel, but also had blue, red, and yellow paint on it. Right in the middle of it was a small round window. It was beautiful and fitted the place perfectly. If anyone had built this today it would feel so superficial.

I got out of the elevator and began doing the last bit of stairs. The stairwell was designed in such a way that it seemed to float, and it was kind of scary.

Finally I reached the top floor were Aly had her apartment. There was a small window beside the last piece of stairs. I couldn't see anything, though.

I took a deep breath and pressed the doorbell. I took a step back and looked around me. I don't remember if I was too inpatient or they were slow, but nothing happened. I waited, but still nothing happened. Just as I leaned forward to push the doorbell again, the door creaked open.

"Hey, man, good to see you! We were just in the middle of a song," Calvin said in an almost winded voice.

I stepped forward and entered the apartment. The entire apartment had neat carpet-covered floors. It was the first thing I noticed.

I quickly got rid of my shoes and walked to the right, entering the living room. Aly was sitting on the couch in the middle of the room with a guitar. Calvin walked and sat down next to her with his guitar. They looked kind of cool.

Aly greeted me from the couch without getting up, and they got right back into their song. I guess she plays other things than the sax.

The apartment was close to perfect. It wasn't too big, but it had space for everything that was needed. The flat was classical as in the sixties, yet still very modern.

She had a big bookshelf, a standing bending lamp and houseplants on the right side. On the left there was the couch that they were sitting on. In front of that there was a big desktop. Beside it she had a big bulletin board. She had printed and written loads of ideas and put them on there.

On the desk there was a huge tray with all kinds of pencils and pens. I guess she was painting as well.

They finished up the song and we talked a little about it. It made them happy that I liked it, but really I was more interested in the flat. Because it was on the top floor, it had a big semicircle roof. Behind the couch there was a rollaway kind of bed and then the kitchen. The kitchen was also straight out of the seventies. All the machinery was retro, and even the kitchen also had the semicircle roof.

This apartment was badass, and the crazy part was that she was living there alone. Her parents must have been loaded.

Beside the desk there was an exit door to a private balcony. It was probably more like a terrace as it was quite huge.

After I had walked around, we all got to talking while sitting on the couch and bed.

Aly moved up to the desktop to show us things on the computer as well. It seemed like a day where everybody was in the mood. We were chilling, and I even learned to play some guitar.

Aly was such an interesting girl, and I wonder why I had never met her before. She was talking all the time and usually that gets very annoying, but not with Aly. It was like she was explaining everything that I had been thinking at that time.

She was into history and global politics and why the world was the way it was. She was explaining how the rest of the world saw Russia and how it really was. How mainstream media and small parts of the elite always plan out things.

She probably sounds like a crazy conspiracy girl, but she was actually backing everything up with facts. She wasn't all about Russia or anything. She just liked to see the world the way she thought it was.

She knew that there was bad stuff going on and that it was all over the political system. We kind of got into talking about bread and circus and how it was all connected. It felt really good, and was my first real time talking about it. It's funny how it just felt completely right talking about it that night.

Many people wouldn't like the discussion we had, but it was honest and like cutting an already open wound. There were things linked to political movements, wars, Cultural Marxism, and other stuff, which she all knew about.

She was special, and I felt lucky that I had gotten to meet her. Politically she had her depression like me, losing the trust in purposeful politics.

She told us about how she had been in a bad car accident around the same time that the world was opening to her. "Opening" was something she called it, and the worst part was that I don't really think Calvin could relate. He really would much rather just play music, but luckily Aly had the baton.

I remembered my own bread and circus down period, and it really enabled me to relate to her depression, as she called it.

She had been hit in a taxi by a car crossing a red light. She was rushed to the hospital and woke after a few days.

The news when she woke up was that she probably would never be able to walk again. She was devastated, and at the same time she had lost hope in the outside world. She had lost her strict religious faith from her orthodox upbringing.

I felt bad for this girl, but now she was all right. It needs to be said that she, by then, was already walking again. Her one-foot kind of pointed inwards when she was walking, but it was more a cute attribute than a flaw to me.

Aly is actually an important part of this story. She played a big part in opening the world of people that I want to fill my life. I had never known them, but when I met and felt her presence, I knew that it was people like her I wanted to be surrounded by. Share the journey with.

There were none of these people in my everyday life. It was like everybody had become numb while serving the machine.

I had some reprieve on Reddit where I sometimes found some intelligent being that I could relate to, but damn it was rare. Thinking about this Friday night I realized how big of a part Aly actually played in me taking this trip. I was looking for her kind, and I thought that I would be able to find them in my drunkenness.

There is, of course, the question of why I didn't just try to grab perfection when it was in front of me. Aly was difficult, and she wasn't ready for me, as I probably wasn't for her.

I had tried to regain contact since that night, but Aly was not reachable, but I think she might get there in the future. I haven't even told the rest of the story and the reason for liking her so much.

She was talking about political governments and how she had experienced how fake both the opposition and government was. She was telling Calvin and me about an old Russian scientist she had met on a plane from Moscow.

She explained how she felt bad for him because he was old, but had theories and a heart to get out there. She explained his theory, and then we discussed it.

It was quite a simple theory, maybe even more just a mindset, in my point of view. He was talking about killing corruption worldwide and controlling birth.

Controlling birth was not something I was particularly fond off, but when Aly explained some of the figures, I could see his and her point.

There are different birthrates for different economies. The problem is that usually really unsustainable economies have the highest birthrates. There is already mass economical immigration, but with the current level and exponential fertility rate, we're looking at a disaster.

All countries should lower their birthrates. Some countries have negative or neutral birthrates, and they should make sure to increase it. Balancing birthrates to a small but secure population growth worldwide is an ideal growth. We have a responsibility to the people who are put on this earth, but not to the ones that aren't.

If nothing is done, Africa will be looking at three billion people on the continent in fifty years. On a continent that already has problems feeding one billion. It screams disaster if there aren't serious political and structural changes coming up.

The old man argued that with the increasing level of robot and computer technology, need for human labor would decrease, and therefore we shouldn't populate like rabbits. We could populate the planet in a sustainable way.

The way Aly told it, this old man seemed like a pal with plenty of ideas. Aly was tired on that flight, which she kind of regretted. If, of course, it's possible to regret being something perfectly natural.

It was bad timing, as she didn't get to hear all this guy's theories and figures. A thing she did hear and could tell about was a solution for corruption and how to prevent it.

Corruption is in every government and country all across the world. Some places have very low corruption, while other have high corruption levels. The way to get rid of the corruption is to make people realize what a real benefit is. A long-term benefit, instead of a short-term benefit.

His solution was this. When we humans were first hunter-gatherers, we all ran around and hunted. It was a tough life, but we knew how to navigate through and survive.

One day, though, someone realized that instead of killing the ox, eating it immediately, all just to chase another, we could breed it.

It's from that controlled agriculture that everything we know as society emerged. Having hunter-gatherers realize something like that is pretty similar to what we need for people who participate in corruption.

They need to realize they hurt themselves as part of that society. Then when people adapt that mindset and realize this, it will only be high-level greedy corruption that is left.

How do you prevent this kind of high society, hidden up corruption much like the one we see in the current Western world? It was simple to the old Russian. You lynch them, humiliate them publicly. Corruption against your own state and people should be viewed at the same level as murder. Corruption probably causes murders, and therefore should be regarded so.

Aly was really rambling away, and I could follow some of the things she had heard from that Russian scientist, though some things didn't make sense. Corruption is so many things, and his way of distinguishing between the seriousness of it is something I would like to see.

It had been a long but interesting talk, well, almost a lecture, as Calvin and I didn't say much. Calvin looked like he regretted bringing me, as I had led the theme of the day away from music. I kind of liked seeing him like that. It was good for him not always staying in that music comfort zone.

Aly found a bunch of pancakes and jam. Apparently Russians have a pancake day, and her mother who had just been over visiting this weekend brought Aly a mountain.

All of a sudden Aly had pulled out some weed that she wanted to smoke. I had only tried it a few times before. Calvin was also game, and since we had smoked together two times, we felt pretty comfortable.

We stepped in the kitchen to smoke, which apparently was how to do it with her. What we learned that night was that Aly's bud was nothing like the shit we had gotten before. It knocked us the fuck off our feet.

Aly picked a movie that she really liked, and we all sat down on the sofa watching the movie on her big ass computer screen.

Calvin still had the guitar and was playing along with the intro music. I was super high, eating a pancake, when this brilliant and humorous film came on.

They Live was the title. It was a brilliant and funny comment on modern society. Being high watching it probably made it a little better as the acting could have seemed very, very bad in retrospect.

Aly had taken the keyboard to the sofa, and she was taking screenshots of everything that she found cool. She was hilarious. The weed only got her more talkative, and sometimes she stopped the film to talk.

It was really annoying, but she was telling such interesting things that it actually made up for being a pain in the ass.

Basically, *They Live* is commenting on consumerism, materialism, and mass hypnosis. The film has some iconic scenes regarding billboards.

Aly stopped the film to talk about billboards and a thought that had emerged in her head. Billboards are things that you cannot avoid. You can look away, but it's not your choice whether or not they are in the public. They are simply in the public space for all to see.

What Aly was thinking was, "Why are you not allowed to say your opinion?"

She was arguing that if you just write the slightest little thing on a billboard, it's vandalism. Of course, it's someone else's property, but why are they allowed to be in the shared public space?

If I need anything, then I will feel the need and go search it. She turned the film on again and we all leaned back to watch it. While sitting there, all I was thinking about was whether this girl was brilliant or mad. Brilliant, I'm quite sure.

She had brilliant taste in movies. *They Live* really hit the spot. It was like the haze of my highness and thinking about the world got me into a state of mind. I wanted a better world for the people, and *They Live* was a metaphor for the few taking advantage of the many.

I'm not exactly a revolutionist, and it's actually sad how politically inferior I feel. Occupy Wall Street was something I supported, but even a movement that big can't change anything. It's really sad to me, but it seems impossible to actually get enough people to protest or strike these days. It's like the world is locked in this perfect state for the upper class. The middle class is just big and satisfied enough that they don't want change. Bread and circus is keeping the entire middle class in place.

Idealism is not a regular thing in ordinary people's minds. They have decent homes and living standards, and as long as the media tells them that that will go away if capitalism changes, then they believe it and will be afraid of change. Really that's how the middle class will always cover for the ultra high upper class. It's what prevents change. I'm not sure that it would create a better society if they didn't, but at least knowing what the rules of the game are is important.

Sitting there watching it, my thoughts wandered off. It was already bad back then, but when smoking weed it almost gets autistic.

The thing I realized was how differently I care for people. That may sound weird, but it's actually true. Being a stranger in need of help, I wouldn't treat anyone differently, but when I hear stuff in the media, it's different.

If some bus crashed far away in a foreign country, it won't really affect me the same way it would if it was in proximity of where I live. Whether that is natural or not is still something I don't know.

I was asking myself how it could be like that. If I heard that twenty some people died somewhere, I still think it is terrible, but it really doesn't hit me that hard. It's really scary, but the media I grew up with made me numb, even to death. That's the small downside of a big and connected world. When the world is your neighbor, then you have a neighbor passing away so often that it becomes everyday stuff.

The traditional explanation for this is, of course, that attachment is bigger to people whom you share culture, country, religion, etcetera with, but it still makes me sad. I know for a fact that some stranger's loss of live will mean more than others, and that feeling is under my skin.

The thing is that it didn't seem natural to me, but was and felt very normal. People are, of course, also very different, and my interest in other people is quite big. I really enjoy being a part of or just observing other existences. Far and wide.

Most of the world is not like me, though. People are different, and people identify with what they know, I know that. I want it good for all people, and I believe in differences. People generally do that, but people always care more for people who look and think like themselves.

It was something that I tried wrapping my mind around, and I concluded that thinking of cultural mixed societies as more complicated is not racist. I'm politically correct, I guess, but I still won't hold obvious opinions.

A large number of people hold onto something, and then when someone who doesn't look like themselves comes around, problems arise.

All this arose from all this thinking, talking, and of course smoking. Talking like this was something that had rarely happened to me before. Of course, I had discussed politics and society's problems a lot of times, but connecting it to the bigger picture and discussing the paradigm was something I hadn't. I imagined how many people might never have experienced it.

Aly had gotten olives and red wine out now. It didn't really go to well along with pancakes, but it was all good. Being high kind of makes you crave everything.

I got more and more into Aly, and she could just go on about all this stuff I was thinking. It even felt like she could read my mind sometimes. Like she was saying things that I agreed to, but that I actually didn't know myself.

This whole story and backlash had dragged the majestic pink sky to the dirty dust of the earth. Aly had been the salt of my earth, but only for so long. A night can feel like a lifetime, but a lifetime cannot feel like one night.

The search for something, anything, like this had put me places, both inside and outside my body. Now I was in a bed watching a terrible movie with Emma.

It's not even about the film and what a film can be and not be. No, it's about life and what it can be. There are so many things it won't be, but why can't we get there? Why can't it be? How do you unlock that secret?

It seems even harder than finding the entrance closet for Narnia. Thinking back, I realized that it was a good memory.

This movie really sucked, but we both loved it. Emma was laughing really hard a lot of the time. Honestly, it really tried to be cute, but it was just so lame. I felt good lying there. I could be myself.

Suddenly this weird mix of feelings was telling me how it was all right to be whatever I wanted to be. Thinking of Aly and everything I had went through inside my head made me realize things. I only have a responsibility to myself. As long as I kept that true, then I could be punk one day and k-pop another. I could dye my hair blue or only play computer games all day. I didn't particularly want to do any of these things, but the liberty it was to be confident with whatever was everything. It seemed like there was so much this world had always told and taught me.

I was and am going to die. Everybody I know or knew will as well. We all knew and told each other that we should get the best out of it. How we only had one life and that we should put it to good use.

What people didn't realize was that there were people putting it to better use. They didn't realize that they were just looking at shadows. That was what I had been surrounded by.

Why I had to go through all this to be able to realize that is still a mystery to me. I think it's because I actually managed to crawl out of the cave. I left the engine room and saw what was outside. A lot of people don't realize that the machine has swallowed them and everyone they know. They are in the engine room telling each other to make the best of life inside the four walls. There was no sky down there, but it seemed that they had all forgotten what a blue sky looks like. I wanted to dye my hair blue in honor of that, but I never did.

I stopped for a second seriously questioning if I was going insane, or if I merely let out everything that had always been trapped inside me. I didn't know for sure, but I know that it felt good. It felt like me. It wasn't pretending and it wasn't pretentious, and so it felt like me.

Emma and I were lying on each of our beds still watching the film. I could tell that it was about to end. It's really easy to predict with the way-overused Hollywood story structure.

While I was lying there, I felt like working out. It's something I hadn't done for a while, but it felt like something I needed to do now. Working out is different from sports. Both are good for you, but sports are more social. I had always played sports, whereas working out was rather new to me. It had not felt like me when doing it, but I wanted to do it now.

Feeling strong, feeling like a man, I really like that. I wonder what kind of person I would have been without sports.

I got up and told Emma that I would go out for a workout. She looked surprised, but it had been a very weird day anyways, so it didn't seem like a big thing.

I changed my clothes and walked down to the beach to do some running and basic exercise. While walking out, I realized how beautiful and nice surroundings I had. I could finish this perfect workout off with a swim in the ocean.

Thinking back, all the different sports I had played had made me a lot of friends. Slowly I had ceased to practice any of them. It had been two years since I stopped with the last. It felt like an eternity, but it was only two years.

The thing I was coming to understand now was that I lacked balance. Sports had been cursed as bread and circus, but really I had misunderstood what it is. It's good and bad. It's circus, but it's also very human. It's like religion, even though I curse it, it seems like something people have always needed. I wanted us to break away from that, breaking away from things that have always been.

That is basically everything the last two years had been about. I felt more distant everyday. I tried to escape it.

It didn't make me happy, but I still think there was some truth in that. Still, it's about balance, because bread and circus is definitely not right.

What I'm saying is that since religion and sports have been around forever, they are probably meeting some needs that we have as humans.

Honestly I didn't know what to think or believe anymore. I was trying to escape something, but I kept being led back to it.

Actually, this was a huge thing to me. Two years ago I had a new world open up to me. It made me discard my old world as superficial. I began exploring the new world and it was very good, yet also very bad. I've closed my eyes to it for too long.

There are things lacking here as well. Looking around at other people had become my tool. After all, it's all we can do. People critical to current society exist, and there are a lot of them. What I had come to realize is that they still grew up in that. They don't want everything to change, they only want a few things to change.

There are a million different thoughts on this world and how it should be, but it was too much for me. It sounds depressing, but I think that I want to stop looking. I just want to live a life that makes me and other people happy. I want to be a good human.

It sounds really basic, but I couldn't find any other good conclusions. You can learn from science, religion, music, literature, everyday life, culture, etcetera, but the sole answer is nowhere in there. It's about finding your balance, which I truly still believe that most people haven't. The outer world had been way too important to me. What I had to think through and experience was companionship, partly platonic, partly physical.

This inner feeling of needing to work out was a small thing, but honestly it was a feeling that I had suppressed. It was a feeling that made me think all the things that I've just talked about.

Sports were a big part of my upbringing. I had tried to escape what I came from, and I think that is what generally made the two last years a less happy time. Not only did I lack the social community part, I also lacked the energy and hormones sports and workouts give you. It's not that smoking weed and talking about the world with two friends doesn't feel better. It's just that I need both in my life. I'm the guy who needs push-ups to feel really well, but I will go sit in the park, drink beer in black skinny jeans while listening to Iceage afterwards. It's who I am, a weird mix of personalities, but I feel that it's a silver lining.

The cold water embraced my body like a mother embraces the returning son. I felt pure, purified in the light of my thoughts. It's crazy the places they can take me, if I give them the space.

The tense muscles relaxed in the dark waves. Two days I had been here, and both nights I had gone in the moonlit ocean. I'm quite certain that it's not the ocean doing it, but there is something here. It's playing with me and my mind. This mind that I've carried with me but used so little.

The amount of thoughts inside my head the last four days says so much about the rest of my life. It feels like I've done more thinking the last four days than I did the last four years. How did I get into this state of mind?

I was thinking that it might have been Emma, but she really isn't in all this. It actually feels very selfish. I'm inside my head all this time, and I suck so badly at inviting her.

The cold water was sliding down my heated body. The sand under my feet still felt warm from the sunlight. I was walking towards the main building. I looked around and everything seemed the same. I looked inside, and everything was suddenly slightly different. When I got in, Emma was actually asleep. Me opening the door was enough to wake her, so I guess she wasn't fast asleep.

"How was your workout?" she asked in a sleepy voice.

"Very good," I answered. It was actually true.

The heated body and tense muscles, the feeling you get from a good workout, is really good. You feel that your heart is pumping, the blood is flowing, and your hormones are awake.

"I finished it off with a swim," I continued.

"Sounds nice," Emma said in her now cute sleepy voice.

She rolled over on the bed in a just as cute a way.

"I'm gonna grab a quick shower," I said, and so I did.

This had been a weird day, but it had made me feel very good. There was some energy that I hadn't felt before. Let's call it the energy of a mind in unity.

I stepped out of the shower and gently dried my body with the smooth towel. I put on my clothes and realized how much I needed to do laundry. When you don't have much clothing it means doing laundry quite often.

I stepped out into the dark room. Emma had turned the lights off, only leaving the small table lamps on. Once again I made noise that made her awaken.

She was beautiful when she was snoozing. I just stood there and looked at her. The light on her face was perfect, and she was just gorgeous.

"Don't look at me like that way, creepy," she said in a cute, funny voice. I laughed, but still felt a little embarrassed. She reached her hand out and moved slightly so that her face wasn't completely covered by the duvet. Even though it was obvious, it still took me a second to realize that she wanted me to hold her hand.

I gently laid my hand in hers and slowly she led me towards her. I sat down on the bed, but her hand kept leading me, and soon I was lying next to her. She slowly lifted the duvet and put it over my hip. I could smell her hair while it was resting on the pillow.

She turned around, lying so she could look me in the eyes. Her hand was still holding mine. She slowly pulled her hand towards her back, but then I took over. Firmly I laid my hand on her lower back and moved closer to her. Her eyes were melting me, just as her lips did when they touched mine.

Nervousness was creeping up on me, but I had the better of it. This was right. Kissing her, feeling her, was magical, like a summer day when you're a kid. I could hear the river flow, the water rinse my heart. I could feel the sun warming my skin, the smell of rapeseed filling my nostrils, as I was running through the field.

The kissing got more intense, then calm again, then more intense, and calm again. All until it got sexual. I could feel her breath, her heart, and her life.

Slowly she was removing my shirt, as I was removing hers. Her skin felt hot against mine. Nervousness was still there, but I was in power. Emma and I belonged together right there.

It all went fairly slow, but it wasn't long before we were both down to our underwear. It is strange how my mind then cleared. I think my curse is that I'm always thinking, in that moment I wasn't thinking. My mind was clear of everything but Emma.

We were holding hands while we were still kissing. The underwear slowly came off, and just as slowly I got on top of her. She was beautiful like nothing else.

Holding both her hands, I moved her arms over her head. We had a firm touch on each other while our bodies were slowly uniting. I began kissing her neck and chest and then her lips again. She softly moaned while she was moving her neck according to my kisses.

She slowly slipped her left hand out of my right and moved it down over my shoulder, chest, side, and hip. I was hard, and she grabbed me to lead me inside her.

I slowly penetrated without ever losing the magical look of her eyes. Slowly our bodies were becoming one. The kisses were only interrupted by our need for eye contact.

We slowly got faster and faster and the kissing got more intense. I had never felt anything like this. I could feel her flesh against mine, it felt like this was all I had lived to do.

She was still moaning softly in my ears as I was filling her with me. She wanted me and I wanted her. My mind was still clear. I wasn't thinking of anything. My hands slipped out of her warm hands, letting them free to touch my body. She laid her arms over my shoulders, touching my hair while pulling me closer. My arms slowly slipped down her perfectly curved body. Her thighs were smooth as silk, but I still got a firm grip around them. I lifted up her legs so I could get deeper inside her

She now moaned even louder as I was coming at her harder. The feeling caught me, and I kept going even faster.

Suddenly she pulled me close for a kiss and the tempo died. She squeezed her hands under my chest and rolled me over.

Now she was sitting there on top of me, holding me firmly with her hands and steadily with her eyes. Her long hair was covering her right breast. She swung her head so the hair went behind and slowly began riding me.

She looked me in the eyes while she went back and forth. With that look in her eyes, she became mine and I became hers. Suddenly she began riding me upwards. I could feel her sliding up my cock and then down again. Every time it went down and

I was all inside her, everything felt perfect. It felt like I was home, that this was nirvana. She kept riding me like that, and I could feel how my load was getting closer and closer to ejaculating.

I tried to squeeze it, hold it back, but it wanted out. Emma was still moaning, as I was getting closer. Suddenly my mind was thinking. I leaned forward to make Emma stop, but she pushed me down with her hands on my chest.

"I'm coming," I said, short of breath. When I said it, Emma moaned and only began to ride me harder. She leaned forward and looked me in the eyes.

"I want you to come inside me," she whispered in my ear. I began moaning loudly as I could feel my cum exiting me and entering her. I ejaculated several times, and each time my body went more and more into cramps.

Emma was now kissing me in a long profound kiss until my cramp-like movements were gone. She slowly lifted her lips off mine and looked me in the eyes. As much as I wanted to say something, I couldn't. I felt perfect.

Emma slowly lifted herself off me, and I felt my wet penis fall on my stomach. Emma came lying right next to me with her head on my shoulder. I put my arm firmly around her, and she kissed me on the cheek.

Only our breaths were breaking the complete silence, yet it still felt like we were talking. Our bodies and flesh were there and it was perfect. Her breath and touch was like a lullaby and slowly it tangled me into a very peaceful mood. We were lying there touching and feeling each other, slowly falling into a deep sleep.

Chapter 8: Facing the path of time

Running on instincts might seem kind of primal, but really it felt so good to me. My mind was clear. I wasn't worried, afraid, or scared of anything in the whole world. Never had I tried that before, and out of all the places I've looked, it was in bed that I found it. How could it be? It wasn't that simple, but how could it be?

I had a bad taste in my mouth. The kind of taste you have when you went to bed without brushing your teeth. Emma still seemed to be asleep. I couldn't exactly tell as she had her back turned on me.

Feeling sleepy, I picked up the phone to check the time. Sometimes I count how many hours I've slept. I know it's stupid and a habit that I should get rid off. No clock is needed to be able to feel if you're tired or if you're ready for the day.

My mind suddenly seemed clear as the morning sky. What the hell happened last night? We actually had sex; it felt unreal to think about.

What the hell was it going to be like when she was waking up? I didn't wear a condom and I came inside her.

All these thoughts just started spinning around in my head. I didn't want to panic, and I wanted to hear what Emma was thinking. It felt good being able to control a still very present panic.

I rolled on my side in order to spoon Emma. Her shoulders were very cold compared to the rest of her body. I grabbed the duvet and covered her with it. She made a little movement and a sound that I took for being a sign of pleasure. I grabbed and touched her breast with my right hand. She sensed and liked it, but still took my hand. It felt so good holding her hand and feeling her heat.

She was asleep while I was busy smelling, touching, thinking, and fantasizing about her. She didn't seem to get closer to waking up, so while I was lying there I had plenty of time to think about last night. I couldn't stop to think about the thing she said to me.

"Come inside me." It must be the strongest words I've ever heard. They had such power, a power that is hard to describe. Being confused was my new thing, I think. Calm and confused, it was like all the despair and anger had left me. My anger is not anything physical, and I guess that's why you might as well call it negative energy. I guess if you surround yourself with the right people and surroundings, then there won't be anger.

Anger is many things. For some people it's physical and outwards; for others it's psychological and inwards. Others might have a mixture of both, but one thing is certain. It is all anger.

Thinking about my own family, father, and people I know, then anger is not a rare thing. Physical anger that is outwards is by far the easiest to spot. Much of my late father's anger came out like that.

Once when I was a kid, he hit me. I don't remember why, but I remember that he hit me and that it hurt. My anger had always been different from his, but at least I was aware.

What was clear to me now was that no matter what kind of anger you have, you can get rid of it. Many people don't know how to and maybe don't realize what they are carrying is actually anger. Also, they don't realize what it does to others.

I didn't until it was all released, and with the way it was released, it seems even more strange and confusing.

Anyways, I'm not going to ramble on anymore. I just knew that I had to deal with things and not waste time. Not wasting time takes awareness. It takes concentration, and that's what I'm striving for. This here with Emma happened, but it was self-chosen just like any anger.

I leaned farther in towards Emma and could smell her hair. It had that special scent. Every person has one, and Emma's was marvelous.

We were lying there naked, and once again the thought of coincidences was bothering me. Out of all the women in the world, she was the one I had sex with. It felt pretty good, and I think our meeting was honest.

As I tried to figure out before, but still not sure that I can. It's funny to think about which people fill each other's lives. The question was, is there a right and wrong way of meeting? Most people get their friends in school. It's the norm, but after all, isn't that just arbitrary names on a paper?

A paper that was once laid in front of some office worker or principal on a random and dull autumn afternoon. Of course, the children shared one thing. They were living close to the school, but that just seems like a weak foundation for all your lifelong friendships, if you ask me.

This has been breaking my mind a little as it is constantly changing. I still recall the time when it wasn't socially acceptable and true meeting people online. Not that I ever did, but now all those same jerks that condemned it are doing exactly that. I mean, couldn't you truly sort through people a lot quicker and with the same distance as everything else online? A distance you can't have in real life and a way of sorting you can't do in real life.

Unless, of course, you want to seem like a total douche bag. What people fill our lives, often it seems coincidental, but is it really?

I wouldn't feel bad meeting a friend online, yet I'm not saying that it is the best way. Really it doesn't even matter what I think about that. I just know that I could be much more honest with an online stranger than a real life stranger.

Also, I just know that meeting a face, not a picture, is important to me. I guess it's another good lesson in life. There is no one answer, and we don't have to fantasize and create one. All I needed was to wake Emma up, talk to her, and appreciate the fact that we were together.

Actually, I want to tell you that I had an online pen friend. It's a funny story, but I'll just tell it shortly. We were in different places, yet so much the same place. It's funny how I, on this very lonely night in my opening period, was looking for something.

I was going through music and just randomly wrote an account on YouTube. The account had uploaded around five songs and some video about David Lynch.

I had been through hundreds of songs that night, but she was the one I decided to write. Maya was the name behind the profile. The funny thing is that we ended up writing for so long, exchanging thoughts, feelings, and stories.

I could be scarily honest with her, and she felt the same about me. I think her motivation and encouragement also played some part in the making of this picture.

That's why life is beautiful. It's so many things. It's a longing girl sitting in her windowsill looking at the setting sun, and it's a lonely boy screaming in the darkest night.

Chapter 9: Some things come all the way to the last end

It became clear to me that Emma and I weren't one of them. Another tear slowly ran down her cheek. I reached out to wipe it off, but she pushed my hand and wiped it away by herself.

Her feet felt cold on top of mine. We were sitting opposite of each other and only having our feet in contact. It had only been five hours of daylight, and it already seemed like the surface of the earth had been scorched by the light.

Looking back at it now, I also realize how much timing matters. I didn't realize these things while living them, but then again, who does? Basically I turned my back on all that I knew a total of two times, and now I was looking at my third. I guess that some people only do one, some maybe none, but I was looking at three.

Basically I felt lucky that I developed like I did. The funny thing was that after each transformation, I felt so lucky and blessed to not being stuck in the old world. I had friends in elementary that I turned my back on. It was the first time I tried it. It felt weird. They are still all the old guys hanging out together and basically that has a lot to do with what I was just talking about.

These guys were put in the same class by some primary school employee. There was nothing special about the way they met, but they didn't think about that. To be honest, we were all just normal kids.

The time I turned my back on them was in early puberty. I was starting to think about girls and how to talk to them. Apart from that, I also just looked for new friends. These guys started to bore the shit out of me. They weren't cool, but even worse, they weren't fun or interesting.

What I later realized was that they also only gathered on things in the bread and circus category. I was looking for new friends, and luckily I found them.

Ironically enough, it's the guys that I've got no contact with today. It was my second time cleaning out the closet, but that's not what this is about. Basically what it's about is timing. If I hadn't turned my back on those guys, then things wouldn't have added up as they did.

Right now I was looking at my third throw over, and who knows if I will be looking at a fourth? The second throw over isn't just about finding out about the opposite sex; no, it's a lot more than that. Basically someone can go from one thing to another, but it's the awareness of choices that matters. It's releasing, that walking away. Leaving someone or something behind sometimes is a step forward.

It's about growing older and wiser and keeping your personality open to the world. Beginning to realize what you need. Also, most people only go from the first to the second level. That whole area of understanding is quite similar. You can build a sustainable life on both of them, and that's why they are very popular.

Still, what people lack is awareness. Most people don't have that that, or they don't care. That's exactly where everything differs, and that's why the question of how to get awareness is the most important.

I don't think there is a single answer to that question, but I know that there is journey that you'll experience if you embrace it. The journey of figuring out what you need for you and the people in your life.

I wasn't cleaning out the closet again. I knew what I was by then, I think. It was all ideas and values taken from everywhere, but I made them mine. I guess that's what you do.

I was talking to Emma about what happened. We hadn't been awake for long, but things were going quickly. Another tear was sliding over her curved cheekbone.

Had I done anything wrong? She assured me that I hadn't, but I had a hard time believing that with her crying in my arms. Emma wasn't being mad at me. Basically we were talking about how we decided the sex would happen.

She thought she couldn't, but something about her was way too fragile for that. She wasn't telling me anything but the fact that she had realized that she wasn't ready for sex.

She liked it, but as soon as she woke up and the spell was gone, something was different. I realized that Emma wasn't that strong after all. It was an outer facade. I soon began to think about this book that I had read. *Existentialism is a Humanism* was the name of it.

It talks about existentialism, of course, but more about the responsibility that goes with it. Personal and integrative responsibility for one's actions. I was wondering how you could take responsibility if you haven't figured out all the inner motivations, stories, feelings, etcetera dwelling in both the conscious and subconscious you. I also remember the front cover of a chair. It was very subtle, but I liked it so much.

It wasn't going anywhere, but I think she just needed time. We were sitting there in the perfect hotel room not being that happy anymore.

My love life is something I haven't talked much about, but it's because I don't find it as being part of this story. I kissed a girl while having a girlfriend. The guilt that I felt was terrible, and I'm glad it was. I wanted to make sure I would never do that again. I would not let myself love someone before I knew that I wouldn't fuck up again. That was basically one of the greatest lessons of my love life, but I didn't know anything about Emma's.

Her crying because of voluntary intercourse with me is not right at all. Something had happened to her, but she wasn't going to tell me. The problem was that I didn't feel like I could help her if she didn't tell me.

I really cared about her, and she needed to get something off her chest. I think that it was by then I knew that I loved Emma. The concern confirms the love of another human.

Love is many things. It's not that I wanted to be in a relationship with her. The thing was that she mattered. She mattered to me and I cared about her. Still, she kept quiet.

I closed my eyes and slowly dazed into myself. I was thinking of that December night, the Christmas vibe and the freshly fallen snow. The sky here was red like an open wound, yet all of a sudden all I wanted was the dark snowy sky. Just not being here, causing whatever it was I was causing.

Emma was so strong, and I respected her for that. Not admire, respect. I realized that I had done that from the very first time I laid my eyes on her. We were equal in everything as we connected there. Like we had finally found the other half.

It seemed so when she finally got up to telling me about her past. It's very personal, and I won't say what happened to her. All I will say is that it's something I wish had not and will never happen to anyone again.

The entire day was very peculiar and weird. It was like time passed while we were in a vacuum. Like nothing went on, but still everything did.

We were in bed all day, and Emma was slowly getting better. I got us some pineapple juice from the reception, and that's the closest we got to sunlight that day.

The window was open, and once in a while we got a light breeze. Mostly the air was thick from the heat, but the ocean breeze made up for it. We were lying next to each other, sometimes touching and caressing each other.

We kept talking about how we felt, but it never really seemed like we got that deep, and yet it still worked. It was like all these scattered conversations made up a really big picture.

I didn't realize it at the time, but I also realized that most things are realized in retrospect. That's, of course, given that one thinks a lot about the actions of the past.

As we were lying there, Emma all of a sudden changed the subject. We had only talked in fractions about our lives, and all of a sudden she was telling me about this thing she once read.

It was about a room that some scientist had invented for a project. It was a complete sound and light proof room. I don't know why she was telling me about it, but I figure she must have thought I found it interesting.

Actually, I kind of did, so she was about right. It sounded really interesting. I tried imagining how it must be to be inside such a room. She was telling me that it made people go completely mad.

I was contemplating how that could be. She said that all the sounds you can hear are from your body, your heart beating, every breath and muscle moving. It sounds scary, but it's funny to think about it anyways. It's something that we do everyday at all times, but it scares us when we get aware of it. When it's the only ambience, we get uncomfortable. It's the sounds of mortality, and we can't bear to deal with it.

I've thought and talked about this before, but the memento mori feeling doesn't really go well with us. I just know that I will always remember that summer whenever it's present. Even on my deathbed when I'm about to flow down the river, then that's what I'll be holding onto.

Memories will be there despite the fact that the wind has carried it away a long time ago. As long as I knew that I found my way and stayed true to it. That's how long I know that there will be a sunny day and I will stay new to it.

We went for dinner in the afternoon. The restaurant was calm even though it had a few people around. Both Emma and I looked like we had just gotten out of bed, which wasn't untrue at all.

I felt that we could kind of talk about anything we wanted at that dinner table. I kept asking her how she felt. I wanted to know if she needed space, or anything else for that matter. It didn't seem like it, but I still considered giving her some.

The nice girl in the reception who was also waitressing came serving our food. Emma said "thank you" in the native tongue again.

Just for a second I thought it was irritating until I saw what kind of reaction it sparked. The girl grew a big smile and got really excited.

She began asking Emma how she'd learned and why her pronunciation was so good. I hadn't realized how excited a language can get someone.

Linguistics are pretty interesting, but still this was on such a different level. It kind of made sense to me, there might be something good about it as well. "It's good around here. I just need to think a little," Emma said.

"That's all right, let's just stay the nights we've planned and see," I said.

Emma agreed, and then we went on to eating some food. The food made the silence less awkward, but I felt a need for having a topic that we could dig into.

"Do you believe in God?" I asked her. She looked rather surprised.

"Do I believe in God?" she asked rhetorically.

"Yes," I said in a mellow voice. She made a long humming sound inciting contemplating.

"I think I do. Yes," she said. It sounded interesting.

"How? The bible?" I asked.

"No."

"Then what?" I asked.

"I don't believe in any of the books. Do you?" Emma asked.

"No, I don't. How are you not in the same boat as me??'

"What boat are you in?" Emma asked, kind of funny.

"The one that says nonbelievers and atheists are on the same side."

"Because I'm not."

"But you don't believe in religion?"

"Not any written religion. I just believe in greater powers. There is a word for it, but I can't remember what it is."

"Greater powers, like what?" I asked.

"I don't know. Karma, afterlife, it doesn't even have to be specific. I just believe that there is more than meets the eye. I mean, there is something that we can't explain, and I don't think we should."

I was actually really following what she was saying. I see myself as an atheist, and I don't really think I could believe in any of the written religions, but I liked Emma's approach.

"I actually haven't thought like you. The written religions are all bullshit, but I hadn't thought of the Twin Peak approach."

You could tell that she didn't get it. She hadn't watched *Twin Peaks*, which was kind of a shame. If you haven't either, it's just a reference to supernatural things happening, but you should still watch it.

"Actually, I don't pay much attention to it," she said.

"To be honest, I try not to either, but it just seems like something I care about a lot," I said.

"I find religious people so irritating at most times. I've met plenty of nice ones, but there is something about the way they go about things. There is something that ties them, and it's just about pinpointing what it is. Mostly it's just cultural heritage, but for the ones that it's not, it's really interesting. I mean, if a god existed, why would he then have made a thousand different religions? It's human history. We have a basic need for fairy tales and existential explanations. Not to mention that it's the best way to control people."

Wow. I was speechless. Emma just literally hit the nail right on the head. I didn't know that she could think and speak like that. Maybe she wasn't so bad after all.

It's funny that such criticism came with her being and feeling down. Honestly, I think most people could speak like this, but so few do.

We quickly got through the dinner and decided to buy a red wine to take to the room. We put it all on the tab again.

We got inside the room with our two glasses. After we had poured the wine, we were on the beds again. It was like the conversations didn't really flow.

I think both of us felt really comfortable around each other by now, but still the mood just wasn't there.

We turned on the TV only to discover that More Movies still was broadcasting horrible motion pictures.

I decided to go through all the channels just to see what was on. They were all in the native language, showing stuff we didn't exactly want to watch.

That's all except one. Until this day I'm so happy that I decided to scroll through the TV channels at that time. It was one of the local TV stations, but the film they had on was definitely foreign.

It was an old film, I could tell. Not only from the black and white, but also just the style. I didn't and still don't know the name of it. It was in French for the most part, but definitely took place in Japan a lot of the time.

There was this couple which consisted of an absurdly gorgeous French woman and rather handsome Japanese man. They were lying in a bed and discussing something. I didn't get a thing of what they were saying, but it was so tender.

I had never ever experienced such a tender story. I sensed that it was a simple story of love, but also something more than that. This couple, it was like they didn't live on planet earth. The way they talked seemed so unlike any real people I know of.

Still they seemed so real and attractive in their misery of longing and loving. Nothing went on in the film. They were just there trying to find themselves and each other.

That might of course be a story I made up. I didn't understand any dialogue, but it was still one of the best films I've ever watched.

Emma was watching it as well. She seemed to like it, and I think it was given that day's very special mood.

Usually it would probably not have been her taste. Watching a film centered on dialogue and not understanding it can sound like a waste of time, but it was anything but that. I can tell you that I dreamed myself away to those Japanese streets, this brutalist hotel, and this one very classic Japanese restaurant.

It looked like the best place on earth, yet still I felt it came to us. The film ended and it made me feel kind of sad. It was like it wasn't finished, like they left Emma and me behind. There was definitely something in those characters, but they left too soon.

I got up and looked for the remote. Emma picked it up and turned off the TV. The room was dark. The moon was illuminating a thin white line over Emma's blanket. It gently touched her face. Her skin was like velvet in the light, her eyes like pearls in the night. She looked like no words can describe.

Life is simple in moonlight. We sat next to each other. I just wanted to be there for her. She didn't want me close to her. Still she didn't want me away either.

Transparency is one thing the moon can't illuminate. Right there in the middle of things, it all seemed liquefied. Were we the only people breathing on this planet that night?

We were lying down, yet not touching each other. Given what Emma had told, I just wanted to do whatever she needed. Being whatever she needed me to be.

Lying there, I began looking around, first at the table then the lamp, TV, bed table, TV, and vase. The room was full of things, yet it seemed empty. Still it felt like there were other people with us there. Like all these things around us contained a bit of the humans that they were made by.

Nothing was natural. The voices of all these people were in the wood. Still, I felt better than ever. The entire search for truth was coming to an end. Really it wasn't, as that is the point. There is no end, and that I have accepted now.

You can say that the end of my search was the realization that there is no end. Everything can be interpreted in different ways. I was so obsessed with finding truth. The problem was that I was looking for it and not creating it. Making it temporary and always changeable is what I have done now.

Truth was not something I was going to find in a doctrine, a paradigm, and then just stick to it. There might be something I read or think that will be valid for me my whole life.

Still, that can surely be seen as meaningless and superficial from somewhere else. That is the beauty of it, in my opinion. Wisdom is definitely a thing that you can read, but the absolute wisdom is something one must strive to provide oneself.

I was looking at the bed table and slowly moved my hand to touch the wood. It was some beautiful tree, and I really enjoyed touching it with my hand. This was a good table, a quality table. That was something I decided, still I know that quality is not completely subjective nor objective. This is something I have been thinking about for a long time and reading about as well.

The wisdom, the personality that one creates out of whatever comes is and should always be changeable. The experiences that will change it will come through everyday life experiences. We can never know what will come and neither how we will react to it.

This is where quality becomes a thing, as it is found only in the present. It is accessible and known to all of us, yet still many haven't given it any thought.

Quality can be recognized before it can be conceptualized, and that is why it is so important. A person can tell whether he or she likes something or not. That's almost no matter what on earth it is.

A person will have an opinion, yet still it won't be a completely subjective opinion. Many people will slowly grow such deep roots that they lose their dynamic form. They lose the ability to let observed quality shape their personalities.

Thinking back, that openness is one of the most important things that I learned from meeting and getting to know Emma.

I could hear Emma breathe a little heavier than usual. The kind of breathing you do when sleeping. I gently got off the bed and walked to the balcony door.

It was perfectly chilly outside. It was so quiet that I could hear the waves from the ocean trying to eat the land. I was wondering if there was an ocean tide under this moonlight. What life would be like after this was all over.

I could hear the cigarette burn as I breathed through it. It was a calming sound. As I sat there looking I suddenly heard a sound.

A door from one of the huts opened up. It sounded like it came from the right side. I became a little vigilant and tried to see if I could see anything. The trees were covering my view until I spotted someone dressed in white walking slowly. Still the trees blocked my view, but I did my best.

It didn't take me long to realize that it was a kid, a young boy in white and light blue sleepwear. What was he doing at this time, was what I asked myself. I realized that it was the boy that I'd seen in the restaurant the other day. I couldn't tell if he was really awake.

I quickly contemplated whether I should do something or not. I decided to just sit and observe him. He was a neat and adorable little kid. It's not that I find many kids adorable, but this one was.

I could have walked down to see what he was up to, but it was none of my business. I would probably also just scare the shit out of him. That's at least how I would have felt if a stranger had intervened in one of my childhood adventures.

He walked inside the main building. It ended up with me smoking two cigarettes and starting really wondering what he was doing.

Just as I was about to decide to walk down and see for myself, he came walking out. It was in the exact same slow and snoozing way. I smiled at him, but he had not awareness of my presence.

He walked back into the hut, and I felt that the day had brought me enough. I silently sneaked inside and as quietly as possible brushed my teeth.

Thinking of how Emma felt, it's weird. She tells me stuff and then goes to sleep. It might have drained her energy drastically, but I don't know. She was absurdly fast asleep though. I tucked in next to her and had absolutely no problem feeling comfortable or falling asleep.

Chapter 10: Marble House

The sweat was slowly exiting the skin on my forehead. I looked over my shoulder while running. They were still chasing us. I don't recall how many people were running, but it was many. The road was hilly with houses on both sides. We all knew it led to the woods.

That was where we were running. The fear had erupted all of a sudden. These guys in red clothes and armor were killing people. With katanas they were spreading the fear and death.

The fear of mortality is the strongest kind of fear. We were running through the tall grass. I looked around and saw people come running from all the streets. The tall grass was still wet from the rain. It caressed my legs for every step.

We soon found shelter under the treetops. The woods were slowly getting darker, like less and less sunshine came through the leaves. Fewer and fewer people were with me until we were only five. They didn't have faces. I don't remember any faces.

The woods were dark. A new fear was smoldering in our stomachs. Something was in the woods, and we knew we had to run from it as well.

It came closer. I couldn't run any faster. I realized what monster it was, a giant dog with three heads. It was closing in on us.

I remember seeing a forest glade in front of us. It wasn't really a glade, as there wasn't any light, but something was there. I could feel it.

We were only three people now, still running for our lives. In front of me I saw a house. There was a house there.

I felt relief coming through my entire body. It was a completely black house, but there was light in two of the windows.

I felt the breath on my neck, but finally we got close to the house. Someone was waiting for us there.

An old lady with a wise and wrinkled face was standing there holding the door. We ran to her and she welcomed us. All short of breath, we got inside. She stepped outside and looked in the dark for a few seconds. Then she turned and closed the door.

"Welcome," she said in a warm and shaky voice. She was happy to have our company. I realized that the entire house was built from black stone. It looked like black marble. In the kitchen there was some wood, and the lady served us a drink from the pot on the stove. It tasted like nothing I'd ever tasted. It was like tea and hot chocolate at the same time. I looked around, but still only the old lady had a face. She could see that we were freezing from being in forest.

"Come," she said.

We all got up and followed her down the hall. She creaked open a door to a massive bathroom. Everything was still made out of black marble. On our left side, a massive hot tub was ready to warm our bodies. Steam was slowly rising from the hot water. The old lady smiled and then walked out. We all got in the hot tub. I leaned my head back on the edge and relaxed.

I heard a sound, opened my eyes, and looked to my left. Emma was up, and I was awake. It took me some seconds to realize that I was back in reality. What kind of dream did I just have? I felt kind of bad from it, like from a nightmare. Emma looked at me.

"Good morning," she said in a slow voice.

"Good morning," I replied.

"I had the weirdest dream," I continued.

"Oh yeah? What was it about?" Emma asked.

"I don't know. It was just weird stuff going on. Some samurais, me running in fear, an old lady, and a house of marble."

Emma looked at me with a weird look.

"That does sound peculiar," she said.

I didn't really know what to make of it. Not what Emma said, but the dream.

"Yeah. I don't know what that was about," I said.

"No, it's hard with dreams. Just let it be. Something might come to you," she said.

I think that was good logic.

"Do you wanna come to the beach?" she asked.

It didn't sound like a bad plan at all.

"Can we grab some breakfast on the way?" I asked.

"Oh yes, we can just bring everything and then eat breakfast downstairs on our way."

"All right." A plan was made.

At breakfast I saw the small boy from last night at the table again. I was wondering what shenanigans he was up to. He looked a little tired, but no wonder with him being up late at night. Luckily he was on vacation. At his age, vacations are all about shenanigans. I like that.

The sand was hot, even though it was still early. The sun was still rising rapidly on the sky. I decided to go for a swim right away. Emma was lying on her towel next to mine, and we both found it good with some sunshine and tanning.

I put in my iPod earphones and began listening to my Acoustic Melancholic playlist, which is one of my favorites. I'll give you a little taste of what's on there. I listened to all these songs that day. The thing is that I listened and still do listen to at least a few of these songs every day. You can play them to yourself to get the sound picture. Music is a very personal experience, and I could have listened to anything. This was just my taste.

Alice in Chains – "Nutshell (Unplugged)"

Iceage – "Plowing Into the Field of Love"

Mad Season – "Wake Up"

Johnny Cash – "Hurt"

The Strokes – "Call Me Back"

The Libertines – "Music When the Lights Go Out"

The Smashing Pumpkins – "Landslide"

Mad Season – "River of Deceit"

Eddie Vedder – "Long Nights"

Bright Eyes – "First Day Of My Life"

Bon Iver – "Creature Fear"

Frank Ocean – "Nikes"

I had been lying there for a while. The sun was beginning to feel a little too hot. I needed another dip. I took out my in-ears and asked Emma.

"Do you wanna come for a swim?" She lifted her head and looked at me.

"Yeah, sounds like a good idea."

We got up and slowly walked into the blue water. It was like cutting the body in half with the cold water and hot air.

We both smiled because it was a little chilly, but there is no other cure than to just dive into the surf. I got up from the water and got on my feet. It felt so good to be cooled like this. I looked at Emma, and she enjoyed it just as much.

She looked so natural and beautiful when she was standing there. We both got into the water again. Just keeping our heads above water and enjoying it.

"Wow, this is the life," Emma said. I agreed with a smile, but something inside of me was telling me something.

"There is something I've been thinking about. Can I ask you?"

"Yes?" She looked kind of nervous in a curious way. Maybe she could sense something in the tone of my voice.

"I've really been enjoying this trip. It's only been some days, but I don't think we should overdo it."

Emma was and looked very surprised.

"Overdo it? Are we?" she asked, a bit defensive yet aggravated.

"No, yes. I don't know. What I'm saying is—"

"Is what?"

"That I've thought about it and I think that it might be time for us to go home."

She was standing there speechless. The water on her face made it look as if it were dissolving.

"But … Are you not enjoying this?"

She looked at me, then around. I was enjoying it.

"I am, I'm just, I think that going home within a day or two is the right choice."

Now she began looking sad.

"You know that I'm not doing this to hurt you, right?" I continued.

The tears were starting to flow down her cheek. She was walking out the water.

"Emma, Emma, Emma, stop." She didn't stop.

I began following her, but didn't know what to do. She was walking fast, but I was hurrying so that I could reach her.

"Emma, come on." When I said that she turned around.

"Come on? Come on what? Why are you doing stuff like this? Why? What is wrong with you? Did you take me all this way for this? It's not like I don't enjoy it and appreciate it, I do, but I regret so badly being dependent on you because you really don't play with open cards."

I didn't know what to say.

"Seriously. I can't be mad at you. You're a good guy, but I don't get you. There is something I don't get."

I was standing there trying to find an answer.

"How do you really feel about me?" she continued.

"I like you. I've learned so much from being around you the past few days. You have a good heart and you are absolutely genuine."

She looked at me in a way that said "what is that supposed to mean?"

"I don't know why I feel like this, but I just think that we can make it home before Christmas, and then we'll still have had a great trip."

She wasn't satisfied with me.

"I get what you are saying, but I don't get you," she said and began walking. She walked straight to our things, picked up her part, and walked on towards the hotel.

I was just standing there completely astonished.

Why did I even say that, why did I think it? I was so happy here. I was able to do most the things that I like and try out how much to do it all. I was finding balance, and I was together with a cute girl that I knew.

I wanted to go home, even despite the fact that I didn't like it. It wasn't my comfort zone calling me home. It was something deep and profound inside of me that just wanted to break up the trip. It wasn't the same feeling from when I asked Emma initially. That was also a feeling that I couldn't oppress, but this one was different.

I walked up to our spot, which was now only mine. I sat down on the towel and overlooked the ocean. There were a few other people on the beach that were all really interested. They wanted to act like they weren't, but I could feel they were. It was irritating and disgusting.

I closed my eyes and looked towards the sun. The sun was slowly drying my face. It was burning hot. I felt like my skin was slowly wrinkling.

I had to sort things out with Emma. I had to reason with her to make her enjoy the last two days. I had to find flight tickets and plan some kind of transport to whatever airport we needed.

I picked up my things and began walking towards the hotel. As I walked onto the path, I saw Harry sitting in the exact same chair as the last time I saw him. He really was enjoying himself. He had spotted me and was clearly interested in talking, if only I would take the initiative.

I walked up to him and greeted him.

"Take a seat if you'd like," he said in his pleasantly rusty voice. It seemed a little less intense than last time, but everything kind of does in the bright sunlight. I sat down and looked at him.

"How are you doing?" I asked.

"Oh, I'm great. Not much, but just enough has happened since we last talked," he said with a smile. He kind of made me smile with the mood he had.

"Yeah, like what?" I asked.

"Today is just a beach day, but yesterday we went to the mountain just close to here," he said.

"Oh wow, how was that?"

"It was perfect. My girl had never been on a mountain before," he said.

"Wow," I kind of answered with my facial expression.

"Yeah, blew her mind, and then she blew me off afterwards," he said with an amazing expression that I won't try to describe.

He obviously found it very funny himself as he started laughing hard. Not exactly my usual type of humor, but he really got me and I started laughing hard.

"All right, all right," I said with the laughing slowly dying out.

"So where is she now?" I continued. Harry still had his wonderful smile on.

"She's in town buying something, whatever. I don't remember," he said with a smile.

"How is your life here going along? I saw your girl leave you rather drastically down there," he said and glanced towards the beach. He could even see it from up here; it meant that everybody had seen it. Of course, Harry had a good eye for human interactions, but still. I tried to tell myself that it didn't matter, and really it didn't that much.

"So what's going on?" he continued.

I looked at him and said, "It's complicated, but basically I just told her that I think we should go home," I said with a bit of insecurity in my voice.

"Well, she must sure as hell like this place if that's how she reacts," he said, trying to be cheeky. I tried to force a smile.

"As I said, it's complicated. Technically we don't even know each other, and I kind of took her as a hostage in my imagination or something," I said.

"Look at me," Harry said. I had looked down without even realizing.

"I don't even want to know the story. Just be honest and do what feels right. If you are in doubt, as I can see you are, then remember to ask yourself why it feels right," he said.

I was trying to comprehend the meaning of it. My brain was on really slow speed. I think he could tell that I didn't quite get it.

"All right, let me make an example and tell you a little anecdote. Through my life, experiences and everything I had to go through, I've had and made many rules. Some I overdid, others I didn't stick to enough, mutual for most of them were that they got discarded. Still I have some, and who knows if I'll invent new ones. The most important rule that I had with me all along is: Be honest. It may sound easy, banal, and very religious, and the most natural thing to be, but trust me, it's not. Let me explain to you what honesty also can be."

I leaned in as he was talking. He continued.

"The other day, for example, I had an encounter with a stranger that I didn't particularly like. He wasn't being hostile, but there was something going on with him. He was, like everybody else, used to people keeping up appearances. We all do a little bit of cover-up for our honesty every day. I've tried to kill mine for twelve years now, and it hasn't felt bad yet. Sometimes people think you are a douche, a prick, maybe even a cunt, but if you are being honest, then you are being the best you can be. You can meet people on a whole new level and it's quite relieving, I can tell you. The only thing you have to be aware of is why you feel the way you do. Is your reality, the one you are being honest about, closest to the truth? Do you get what I'm saying?"

I think I knew what he meant.

"I think so. I'm always honest whenever I open my mouth," I said.

"And what about when you don't? Are you honest then?" he asked. I felt like I was being honest most of the time. Actually, all the time, a lot of things I didn't say out loud, but that wasn't lying in my book.

"I keep a lot of things and thoughts to myself. That's how I always have been," I said.

"Good, that's good. Still, I think that you keep too much. Honesty is not only telling the truth. It's also about opening up. I don't know your problems or imagination, but just be open and honest. You have a good heart, kid. You just need to know how to protect it, so that you can open it," Harry said in his very pleasant voice. It's funny how he was being so intimate with me, and yet not intimidating me at all. He was just brilliant in his own way.

"I think I know what you mean now. I mean, I know what you mean," I said in a thankful voice that made Harry smile. He was a funny guy like that. He just energized off being a genuine guy, helping out and sharing a bit of wisdom. It's funny how he still was kind of a stranger to me, and still I feel like the conversation we just had was deeper than any conversation I ever had with my dad. I had stood up and was walking towards the room. It's funny how both of our conversations had been so short but important. It still shows a lot, I think.

I don't know if the things Harry was talking about applied to me, but I do feel the part about honesty does a little. The part about knowing why you think or feel something. The worst part was that I couldn't figure out why I felt like going home. It was just a gut feeling, but they are, after all, the strongest feelings I have.

On the stairs I met Emma. She was on her way down.

"Hey," I said. She still looked kind of hurt.

"Where are you going?" I continued.

"I'm going to town. I'll be back tonight, but I just need a little space."

I had done the exact same thing. I didn't know how she felt, but what she wanted to do was perfectly cool. I wish she would want to talk, but it wasn't exactly weird that she didn't. She walked down and turned around the corner.

I leaned back and fell onto the mattress. The thick, hot air made me feel moist. I was lying there looking at the ceiling thinking about how everything went down. What went through my head? Was it an obsession or just a desire? Did I love Emma? Why did I feel like going home so badly?

I took my time to think. Trying to make sense of everything. I was thinking of how the world was opening to me like this. Was there something else, more than meets the eye?

I've never been religious, but just for a short time I was making myself believe that someone had controlled me. No one had, it was just my motivations and myself.

Reality can be really beautiful, but nowadays we grow up in a world built upon logical thinking. Logical minds have a really hard time being religious, and thank God for that. There wasn't any divine intervention or big plan. Sure there was a bigger picture, but it was myself navigating in it.

Emma had put her passport on the bed so it was easily visible. I found my own, took my phone out, and began looking for flight tickets.

I don't know what it was with this country, but flying was extremely cheap. It still costs quite a bit, but really I didn't care.

That voice in the back of my head was bothering me again. Honestly, it was a lot of money spent in five days, but there was nothing to do about it, and it was well spent anyways. I don't want money to affect me like that.

I booked the flight tickets and put down the phone. Now it was done. We had to leave.

Now I was lying on the bed again, thinking. Slowly I was gliding into my poetic mood. I hadn't been there for quite a while, but I was getting there again finally. I found a pen, some random paper, and began writing. When the pen hits the paper and the ink is coming out, my mind gets clear as a morning haze. Nothing is really in there, but somehow I still feel downed when it ends. It scared me a little, as I know what my poetic mood means. It's not in my most blissful moments that it's best.

Once again I was listening to the melancholic acoustics playlist. Smashing Pumpkins version of "Landslide" was my choice for now. It fitted my mood perfectly.

It's the sad dance of the old lady and the orphan left in the park, yet it's also the summer sky and mating fireflies. The ceiling in that room wasn't dreamy, yet neither was I. I had been so eager to come out here. I had enjoyed it, and now I was putting it all to an end.

The heat made me feel like snoozing for a while. I had no obligations and plenty of time, so that's what I decided to do. I woke up a fair bit later and still without a sign of Emma. I went onto the terrace and looked.

Impatience began to grow. She probably hadn't even been gone for that long, but it still felt like enough. I figured that I could shorten the waiting time by working out a bit.

Changing clothes didn't take long. The feeling I get from keeping my body healthy is so treasurable. It makes me feel like I ought to. When I can finish it off with a swim in the ocean, it's like nothing else.

I'd gotten back in the room, and fully dressed I was sitting on the bed feeling impatient.

What was she doing in town? Maybe I could go find her? I discarded those thoughts. She left to get rid of me, and I didn't want to be that stalker kind of guy.

Still, they came right back. I decided that I could at least go to town to find my own place. She couldn't accuse me of anything if I was just looking for my own place. The afternoon sun was a little more humane, yet still not at all. I was sweating so much that I'd completely ceased to care.

The town was quiet under the sun. People had crept in the shade or in the water's edge.

I was partly looking for a beer and partly for Emma. Honestly I don't even know if I wanted to meet her.

I walked into a rather big café, which also served as a bar. A big team of waiters awaited me, and this one girl escorted me to a seat.

It was an all right place for a beer. I sat there and overlooked the ocean from a distance. What was to come of all this?

I pulled out my pen in attempt to write a poem. As I hold it here in my hand, now I know what rubbish it turned out to be.

I can rarely sit in one place with total calmness in my mind, but that night I did. No distractions or urges for anything came by. I wonder if it was a sign of adulthood. I still don't know.

The sun had set over the ocean, and the night was creeping up on all of us. More people had come in the place. People were chattering, eating, and drinking. I was lonely at my table.

Watching the road and the ocean living their life. I liked the kind of music they played in here. It was some type of funky jazz.

At one point I looked over my shoulder to discover two women dancing. I couldn't really grasp nor understand it at first. They were old, probably about the age of my grandmother. They were at their table in a more discrete yet very public part of the café. Easily visible, they still moved their old hips like they were young as a cherry.

I still remember the feeling they gave me. It was a feeling of rootlessness and aging. It's not a beautiful cocktail. I know how they say age is just a number, but sometimes it's not. Some things are just better the way they were.

I didn't stare at them, mainly out of politeness. After all it hadn't been that long since I experienced it myself, yet still I swore that I would never grow sixty and act like I was twenty.

It was everything that it came down to. It kind of reminded me of the tram ride I had with Emma, yet this wasn't close to being as bad of a case.

I'd finished a couple of beers and decided to transition into a drink that was named after the bar. It consisted of gin, lemon, sugar, and ginger ale. It was quite the tasteful drink.

I'd also asked the waiter for some paper, and luckily they had some A4 in the back.

I briefly thought of Emma and that she might even be back at the hotel by now. I put the pen to the paper and dragged it across. I wasn't thinking, but something was coming out onto the paper.

All of a sudden I could hear the line "Can we get much higher" in the speakers. A new song had come on, a song I remember very well. I used to listen to it every day on my way to school. It was when I would still listen to music like that.

When it began playing, it was like it dragged me back into that time. It was a song of stupidity and depression.

For a brief second I considered asking if they could change it, but then I realized that this song of sorrows shouldn't be what I made it.

It was good that it reminded me. It reminded me to take it into my own hands and make it a song of overcoming everything. All my lack of will and hope in everything. My general depression and its tune had to be changed.

All of this I tried to fit into a poem. I decided to write it on my phone instead of the paper. Did you know that depression turns into eternal when spelled wrong in the auto correct? It made me smile.

The song was fading as I downed the last sip. I had to leave. I got out on the street and the air was still thick and hot like earlier. A few mild breezes were coming in from the ocean, but it wasn't enough.

I was standing there on this quite trashy yet so charming street next to the ocean. Suddenly I got this picture of Emma in my head. She was in a bar flirting with some guy. I could see how he was leaning in and making a move on her. She was being discrete but open to the compliments.

I tried to get it out, but some part of me really wanted to go down that road. I was thinking. Whether to go back to the hotel or begin walking around the bar area looking for her?

It felt weird that I had some part of me fighting another, like there wasn't unity in my brain anymore. It wasn't just a regular decision. I wanted to go back to the hotel, but some voice inside my head kept saying that she wouldn't be there. She would be out with some guy doing whatever.

I walked down towards the ocean and turned left. I tried excusing my behavior to myself. It was pathetic, and yet my one leg still kept coming in front of the other.

I was basically already in the bar area and walking around. There was a fair bit of people, but I still felt comfortable. I wasn't frantic or anything. I just wanted to find Emma.

I still remember some of those faces in the café. Beautiful couples, old men, people laughing and staring into the night. Everything seemed to be there, yet not what I was looking for.

When I had finished up the main street, I was seriously thinking of walking back to the hostel, yet my urge to check out some of the smaller side streets was too big.

I turned right, walked slowly, scanning every café, bar, and restaurant. One girl with golden brown hair caught my attention. Her hair just the same liveliness as Emma's, despite the glance, it quickly showed that it wasn't her.

As I got to the end of the street, it felt like the, whatever part of me it was, didn't have the better of me anymore. I turned away from the jazzy house and human humming of the bars and began walking back towards the quiet hotel. The voice was still in the back of my head, trying to play games, but I did control my own body again.

The walk home wasn't long. When I arrived at the hotel, I was surprised to see that Harry wasn't in his usual chair. I was still thinking about some of the things he said. That man was a weird acquaintance, yet still a very pleasant one.

As I walked up the balcony, our room became visible between the trees. Emma was sitting on it. The lights lit in the room behind her.

She had noticed me as I walked there. I looked at her as I walked, not once did I look down or away.

When I got up to about five meters from the balcony I stopped and looked at her. She was staring at me. Her hair was lit beautifully from behind, and with the ocean breeze on her face nothing seemed so bad. She wasn't just any girl. I liked her, but why did I want to stop traveling with her?

Looking in her eyes and having them look at my heart alongside myself, I still couldn't figure it out. I was looking for any sign in her face, but the stare just continued.

Slowly we got to a point where we both knew. Emma turned around and walked into the room. I'll never forget the sight of her disappearing through the door.

I walked into the reception, awkwardly passing and greeting the reception lady before going up the stairs. I slowly pushed down the door handle. The door was unlocked. Slowly I pushed it open. It was to the sight of Emma standing and looking straight towards me.

"Hey," I said in a relieved voice.

She didn't say anything. I got in and closed the door after me.

"I got so worried about you today that I couldn't stay here," I continued.

I could tell by her looks that she wasn't really mad at me.

"Worried. Why would you get worried about me?" she said.

I think borderline jealousy might have been a better word for it, but being worried sounded a little better.

"I don't know. I guess I just really wanted to talk to you. I didn't mean to tell you right there in the water in front of all those people."

"I don't care about all the people," she said.

"All right, but still I just want you to know that I've booked our flights, but that it's not a sign of any bad vibes."

"I've been thinking about this a lot today. I don't think I understand you, but I respect whatever you say. I think it's weird that we went all this way just to spend five days together. I've enjoyed them, so I'm not gonna complain. I just really hope that I can get my job back."

I got really glad when she said that, everything except the part about her getting her job back.

"I'm glad you think that way. Honestly, I don't know why I feel this way. I really like you, and never meant to make you part of this circus. I just have this gut feeling, it's the same feeling that made me ask you in the first place. I have to trust it."

Emma had a confined look on her face. She knew I was being honest and being me, however weird that must have been.

It actually felt like she kind of knew me by then, as she didn't seem to judge me in any way. I think that it's a very good thing that she didn't.

Most of the time Emma and I spent after I told her that we were going home was weird. It had some slightly different feel to it.

I had gone to the reception and asked for a bus to the nearest airport, which was the one our transfer flight was from. The receptionist advised taking a taxi, so I took that into consideration.

Now we were going to spend Christmas at home anyways. When I began thinking of that, I could see my mother decorating the Christmas tree. She was probably not this year, as I had made her and everybody panic. It was actually quite a bad situation. I didn't wish for it, but I single-handedly made it happen.

For the thousandth time I was thinking of how I was going to deal with the parent interrogation when I got home. I began thinking about Christmas and how nice it usually is. It's the time of year that has always been reserved for family time.

I don't know how most families do it, but every second year we celebrated Christmas with my father's family and every second year with my mom's. It's not like they didn't get along, but it just doesn't feel family-like when we were all together.

Birthdays are the times when we all get together and it has and probably will always be really awkward. My father's big brother came celebrating with us every year, as he didn't have a wife, girlfriend, or kids. We were his closest family. I didn't mind having him around; to be honest, I actually kind of liked it.

He was very peculiar in some ways, but pretty relaxed, smart, and fun to talk to. He was a history and linguistics teacher, and as I said, quite a strange man. I had a lot of respect for him as he was an idealistic man. He believed in compassion, democracy, neighborly love, and hard work. He was the type of man who never skipped a day of work and was still a hardcore conservative, social liberal. I really admired that.

He was teaching at a type of middle school, I think. I really can imagine him being very overqualified, as he was one of the people with the most historical knowledge that I ever met.

With all this being said, he sounds like a pretty decent guy. He definitely was, but something was off. He was also a crazy nostalgic.

The thing I didn't understand was that he kept so much to himself. I guess that's just him, but it's now from this terrace that it really strikes me that the adventure of life is in other humans.

Yes, it's true. I'd moved on to the balcony to smoke a cigarette. The vibes between Emma and me were good again.

So he was with us every year. That year it was with my father's family. That meant that my grandmother and her sister would come. That is my father's mom and aunt. They were both widows, and together with my father's two brothers counted as the family. They also had a sister, but she always celebrated with her husband and their family.

So we were not a big family, but still big enough to have the clichés going. My grandmother and her sister were both daughters of a reverend, which meant they had a much more strict upbringing religion-wise. That also meant that they wanted to sing every hymn walking around the Christmas tree, which I remember finding so annoying as a child.

It was torture, being a little present-eager child having to sing at least ten songs of worship to God. It all paid off in the end though. My father's family was pretty well off, and that of course resulted in very nice presents.

It was so funny how faith equaled consumerism for me back then. Thinking that made me think of the couple who sat next to me in the bar the night that I met Emma. It felt like so long ago.

Anyways, that was how it was like celebrating Christmas with my father's family. My mother's family was different; not worse, just different.

The family wasn't so well off, but it seemed that they always managed to find money for decent presents anyway. It was more about the cooking, though.

To be honest, I really enjoyed Christmas with both parts of the family. As my grandmother and her sister had their thing with the hymns, my mother's father had his with the storytelling.

He had these few different stories that he went over every year like we never heard them before, and we all reacted like we never heard them before every time. It was the social norm.

It was stories about how he grew up. They were a very poor family, and he was a lone son, which was rare at the time. The family was poor, and he was sent to work at age of thirteen. He rode his bike twelve kilometers to and from work every day and went for sports afterwards.

Things like that may sound annoying, but in some weird way I enjoyed them.

There was this one other story that he always saved for when the children were unwrapping presents. It was about a Christmas he celebrated sometime in the late forties, and how all he got for Christmas was an orange.

I guess we all got the moral of how privileged we were, but to me it always kind of drowned in wrapping paper. I was all very far away from that Christmas now, and it kind of put it in to some kind of perspective.

I remember his stories, and I think the most important message I got was how they learned to find quality. Today we have so much quantity that we've almost forgotten what quality is. What it means and that it's everywhere if only we learn how to look.

He also talked about the bible and reminded us how far we had gotten away from it. He was funny since it didn't seem to bother him. He just liked to remind us all. He had read it, but then again he was eighty, and it was the thing of his time.

I still remember Christmas four years ago when he told me about the origin of the bible. I remember being totally bewildered and not believing his facts, but I looked them up and they were true.

The bible was written several decades after Jesus passed away, which means what people take for the word of God was handed down verbally for a considerable amount of time.

On top of that it was only put together finally some three hundred years after Jesus died. Someone in Rome basically decided what text got to be in there and what text didn't.

That people took and take that, and any other book for that matter, as the word of God is quite a mystery to me. I mean, there is without doubt something mysterious and spiritual in this world, something we can't explain, but those old books?

I liked my grandpa and looked forward to seeing his face again. Stories like that are important, and that's another reason why Grandpa is important.

My cigarette was done, and it whistled as I twisted the bud against the surface of the ashtray. I took a look at my hand. Sometimes I think it looks really good. The smooth nails and light tanned skin.

I got inside and began talking to Emma again. I told her about the plan of getting home. We had two nights of sleep left before we had to go to the airport. Our flight was quite early in the morning, and it meant that we had one real day left.

Emma was rather constructive about our last day with everything taken into consideration.

We both jumped up in the same bed and began discussing what we wanted to do. Neither of us was keen for anything dramatic. Just a long day at the beach finished off with a good dinner. It wasn't anything fancy, just a perfectly normal day in a girl-boy relationship.

It's now that I realize how much perfectly normal days filled with perfectly normal activities can matter. It made me feel alive, human and motivated. There is a nice Japanese word for it. I found it a while afterwards, but it describes the feeling perfectly. Yaruki, I got it back during those days. Yaruki, possibly my new favorite word.

As we were lying there talking, I felt the urge to kiss her silky lips. I could still smell her scent, and it straight up made me want to crawl on top of her. I hadn't been like this before, but Emma surely had awakened something in me. I was holding back, though. If anything were to happen it would be on her initiative.

With the way she had reacted the last few days, it would be fucking disrespectful of me to try anything. Emma had sat herself up in the bed. I did the same as it felt weird lying next to her when she was sitting.

"So what do you want to do for the night?" I asked.

"I don't really know," Emma said.

"Well, we can watch a movie. Go for a late night swim?"

"Nah, I don't feel like either of those things," Emma said.

I was thinking a little. What else could we possibly do?

"Do you wanna go to town for a drink?" Emma asked.

"Well, if you want to."

"I don't know if I want to. I'm not tired or anything, and the bar area seems rather nice."

"I was just there. It is."

"We could always just do one drink, right?" Emma said.

I agreed, and then we decided to walk back into town. The night was still warm and full of vibes. Light and dark souls were hanging around the bars.

Emma and I picked a really relaxed place that played the kind of deep house anybody and everybody does at this point. Don't be mistaken. I like electronic music, it's just that most people just listen to it because it's the new thing.

Emma and I had been very secluded throughout the days we had spent together. We were open to the world, but didn't really talk to many other people. It changed that night after we had a few drinks.

Inside the bar there was a ping-pong table and about eight or so people playing. We started by talking about how we never got to play at the hotel, and soon we were playing with all the people there. They were all really funny, happy, and drunk. Mostly tourists and people traveling, the kind of people I hadn't met a lot of in my life.

Emma didn't feel like playing a lot. It seemed to me that she, like me, was better in smaller constellations, smaller groups with fewer people. Still, the drinks had loosened us up a bit, and we were chatting.

"So how do you two know each other?" one of the guys asked. Both Emma and I heard the question. He kind of asked us simultaneously. I remember not feeling the will to answer truthfully.

"We've known and dated each other for a long time," Emma said.

I got so surprised that I almost blew our cover. I guess it was only given to the guy's drunkenness that I didn't blow my cover.

Afterwards we went back to playing and chatting, and I remember it as a good time. After an hour or so, people stopped playing. Emma walked over to me and asked how I felt.

"Like going back home and taking a swim in the ocean," I said, being completely honest.

"Let's do that," she said while she looked me in the eyes. We thanked all the guys for good company and began walking back home.

Thinking back, it's funny to think about. We needed that outer influence to get close again. Like the experience of the stranger made us bond or something.

We had reached the end of the town and gotten onto the tree covered pathway. Suddenly I stopped walking, grabbed Emma's arm, and turned her towards me. She was surprised, but everything went pretty fast.

My lips touched hers, and she didn't resist one bit. The moon was lighting us carefully through the treetops while the mermaid sang us lullabies about joining her in the water.

Nothing could touch us. I felt that Emma liked me holding her firmly. She wanted that. I don't recall for how long we stood there kissing, but it was enough to make me forget about the fact that the earth was moving.

At one point she grabbed my hand, and we slowly began walking back to the hotel. The rest of the night was the most sensual. We didn't have sex, but we ended up kissing and cuddling all night. She felt something for me and I for her, despite the fact that my feelings were confused and partly scattered.

The time was 09:17 when I looked at my phone. It was our last real day under the summer sun. Emma was still making the night stretch a little further into the day. The night is, after all, relative these days.

I logged into the phone and opened up Facebook. I would kind of like to say that I did it less, but I was addicted.

I had an overwhelming amount of messages compared to the usual. I opened the message inbox, but just in the last second before I opened any of them thought a second time. Facebook saves and shows your location. I didn't want them to know where I was. The people who were writing me were my brother, sister, Calvin, and a couple of other people from school. I hadn't thought about it, but I guess even they were wondering about my whereabouts.

One message was from Aly. Despite the fact that I never talk to her, she will still send me articles that she knows I will like, articles on the state of the world and stuff similar to that.

Even though she wasn't a part of the people looking for me, I still wouldn't let anybody know about this place. I wanted to come back home and not tell anybody where I had been.

I closed the messages and scrolled the news feed. As usual it was just filled with brain-dead infotainment, entertainment, and half are dishonest stories like 95 percent of all other media.

It's not even subtle anymore. Every media company has such obvious agendas that I can't even bear to watch it.

I put my phone on the table in my fragile attempt to refuse cultural indoctrination. I slid out of bed, grabbed my iPod, and stepped onto the balcony. The increasing light of the rising sun fitted my mood quite well. I put in the headphones and put on "Wake Up" by Mad Season. There is nothing like a morning with Staley and the bros.

I was sitting there trying to construct some lines for a poem when suddenly Emma opened the door behind me.

"Good morning," she said and sat down next to me. She didn't kiss me good morning, but I didn't find it that weird, as we both seem to work best under the spell of the night. Everything past the blue hour till the sunset was our prime, and I don't even think of it as a pity.

The chatter was casual, and it didn't bother me. I remember this clearly, as it fascinates me. Emma had some spell that for a while kept me there in that world. I didn't feel like I wasted time talking about nothing. My mind, ideas, and actions weren't progressive, but it didn't bother me.

We went for breakfast and enjoyed it quite a lot. The fresh fruit there was amazing. The ocean was waiting for us to swing by and enjoy ourselves. We decided to locate just a little bit farther down the beach. It simply gave us more privacy, yet still it gave me déjà vu.

I don't know how she could get so upset just twenty-four hours earlier, and then be totally content with the situation. She had some crazy compromise skills.

Given the heat, an immediate dip was a necessity. The water was nice and chilly, and it felt good to get our feet out of the warm sand.

When I was back on the towel, I really didn't feel like music, nor did I feel like movie soundtracks. I was going through the iPod library to find something that suited my mood.

I found something that I hadn't used in a while, "A Song of Ice and Fire" audiobook. I was halfway through the third book, and it was exactly the kind of stuff I needed. A good narrative while my body and face felt the heat from the sun. Emma seemed to be totally fine with me being in my own world. That's another thing that was so peculiar about the entire trip.

It seemed like the most normal thing in the world.

We fell into each other's worlds like it was nothing. I wasn't a madman, it was just how it went down. Still I felt this repellent feeling inside me. The same feeling that made me want to go home.

Today I know that it was the right thing, but back then it was different. I didn't realize what sides of myself that I was discovering.

I was attracted to Emma, but as persons we would never work out. That's what I slowly felt, but didn't realize. Emma started out not being attracted to me, but now slowly she was growing more and more fond of me. We had both been lone souls, and maybe that's what I sensed in the first place; yet still not all lone souls are looking for the same path.

I didn't want her so badly anymore. It's funny how I lost the feeling more and more. She was perfectly attractive in every way, but I lost it.

For a while I thought that maybe we became too close of friends, but that is just rubbish. I cared about her, liked her, and loved the way she looked, yet still I didn't want to be with her.

I pictured her being with other guys. I really hadn't experienced jealousy before, and I felt so pitiful. It was the first time I felt like a stupid patriarch, yet probably also the last time.

Literally I was giving myself a beating. I'm telling you, with friends like this, you don't need enemies.

Thinking of Emma being around others, yet still not wanting her myself. It was a pathetic complex and luckily it only lasted a short time after the travels. I wasn't a patriarch or anything, just a boy needing to learn a lesson. Needing to know and be honest with myself. Learning to live in the moment, just for a moment, yet still not base everything on that moment.

The day at the beach was coming to an end. In that heat you can easily skip lunch and just buy a few fruits from whoever sells them. Dinner wasn't for another hour, but we decided to go back to our room to get ready and relax a bit.

Emma was the first to take a shower, the logic being that she would need more time than me to get ready. I was lying on the bed relaxing and once again checking my phone.

I had so many texts from my mother and family in general that I could barely stand to use the phone. I felt guilty, but at the same time some kind of feeling was growing inside me. A feeling of wanting to stand up and being honest. All of this was my own decision, after all. I had enjoyed them, I was even proud of them, so why shouldn't I be honest about them? It was easier said than done, but still I felt determined.

Emma coming back from the shower interrupted my thoughts. She had a towel around her body and another wrapped around her head. Steam was still coming off her skin from the hot water. Her face looked so clean and natural. She was beyond beautiful, at least to me.

I got up and jumped in the shower. I'm quite quick at getting ready, so it wasn't long before we were both ready and looking at ourselves in the mirror.

We looked quite good like this, next to each other and stuff. I'd spent a bit of time getting ready compared to what I usually do. It seemed to have paid off and reminded me that a little extra time in the morning might be worth it.

I mean, I've been opposing the narcissism of my generation and I still am, but spending time looking good can be justified. I'm not obsessed with how I look, neither with other people's opinion on how I look. I just like to look good.

At first I had actually imagined us to be dining at the hotel restaurant, but when we talked about it I realized how much we needed to go someplace better. Emma told me that she had seen this restaurant in town that she really wanted to go to. Apparently it was quite expensive and one of best in town. Good thing was that I didn't care.

We walked down through the reception, and the sweet girl at the reception desk actually complimented our looks. It was nice of her, especially since we knew that she meant it.

That's what made her really good at her job as well. She was honest, happy, and genuine. She hadn't said stuff like that before, and that's how you know she actually meant it. Of course we thanked her, but I topped it off with a small compliment towards her as well. It was a little out of place, but I could tell that it landed well with her. I don't remember how Emma felt about it, but honestly I didn't care.

As we were about to walk onto the ocean side pathway, we came by Harry sitting in his chair. Of course it was with a smile and a cigarette in his right hand.

I greeted him and decided to introduce Emma. I felt like she needed to meet that very strange gentleman.

Harry moved the cigarette to his left hand in order to give Emma a handshake. He made some statement about me, which by his delivery felt like a joke, yet it wasn't. He just made me look good in front of her, and that's just another reason that he was a true lad. He was probably not even doing it to make me look good, rather just out of honesty.

Emma felt a little strange about meeting him, but I think that it was in fact more her amazement over me knowing him that shined through. If the circumstances hadn't been as they were, it might have been a little weird, but guess what. Everything is weird when everybody wants to look alike, that's the thing.

We think we live in this special age of individualism, and we do to some extent. Still people don't realize how much they all want to be the same.

The truth is that if you really want to discover anything that's spiritual, philosophical, or deep, you will be considered pretentious. The good life generally seems to be perceived as being a money-seeking, conforming person. It's about being a person who perceives himself or herself as special, yet doesn't do anything with just a little edge.

People are in this weird status quo where they kind of know about everything, yet they are a little scared of everything. No one is being idealist, most have short attention spans, and are afraid of being honest with themselves and the world.

You know how historians always categorize different ages as periods? Everybody kind of knows the most important, the only thing we don't know is how long the current period will be.

The thing I've noticed is that people think it doesn't apply anymore. That we live in a progressive age that can't be defined. Let me tell you, we don't.

The current state of the world has been like this for a long time. Like you, I can merely make assumptions of what our age will be called, but maybe something like the Narcissist and Anti Idealist Rat Race age. The age where everyone was special and politically correct, yet no one truly fought for anything. Where everybody wanted to get richer, yet more people got poor.

The age where everybody looked so much at pictures and mirrors that they started hating or loving themselves in an absurd way. The age where only a few could read a book back to back, and people checked their Facebook before brushing their teeth in the morning.

Yes, that is our age. I'm not saying that everything about my generation is bad. All I'm saying is that I wished Billy Corgan had kept his hair.

Jokes aside, it really bothers me. The current state of the world is an honest concern with me. I'm not saying everything about it is bad. Most of the things that the Internet brought with it are good. I endure them, still I just think that we as a general public don't understand how to filter information and use new technology in general.

I guess a twenty-year delay is a natural thing, yet it's still bothering me nonetheless. To be honest, I really learned a lot of things from those days under the sun. Another thing was seeing things from the outside.

I should probably get back to telling you about the dinner Emma and I had, but let me just ramble on a little more.

Seeing things from the outside. What does that mean? It's something I never tried during those days, but it came in the aftermath of those days with Emma.

It's basically just being an observer through your senses. Like watching a movie through your eyes and ears. Not judging, just looking. Looking without any presumed, preconceived idea. Just observing with one's eyes and analyzing the data coming in.

One of the things I understood to see from the outside was the rat race. The rat race of education and life in general, the fear of being a failure, not having a career, and therefore not living up to society's expectations of you.

The rat race of rushing through life and forgetting what enjoying simple things means, just like my grandpa talked about. The balance between quantity and quality. Looking for true enjoyment in life, instead of buying some idea represented to you.

Yes, I admit that I, as everybody else, base my ideas, beliefs, identity, personality, and dreams on bits of pieces of others. Yet still I refuse to believe that everybody needs the life that gets advocated at the moment.

I'm not saying that everybody needs a trip into the wild. I'm saying that you just need to think, and rethink.

I don't know what made me think all this. Maybe the fact that I had doubts about this trip because of all kind of norms.

Briefly I was even afraid of falling behind in high school. Fucking high school? It's not like it's going to affect the rest of my life. How much more useful stuff had I learned in this past week?

It's not like you can weigh knowledge like that, but it surely seemed like someone had made me look at education and life in a very special way, but not only that. It seemed that something had made everybody lie to each other as well. It seemed very well orchestrated.

Well, maybe not, maybe this was the way of life now. I couldn't really figure out if I was being a madman in a normal world, or a perfectly sane person in a screwed-up world.

Well, maybe no one had lied. I mean, if you lie, it implies that you know the truth. Maybe it was the best thing to do. It was what the system of the world needed. The rat race was just a part of the truth to them. Maybe it wasn't a rat race for them.

When there is no real alternative, then it's just the way of life. To me it was a rat race, and I know that there is an alternative.

That's how it seemed to me, at least. It was, of course, also something I first realized when I finally got out of the picture and saw the frame.

That's when I realized what my own senses told me. We get told so much that we often forget our own senses. Maybe we aren't even that good at using them, but just listening to your own senses, forgetting everything that you've been told, really helped me.

I don't even know anymore. I guess there probably isn't even an alternative answer. There is no alternative route. The only thing possible is to fix the current, and that is definitely not easy. I don't even know.

I just know that it didn't seem like the happy life to me, and therefore I would do everything within my grasp to shape my own alternative, yet still within the system.

That was a lot of rambling. Well, it is after all what fills my head most of the time. Honestly, those days were the first time in my life that person-related issues took up most of my brain activity. I think it was very good of me not getting too one-sided. I already was, but seeing the other side kind of balanced me out a little.

Emma had made me a kind of person that I hadn't been for a long time. That was her spell. Her spell was also that her candlelit eyes were like the top of the lake reflecting the setting sun.

The restaurant that she had in mind surely was a nice one. All along the walk we had been talking about Harry. She found it quite interesting that I had talked to him, and I actually enjoyed telling her about him. He was kind of special to me, and I think Emma could feel it.

Now we were in the middle of our starters and talking about tomorrow. Emma was asking me about how I thought it would feel getting home. How our relationship would be under the hometown winter sky.

I couldn't answer her at the time. Honestly, it felt more like she was trying to persuade me to stay by some kind of backwards persuasion technique.

It wasn't, though, she was just being straight-up concerned. At the time I didn't really have the balls to tell her that I had mixed feelings about her. I admired and respected her more than I loved her, but how do you tell a girl that?

The dinner was like nothing I ever had. The food, wine, waiters, and surroundings were all out of this world. The crazy thing was that it was only at the price of a regular meal at a decent restaurant back home. This country really was way cheaper.

Our topics went from talking about feelings to being quite ordinary. I tried to talk about the Facebook experience I had earlier, but it seemed that the amount of messages I had received interested her more. It wasn't exactly what I wanted to talk about, but it was quite a big personal matter, so we discussed it.

Honestly, it wasn't so bad, but I had to be careful. I didn't know how it was going to play out yet. I felt like being honest, but what I said now and what I would end up doing could be two very different things. What I told Emma I would do said a lot about my attitude about our relationship, or at least about me as a person.

I decided to tell her that I had no regrets, and that I was going to be honest about the trip, only leaving out a few unnecessary details. I wasn't sure that I had the balls to pull it off, but I said it anyways.

To this day one of the things I regret the most is that I don't have any pictures of that beautiful girl sitting there in the candlelight. Her hair gently covering her shoulders and freshly tanned skin. It was a dreamy moment that passed and only a picture could have kept it through eternity.

I had always felt like I didn't need to take damn pictures of everything. Pictures and films are made as art, memories I keep inside my head. That's what I used to say. It was bullshit now. Some things are essential to have pictures of.

There is loads of beauty in the moment and it's better captured and printed through light. Maybe that is the art, and that's what I had misunderstood.

Again I'm not advocating living life through a lens, but I guess that reading my thoughts already have made clear that balance is the key in almost every matter in life.

The moment was gone, but my memory wasn't. It is all I have now, and it's what I'm telling this piece of life from. I hope it's enough.

A funny thing just came to my mind. Don't we almost always remember faces in photographs today? Not always, but with most people that we don't see often enough. I wonder how it was before 1820 or whenever photography was invented?

Honestly, I couldn't care less at the time, but funny facts like that always interest me nonetheless. I was just really satisfied with the five different photographs that I had managed to snap of her. One in particular had her very distinctive smile on it.

Usually I would have poured the red wine empty, but in this restaurant it was the waiter's job. We made a toast to the trip and coincidences.

The main course was about gone and neither of us felt like dessert. It was just about enjoying the wine and this last evening.

My brain was beginning to play tricks on me again. It wasn't wandering off with my consciousness as usual. No, it was thinking about staying because everything felt so nice with her again.

That's when I thought that I was a madman. Once again I was doubting and changing my mind, yet only for a brief moment. The feeling of going home was still inside me. I just had to look.

Still, I couldn't figure out what it was. It wasn't that I was afraid of commitment, neither was I afraid of change, and I definitely didn't miss my comfort zone.

I still try reasoning and think that I might just have felt the change I needed. I don't know, and I don't know if I ever will.

The waiter handed me back my MasterCard. We thanked him for good service and food and got up from our chairs.

The wine was working pretty well. Emma didn't pack too much weight, but she still held her liquor really well. Our conversations this evening had been good. We weren't disagreeing on many things, but I had also purposely held back on topics that I knew we would disagree on.

Emma really was quite fond of the regular life. I'm not saying that I'm super progressive or anything. I just don't think that the square life is the happy life. The reason for Emma thinking so was that she had never had it, or that was at least my theory. I guess it's a pretty common thing, wanting and idealizing the things you don't have.

Purposely, I had also tried to go closer to her little by little. Instead of just disagreeing, I tried to take her viewpoint and go from there. I don't think it's bad psychology.

We got out of the restaurant and all it was about was just enjoying the last bit of time together. The stripper and the confused adolescent were quite different. It was like they were blessed, granted a gift to dream together.

She wanted to hold my hand, but it made me feel bad. Deep inside I wasn't feeling her, still I was so attached to her that I took her hand. What else was I supposed to do?

We chatted quietly as we meandered down the street. The orange streetlight and distant jazz made a perfect ambience. We both decided that we wanted to go back and sit on the beach. A moonlit beach is not the worst place for conversation.

On the way back we talked about how weird and crazy the days had been. Emma couldn't hold her laughter when we started talking about the assault. It wasn't funny, but quite absurd. More or less it was the entire situation that was absurd. It made me laugh as well.

Chapter 11: The more or less coincidental actions and possibilities of a young man and woman.

London Grammar was softly playing from the cell phone. Neither of us was talking. We just sat there quietly enjoying the sight of a vast ocean together.

When I think about it, I'm quite certain that it was happiness. It was a fragile happiness, but it was happiness nonetheless. I know it may sound weird, but I tried not to send any sexual vibes, as I didn't want to give Emma false expectations.

It may sound cocky, but thinking back, it was basically all I had done, but my confused brain really couldn't see that back then.

It frightens me that I was so blind. It's a thought that's stuck with me. What matters? May I possibly still be blind today?

Emma suddenly got up, walked in front of me, and sat down again. She was looking me straight in the eyes, and I quickly sensed that she wanted to discuss something serious.

"I think you know that I don't understand your motivation for any of this. I'm really glad that it happened, but I'm still not sure why. I think there is a purpose for everything, that it'll work itself out, but I need to ask you one thing. How are things going to be between us when we get back?" she said in just as serious a tone as I expected.

She was sitting straight in front of the thin white line that the moon painted on the blank water. The white light was painting a white frame around the edge of her face. She truly looked like an angel.

"I know. I think you've sensed what honesty means to me, and that I have and always will answer you honestly. I don't really know. If I truly knew why I asked you I would tell you, but I don't. I know that I find you gorgeous and attractive like nothing else. I love the way you act around people, but I don't know how things will be back home."

She definitely had mixed feelings about my answer. I had never intended to be any kind of savior, but I sensed that she slowly wanted me to be. It felt like she idolized me a little, but I figured that it wasn't weird as she had never seen me in everyday life.

"Do you want to be with me?" she asked. It couldn't get more straightforward than that.

"Be with you how?" I asked. It was a stupid question, but I wanted to be sure.

"Like be with me? When we get back there?"

"I don't know," I said. I could see how it crushed something in her. I felt pity for her, but I needed to be honest.

"I don't know how I will feel or how the world will look, but I think we should keep seeing each other. See how we feel," I continued.

Tears were already starting to flow from her eyes.

"I'm sorry," I said. She wiped away the first tear.

"All right. Let's just not talk about it then," she said and got up.

She walked down to the water, and I quickly got up and followed. Of course she didn't just want to stop talking about it, but I didn't know how to handle that kind of passive aggressive rhetoric.

"I'm not saying that I don't want to see you. Can't we just please forget about it and have a good last night?" I said.

"No, you don't, but you don't know," she said.

I understood her, I really did, but what was I supposed to do? I know that I sounded and acted like the most ignorant fucking douche bag, but honestly it all came out of confused feelings and acting on impulses. Since then I've become way better at thinking the consequences of my actions through.

Just like my grandmother had always told me. It's still like playing chess, though. You can think so much ahead, but there are more potential consequences than you can ever imagine. Still, there are obvious ones to avoid, and that's what you do.

"I can't tell you something I don't know. How do you know how you will feel about me back home?" I asked.

"I just do. I feel what I feel inside," she answered like it was the easiest thing in the world.

"Don't you ever doubt it?" I asked.

"Not really," she said.

"See, that's where we differ. I do that all the time. It's not that I'm trying to hurt you. I'm just insecure or something."

I had finally found the right argument. I could tell by her expression that she accepted the answer.

"All right," she said in a low voice. She was looking down in silence.

"Let's go for a walk," she suddenly said in a slightly more uplifted voice.

It ended up being the longest walk that we had done together. Once again, life was quite simple in the moonlight, and there wasn't a need for many words.

The sand was soft and the ocean was mellow like a mother with her newborn in her arms. We walked closely, yet without a touch. Like steam, the alcohol slowly left my body.

Upon returning to the hotel, nothing felt the same. There wasn't anyone anywhere in sight. Passing Harry's chair, it didn't quite feel empty. I looked at it and felt some kind of weird presence.

"What's wrong?" Emma asked. I looked away from the chair.

"Nothing. Let's go," I said, still having goose bumps. That was a weird feeling. What was it that he told me again?

I didn't recall before Emma and I were sitting in each of our beds again.

"So this was our last night. It feels strange, doesn't it?" Emma asked. I took my time to think. The way she asked made me wonder.

"It does. Do you want to sleep alone?" I asked.

I was asking her as straightforward as I could. It was mostly due to the fact that I felt like getting on top of her and kissing every inch of her beautiful body. She knew how I felt, so I figured that it was an all right thing to ask.

"I don't know," she said.

It was basically my morals and logic fighting my instincts.

"I don't think I need that right now," she said.

Something inside me made me move anyways. I got right next to her and held both her hands in mine.

She was looking at me and I at her.

"What is it that you want? You are confusing me," she said.

It kind of caught me off guard. It was straight-up mean of me to try to kiss her. She really couldn't separate it. I didn't really want to go all the way with her, so hitting on her is mean. If we both had felt casual about it, then it would have been very different.

My logic got the better of me again. I stood up and walked across the room. I turned towards the balcony door and used both my hands to pull back my hair as I looked into the darkness of the night.

"I don't know, Emma. I don't know." I turned around and looked at her. A silence occurred. It seemed that neither of us could vocalize our feelings. I almost felt deluded; this definitely wasn't why we travelled all this way.

"I just think we should sleep in our own beds," she said.

"Let's do that then," I said in a tired voice. The wine had worn off and it had left me quite exhausted.

I went to the bathroom to brush my teeth and take a good night leak. While I was standing there brushing my teeth, I held eye contact with myself. It feels so good and intimidating at the same time.

There's something about mirrors. Another thing is that they always remind me of the *Taxi Driver* and *La Haine* scenes. God, I love those scenes. There is something self-connecting in a mirror.

We were both finally under our covers and had all the lights turned off. It was like we both anticipated the other to say something, yet neither of us knew what to say.

"Good night," I said in a low voice.

It took a while before Emma answered.

"Good night."

"Sleep well," I said.

"Likewise," she said.

I knew that I could have opened a conversation with her there in the dark, but I decided not to. I couldn't really handle anymore. The last day of our trip was over.

I don't know how long Emma kept awake, but once again I was the first one to open my eyes in the morning light. For a second I panicked, as I didn't wake to the sound of the alarm. I looked at the time and realized that I just woke up really early. The alarm wouldn't ring for another forty minutes.

I decided to put on some clothes and walk to the reception. Making sure a taxi would be ready for us in ninety minutes wasn't the worst idea.

I decided to change into swimming clothes so that I could take a morning swim. The receptionist looked exhausted, but it was no wonder with their twenty-four-hour reception. It wasn't the same girl as I had seen at most other times, but she was just as helpful as the other.

The morning swim felt really good, but I felt kind of nervous inside. I was nervous about going home and nervous about how the day would be with Emma.

The swim made me feel fresh, but it didn't change anything. I got back to the hotel room and found that Emma was already up and going. We both packed our stuff and got ready quite quick.

There was a peculiar mood of not talking and just working to get ready. We had about half an hour for breakfast, and it sure was a silent one. We barely talked during the entire thing.

When the taxi arrived, it felt like the biggest relief. We got in and nothing felt particularly magical anymore. No one in the car talked, it was complete silence.

The road behind the hotel, I hadn't even seen it before departure. It was very beautiful out the back as well. We pulled away from hotel, and I looked out the back. I remember thinking that it was probably the last time in my life that I would see that hotel. It's not exactly the kind of place that you come back to.

I looked at Emma and she looked at me; still no one said anything. The road was disappearing under the car, and the city was slowly getting ready for another day as we rolled by. We had exited the city and were now driving on curvy roads outside the city.

As we drove around yet another curvy corner, we saw a big truck blocking almost the entire road. The driver slowed down and drove onto the left side. There were police on the scene and they were leading the traffic. I looked out the window and saw a motorbike that was totally demolished under the truck. There was a big pool of dark red blood on the asphalt.

The color of death, and that's what I saw. There was no body, but someone had probably just passed away on that exact spot. It gave me that chilly feeling of mortality.

I wondered who that person was. Where was he going, who was he thinking about? It made it all seem pretty senseless.

I looked at Emma and could tell that she felt something similar. We never saw the face. All it was to us was one minute of inconvenience and the unpleasant sight of a blood pool.

That is what it was practically. In reality, it was more than that.

The car kept being completely silent. The only thing that changed was that we all seemed to be in deeper thought. memento mori maybe; might have only been me. I tend to let my own feelings matter in the way I see the world. It's natural, but as I talked about earlier, it affects how you see a lot of things.

We arrived in the airport and got out of the taxi. It was our last stop in this country. It felt kind of good to be back in a non-place for some weird reason.

We walked in, did check-in and everything. It went quite smooth, but we didn't talk much during any of it. We weren't strangers to each other, yet we didn't know how to speak. I still felt comfortable around her, but it was a weird and undesired way to end the trip. I didn't realize how much was on me back then, but I do now.

We were in an airplane again. It was about twenty minutes before takeoff. The flight would only be two hours, and then we had to change flights. We had gotten two window seats, which was quite comfortable.

I was looking at my phone and reading through the text messages from my mother. Once again it made me feel bad, but it was now that I had the chance to be honest. They would probably never understand, but I decided that I wanted to be honest no matter how freakish they would possibly find me.

If I wrote a text now, then they would have time to prepare, and I wouldn't have to explain everything when I got there.

Briefly I wondered how Christmas was going to be now that I was going to be home anyways. I was even going to be home in time for the last school day. I surely didn't plan to go, though.

I considered just keeping my whereabouts a secret, but what I realize now is that it was part of the trip that I grew balls to actually tell the truth.

I began writing.

"Hey Mom, I'm sorry for whatever feelings I've put you, Dad, and the rest of the family through the last few days. I did not intend to make you nervous, but it was something that I had to do. I've done something that I don't think you will understand, but it was important to me, so I don't really care. Last Friday I was drunk and dreamy. I was walking around town as I usually do, except this time my wanderlust got to a point where it had never been before. I know you've noticed the changes I have been going through the last few years. Probably even all my life. I just want you all to know that I feel good now. I have been looking to understand which leg to put weight on. I ended up in a strip club and traveled with a girl that I met there. I convinced her to go, and I learned a lot from being with her. Writing this, I almost think that I sound deluded, but how can that be when I feel so good? I've come to realize that not everything about my upbringing was particularly good. You might think that this is crazy, but I learned so much in so little time. I feel happy, despite still being confused. I don't know when we can talk face to face about this, and I still feel bad about the fact that I chose to write you this. Better written than hidden, I guess. See you tomorrow and once again, I'm sorry!"

Then I pressed send.

Luckily it's just one click and it's done.

Having the thoughts coming out through my fingers was a really special feeling. It was a way of realizing reality for me. Realizing how this weird, short trip had taught me so much. Some of it I can't even vocalize. One thing is for sure. It's under my skin now.

I was anticipating a response. Something like "Are you crazy?" or something even worse. For a second I was wondering if she had a stroke. What could she even answer? Usually I'm not this honest with my parents. Honestly, I'm barely this honest with anybody.

The seat belt sign came on, and I turned off the phone. Honestly, there was no use in keeping it on anyways. The message had been sent, and it was all that mattered.

While I sat there I had my doubts. I knew that my father would never understand, but I had my doubts about my mother. Did it really matter? It was, after all, my life and time that I had used.

Of course it mattered, but I didn't even know how to justify things anymore. What I knew was that I knew what mattered in life. Fuck the rest.

We had changed flights and were now on the last bit of travels. I was looking at the screen in the seat in front of me. It showed our location, route, and destination on a map. The world really is small nowadays.

Honestly, I don't really feel like telling you where all this happened, as I don't think it really matters much. It could have happened anywhere, well, in essence, not in reality. I'm just saying that it doesn't need a label. Emma and the story do not deserve that. Better on a branch than stuck in a lift, right? If you feel it you feel it, if you think it, you think it.

The skies look even more beautiful from above than underneath, and sun always shines up there.

My mind and line of thoughts were like the web spun by a spider in the early and cold winter dawn. It tangles around in so many directions, and when it's finished it freezes never to change form again. Then you live on that platform, that frozen web. You keep going around and around on that web, getting saddened. At least when the web turns out like mine did. It was these thoughts that I had come to.

I wondered why this trip even happened. It was me and my thoughts that were frozen, and I realized that I had to open up again. Well, that was really how it was, a frozen web. I don't know if everybody comes to that point. I don't know if it's time, adulthood, growing up, or if it was just me.

My hands looked unreal. It really seemed like my line of thoughts and my entire idea of a life platform had been spun out and frozen. All to get melted and torn apart again.

Emma hadn't looked at me for at least an hour. Today I feel privileged that it played out as it did. It's the thing with utilizing a lot of coincidental possibilities. There are so many things you don't know. I liked her, yet there were still so many things that I didn't like about her.

When I'm being honest with myself, as I try to be most of the time, then I actually think that I could've been married to that woman today. If not for the coincidences and the feelings inside me dragging me around the arena.

It may sound stupid in your ears, but I had some very vivid feelings for that girl. I still try to solve the puzzle it is to know what feelings drove me so badly towards her. It had barely been a week and I was feeling like I did. I had been around a fair bit of the circle of love in just one week. Had I changed in any way? Not really, but I think I had learned something.

We've come to the point where I want to say farewell. I could go on for a while, but I think the rest of my and Emma's story isn't that interesting. Maybe it is, but this story ends here. The thing is probably just that I don't like things to get drawn out. There's simply too much stuff out there for that. I could go on, but I would like to end it soon. I think the story has told everything that it needed to. All it has to do now is go and stand with all the other stories. Serving the way, they do.

"Please fasten your seat belts as we will land momentarily."

It was a bit weird that he announced it over the speakers when the seat belt sign had already been on for a good ten minutes.

I didn't mind much. We were on the ground. The time difference meant that it was at quite an inconvenient time, but it was part of the rules.

Soon I would be going back to my life, as Emma would to hers. The question was if it was going to be the old life, or if we would actually manage to change things.

I'd become a whole lot wiser in less than a week, but could I put it to good use?

The landing was smoother than I ever had before. I looked out at the runway through the little round window. The snow was almost gone. It had melted and left dark and moist earth behind. It most definitely was a memorable December.

Each Christmas has its magic, but that year was just very different. It's funny how the air smells differently, how quick things go back to normal. You may wonder whether Emma and I stayed part of each other's lives. I don't really want to answer that. Whatever you find best. I'm just glad we became part of each other's stories. We shared so much, did it vanish or did it grow? That's what I wondered being back in the snow.

I stopped smoking, by the way. It feels really good. Now I'm thinking of this other place. Did this already become too long? I don't think there is more to tell. Well, there definitely is, but I think this sees fit.

My yaruki came back during those days. It was in a different form, but it was in less than a week and it made a difference. I think traveling made me a storyteller, or am I really a storyteller for telling a single story? I won't try to answer that.

I know that I look at people differently now. When I first walked the streets, they seemed strange. Then I realized that they all seemed alike, and it was me that was alienated. It took quite a long time to recover, but I'm still certain that it was a better human that grew from that cocoon.

I've enjoyed telling this story and hope you gained something from reading it. Now it's time to listen. There should be plenty of other stories out there. Take care and remember: it's not so dangerous out there after all.

The end.

9 788879 175705